# Sport & Leisure

# TOM TRONDSON

Black Rose Writing | Texas

First printing

This is a work of fiction. Names, characters, businesses, places, events, and incidents are either the products of the author's imagination or used in a fictitious manner. Any resemblance to actual persons, living or dead, or actual events is purely coincidental.

ISBN: 978-1-68513-615-4
Library of Congress Control Number: 2025932904
PUBLISHED BY BLACK ROSE WRITING
www.blackrosewriting.com

Printed in the United States of America
Suggested Retail Price (SRP) $21.95

*Sport & Leisure* is printed in Garamond

*As a planet-friendly publisher, Black Rose Writing does its best to eliminate unnecessary waste to reduce paper usage and energy costs, while never compromising the reading experience. As a result, the final word count vs. page count may not meet common expectations.

Poem "Autumn Begins in Martins Ferry, Ohio," by James Wright, Above The River: The Complete Poems, Wesleyan University Press Edition, 1990. Used by permission.

# PRAISE FOR
## *SPORT & LEISURE*

"In this rousing, expertly layered story set in the northern grit of Minnesota, Trondson has crafted a novel somewhere between the meticulous blue-collar eye of Bruce Springsteen's *Nebraska* album and the loveable losers seen in a Coen Brothers movie. *Sport & Leisure* is full of losers and fighters, problems and promises, and serves up laughs to accompany a reflection on loss and love."
**–Todd Smith, author of *Hockey Strong: Stories of Sacrifice from Inside the NHL***

"A page turner… realistic, thought-provoking… a novel steeped in a vivid sense of place and culture… women confront men, men confront themselves and each other, and life goes on."
*–Midwest Book Review*

For Tye and Finn

# Sport & Leisure

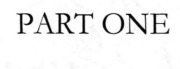

# PART ONE

*"I live now only with strangers*
*I talk to only strangers*
*I walk with angels that have no place"*
**–Bruce Springsteen**

# GLORY DAYS

Traffic is infrequent this far north. Out the windshield the sky is rusty and glinting. Rain hangs on the horizon like the tentacles of a great jellyfish. Ken Solberg sits inside his F-150 with its sporty rims and tinted windows. He and his dog and a twelve-pack of Moosehead. He's a couple hundred miles from the Canadian border. This is his backyard, these winding old roads, this north country, what they call cutover land. He passes a farmhouse set on a rocky exposure. In the yard is a massive tree. "That's me," he tells Dimley, curled up on the passenger seat. His gray whiskered lab gives him an odd stare. "What? I'm just saying."

His thoughts are like the bugs exploding on the windshield. He peers into the encroaching darkness and sees himself by the side of the road. Him age eight lacing up his skates, hand-me downs from his brother. Then he's older and cartoonishly tall. He towers over everything— teachers, girls, the puck. Ken sees himself circling for a face off. He hears the screaming fans. He was like that with his fists, that hunger to be heard.

Springsteen plays on the stereo. This is the music of his youth. The Boss with his clenched fist and blue-collar anthems. He wrote songs about the workingman and muscle cars, couples in way over their head.

His smartphone lights up on the dash. *You good?* the text reads.

"Call Brandon," he tells Siri. The moment his son takes the call he gets choked up. "I fucked up this time. What if it's over? What if she says—"

"—Slow down, Dad." Ken chugs the rest of the beer. "You drinking and driving?"

He reaches behind his seat, drops the bottle in the box carton, and grabs another without missing a beat. "If I'd wanted a lecture I'd have consulted your little brother."

"Will you at least pare down the drinking until you get to Grandma's?"

He glances at the speedometer while prying the cap off using an opener on his key fob. He's shooting up a back-ass, two-lane country road with birch trees and deer warning signs. Shit, he's doing a hundred.

"How'd you know I was going there?"

"Me and Jeremy guessed. I'm jealous you didn't invite me."

In his mind's eye he sees those jaunts up north, camping under the stars with his eldest boy, until the storm weathered back home.

"You seen her?"

"Nah. You two sure trashed the place."

"Text me when you do. And Brandon?" He feels that gob in his throat again.

"It's going to be okay, Dad."


The music turns majestic. Like an American flag rippling in the wind. That's the beauty of Springsteen—his songs are like caught fire. They're the balm against a cruel world, his problem solver and old friend, how he blows off steam. They remind him of America—bottled up one moment, the next like fireworks on the 4ᵗʰ of July.

It's dark like it's never dark in Minneapolis. A northern night sky has a color all its own. A black that tears straight through you. Ken feels like he's near some end and there's nothing he can do but keep moving for fear of getting in its way. Deep cuts from *The River* play. The songs merge and recede then merge again. The headlamps shoot great sheets of light on the road. He is ten miles from Floodwood. He's three hours in. Three hours from the city and his life there. He passes another old tree, this one black with tumors and knots. He sees it in the high beams then it's gone. Ken has a thing for trees. You might call it an affliction. He sees them and walks among them and they touch him like old teammates or lost souls.

*Their sons grow suicidally beautiful*
*At the beginning of October,*
*And gallop terribly against each other's bodies.*

His imagination throws him into the city on the lake Longfellow coined Gitchee Gumee. Him a student-athlete with a mean streak. Freshman year he'd taken a class—*Big Woods, Big Water: Nature Writing in America's Heartland.* They read Sigurd Olson, Bill Holm and Robert Bly. The professor, a woman named Downs-Miers, had wild hair and wore long antiquated dresses in green velvet. She was the best teacher he ever had. She'd run lines of poetry off the top of her head and the images came alive like the Catholic rocker from New Jersey.

Near Chisholm, the console lights up green, a call coming in. "Hey," he says, answering it.

"What happened?"

*What happened was I was confused. No, I was bereft, lost at sea, weak like men can be.* "We thought it best if I go to Grandma's."

"How could you do that, Dad?"

Ken sees his wife's face. That look she gave him in her spiffy new dress. "I love your mom. We got sidetracked is all."

"That's what you call it? Sidetracked?" Jeremy says. "Fuck you, Dad."

The line goes dead.

A car is coming over the hill. Its headlamps splinter like tiny fingers groping in the dark. He fumbles with the phone. He needs to explain things to his youngest son, get things straight. What can he say? That it didn't mean anything. That they should pretend it never happened. The headlamps are nearly on him when Ken closes his eyes and let's go of the steering wheel. *Take me. Take me and do not hesitate. Be swift and clean. Send me into the deep dark abyss.* He feels the truck drifting into the opposing lane. The oncoming car's horn sounds like a dying bird. Or an incantation.

The car passes through him like a spirit. Then nothing. Then nothing but the Ford soaring along. Then he is up over the hill with tears in his eyes.

The afternoon practice comes to him like these things do, draped in shame and guilt. He'd called the team in. "Commitment is everything," he told his players. Steam rose from their helmets. They had their gloves off and were messing with bangs or chinstraps. "Forget talent. Forget genes and smarts. Do the work, fellas, and everything will fall into place next year at State." Ken was standing on the ice with the varsity squad when his phone pulsed in his pocket. *Squeeze Box?* It was code. He smiled at no one kid in particular. Then his heart sank. He had what you call a lucid experience of the mind. In that instant he saw his whole pathetic existence crumbling. He had to get out, now.

"Coach?" It was his captain, Showalter. "You okay?"

Straight home he went with an awful feeling in his stomach. Like it was important he hug his wife and tell her he loved her. He found her alright. She sat on the stoop dressed like she was heading to a fancy party on the brightest of summer afternoons. Strewn on the lawn were his clothes. His sweats and flannels, his orange hunting vest, his socks and underwear. Even the black suit he'd gotten for his dad's funeral. Ken's wardrobe lay scattered on the yard and hung from the trees like the debris from a plane crash.

His wife had gone inside by then. He found her in the den. The room looked worked over like in a TV detective series where the perp turns the place upside down searching for drugs. Kimberly stood in the mess holding *Back in Black*.

"Andrew gave me that for my tenth birthday."

She snapped the record in two. Then she reached for his stereo receiver. He heard himself scream but she'd already yanked the box from the electrical outlet and hurled it toward the brick hearth. Furious, he charged his wife and got hold of her wrists. He was aware of how thin and fragile she was. How he could toss her across the room like she had his stereo. Kimberly fought and cursed him. She said she hated everything he stood for. Then she collapsed on the couch. Ken didn't know what to do or say without making it worse. Instead, he got a beer from the kitchen and drank it on the front lawn. Then he picked up his clothes and went looking for his wife again. She was in the bathroom applying bright red lipstick.

"I want out," she said.

His gaze found the dress. "You're overreacting."

"I don't want to see your face or stupid truck ever again."

Their eyes met in the mirror's reflection. "Fine, I'll go to my mom's."

He packed without thinking—underwear, socks, shorts, T-shirts, jeans, a couple flannels. In the garage he took his golf clubs and fishing gear then unlocked the gun rack and grabbed the 12-guage and some ammo. It was quiet when he reentered the house. Strange, even, like he was trespassing in his own home. He called out his wife's name, but it rang false. Then he heard the front door slam. Ken caught up as she was getting into her Acura.

"I know you're upset," he said. "But can we talk this through?"

"Maybe I have a friend, too. Have you thought about that?"

His eyes found her legs again. They were strong from the cycling kick she'd been on the last few years. Seeing them so tan and muscular got him in his core. "Kimberly … come on."

She slammed the car door shut then burned rubber down the drive. Ken stood in the driveway of the house where they'd raised their boys and hosted Vikings parties and grilled beer-soaked brats and watched *Seinfeld* and *Game of Thrones*, where they slept and ate meals and sometimes made love. She was gone, out of sight. On her way somewhere in her tight little dress. Did she really have a special friend?

He went back into the garage. This time he took the Glock.

***

She saved him the night they met. This was the winter the Buffalo Sabres farm team released him. He'd returned to Duluth to make money and work on his game while his face healed. He was seeing an undergraduate. Maria was from Cloquet and majoring in Sociology. She brewed tea, highlighted her textbooks in her methodical way, and made love to Ken with a motherly sensitivity. As if his pleasure was more important than hers. He liked Maria. But if he came clean about his feelings, he'd have admitted he saw her more like flyover country until his cheek healed and he headed back east.

There was things Maria didn't know about. Like Patricia in Minneapolis. Patricia had even more problems than Ken did. One night when the team was in town he knocked on her door unannounced. She was drunk and accused him of taking her for granted. The bottle she threw at his head exploded on the wall. He thought *fuck this* and left. It was snowing outside. Big fat snowflakes that fell out of nowhere and stuck to your clothes like lint. Instead of heading for the hotel bar, he walked across Lyndale to the neighborhood on the hill. The houses there were turn-of-the-century regal with huge inviting porches and steep roofs. He was thinking about his life. He was having a real serious go inside his head. What was he doing with the likes of Patricia? And shouldn't he tell Maria the truth about his feelings? He made a decision. He would turn his life around. No more fucking around. His only focus would be the big leagues. Once and for all he'd make his dad proud. He touched where his cheek felt delicate and spongy. Then he started down the sidewalk in the snow.

At the bottom of the hill was a group of students smoking outside an apartment hosting a loud party. Ken ducked in out of the weather but soon realized Depeche Mode and clove cigarettes wasn't his scene. He was about to leave when this young woman walked up holding two beers. She hadn't yet said hello when he felt something bloom inside him. She wasn't like any girl he'd ever met. She wore dark clothes and her head was shaved close to the scalp on one side like the punk rockers in Uptown styled it. They talked by the big window overlooking the street. It was magical with the swirling snow and him struck by her beauty and intelligence. She didn't even ask about his cheek. If there was a time in Ken Solberg's brief, chaotic life when he held his breath and prayed to God, it was when she went to get her coat. When he saw her waiting by the door that thick shell around his heart, that protective seal he'd fashioned out of necessity and survival, began to crack.

They left in her car and drove the frozen city in a snowstorm. He played her the mixed tape he took everywhere. He had her pay close attention to the Springsteen songs that meant the most. They went to her dorm. Sometime around dawn, while Kimberly slept, he realized two things about his future. Either he'd marry this girl and make a break from the past for good. Or he'd stick to his original plan and kill himself before the year was out. Whichever came first.

***

Everything falls into place when he drives past the International Falls city limit. This is the town he was reared in. Where he went to school and lost his virginity, where he first fell in love. Rolling down Third Street he gets his first whiff of the paper mill's mushy cardboard smell. Boise Paper has a constant noise coming from its belly, like a force pulling you in. The mill was a way of life for the Solberg clan. Grandpa Les was a river rat, lumberjack, then a tugboat operator. Ken's father ran a dumper that dropped chips into the blowers, operated a big Hy-Hoe 580, then got a job in the Insulite division, making wood byproducts like Durolite and Acoustilite ceiling tiles. Even Ken and his older brother got summer jobs hauling pulp wood. In the 1970s a guy working at the paper mill made a decent salary. Enough to put a down payment on a home, have a lake cabin and maybe a hunting shack in the woods, plus a little change in his pocket come quitting time to camp out on a stool at Swede Charlie's or the Border Bar. Since then, so much had changed. The mill was still Falls' largest employer, but every year more and more workers were being replaced by improved automation.

He slows at the bandshell where he first copped a feel up Melody Fillman's shirt. He thinks about the places they used to go, "Hungry Heart" blasting from the stereo, looking for a place to grope each other in the dark. Last he heard Melody was divorced and singing in a band. He sometimes wondered how it would play out if he saw her in town, what emotions might surge through his veins, if something still burned between them. Soon he's driving down Ninth Street, past the church and under the big lazy trees that hang over the street. He parks next to the curb then leans his big self over the console and gets a good look at the house he grew up in. Yard's cut and the stoop light shines gold. He texts his best friend Cal Johnston. *Golf tomorrow?*

*Shit, brother. You in town? Let's make it two. And Ken? You know what time it is?*

He and Dimley climb down from the rig with their old achy joints then take a long gratifying piss on the side of the house. Ken stares at the night sky with a smile that's unrecognizable considering the day he's had. His life is upside down, his marriage probably fucked, but he can appreciate the magnitude of the cosmos lit up like a pinball machine. "They don't make em' like that in Minneapolis," he tells his dog.

Winter was the best. Winter meant the outdoor rinks were open. Every neighborhood had a team. Carson Lupie, Kerry Park, the Rainer Rats. The biggest rivals were across the river in Fort Frances. Night hockey. The way the streetlights threw a romantic brilliance over the rinks. Dads standing around in work coats and jeans, their breath mist-white and vaporous. The whoosh of bodies hurtling down the ice, the hard *whack* the puck made ricochetting off the boards, off hockey sticks. The girls bundled up in parkas and making eye contact when you glided by. The promise in those gazes, of better days.

Hockey was Ken's way out. This became clear after everything that happened. Though it meant getting stronger and working on his skating technique. It meant cutting back on alcohol and drugs. It meant packing up his belongings for the long, lonely drives east. Places like Hershey, Pennsylvania and Rochester, New York. If a player was lucky enough to be called up. The fights he was in. But that was his role. He wasn't special like his older brother was. Ken Solberg was a team's bruiser. The goon who protected the special players. Guys like Andrew. And he was good in the role. If Derek "The Dethroner" Delone didn't throw the perfect punch and his cheek didn't collapse like a sandcastle, who knows how far he would have gone in the big leagues?

Wound up after the long drive, Ken digs out his fleece, grabs a tepid Moosehead, and walks across the street with Dimley. He parks it at the picnic table by the old rink and pops off the cap. What a fucking day. Did Kimberly really meet someone tonight? Or did she get drunk, Uber home, and pass out on the couch? He tries to imagine a man she might fall for. But he can't. He's too close to it—his feelings are too cloudy. All he knows is he deserves feeling like shit because he did this to himself.

Guzzling the beer, he notices the fur on Dimley's back stiffen. Ken turns, hearing the swing set creak. Out of the darkness walks this man with a pronounced limp. Him and his old dog. Ken stands with his hands hanging low by his sides. At the University of Minnesota-Duluth where he played hockey, the announcers calling games introduced him as Ken-Forcer, as in *Ken Solberg, the Enforcer.* He lived up to the nickname best he could, fighting anyone, hockey game or not. He feared nothing, not pain or injury, not jail time, not physically injuring another human being beyond recognition. And here comes this gimp with his sad looking dog. They meet in the clearing. The dogs approach each other with a similar distrust.

"I saw you and thought, there goes a man in need of company." The man pulls at his knapsack straps as if he's making sure his few possessions are secure in case a speedy exit is needed. Ken glances at his watch though the time doesn't register in his head. "Me? I don't believe in time. Time is arbitrary. It's a number that pops in your head. It don't mean nothing in the long haul."

"What's the dog's name?"

The man brightens. "This old girl? Beatrice. She's named after my one true love," he says. "Are you ready for the end of the world? Me and Beatrice, we got it all figured out. We're heading north. I got this for protection." He lifts his hooded sweatshirt. His stomach is flat and corded, blue in the moonlight. A sheathed knife with a leather handle is shoved in the waistband of his jeans. "I'll fend for myself. Bear, water moccasin, beaver, what have you."

He's all gristle and madness. They are everywhere these days, the homeless, the destitute, the mentally ill. They stand on street corners in crazy-shit weather with their placards that break your heart if you have the courage to read them.

"What about you? Why are you out on a night like this?"

The question shakes Ken to his fundamental core. Was it only this afternoon he spoke to the team about commitment? Is his world already that far gone?

"Wanna see it?" Out comes the knife, a silver gleam in the moonlight. The man runs a finger down the blade. "She's sharp. Oh, is she ever." He gets in real close like he wants to tell him a secret. There's a smell coming off the man that's a mix of sour piss and body odor. Ken stares at the blade. One false move and he'll seize the man's wrist and beg him to cry mercy.

"Spare any change for a fellow seeker?"

Ken takes a step back and grins. There is honor among thieves. There is karma. Out comes his wallet on this most peculiar of days. He hands him a ten spot. Which has the man smacking his lips and holding the bill up to the moonlight. "Much obliged," he says, slipping it in his pocket. Same goes for the knife, stowing it away. "Per chance, can you point the way to Canada?"

"Follow the road into town. You'll see the border at the end of the bridge." Ken stares at the mangy dog. "You got a leash? They won't let you cross unless the dog's harnessed. Here take mine." He bends down and unclips Dimley's lead. Then he takes off his jacket. "And you'll need this. It gets mighty cold even in the summer months."

The man bows his head accepting his gifts. "I wasn't always like this. I was married. We had a kid. We lived in a neighborhood like this. Well, we better be getting on."

They move off, one limping, the other with a delicate prance. Then Ken and Dimley walk across the lot toward the far stoop light like it's calling them home.

\*\*\*

Voices wake him. For a moment he's not sure where he is. Then it comes to him. He's in the bedroom he shares with his older brother with the KISS poster and *The Hardy Boys* collection, the cheap stereo sitting on concrete blocks. The sheet is bunched up near Ken's chin. He's eleven years old and staring at the dark clouds out the window while his mom makes him breakfast. Andrew's dressed and out the door for his morning skate. He hasn't been asked yet. His older brother says give the old man time. He calls him that, old man, which cracks Ken up. Andrew is really, really good. Twice a month he trains with the state's best junior hockey players in St. Paul. Scouts from the North Stars and the best college programs in the country have contacted Dad. About Andrew's future. About him one day playing for his country against their sworn enemy, the Ruskies. Andrew's on a weight program, controversial as that is. Or that's what Cal says. His father, being a doctor, doesn't think eighth graders should do deadlifts and bench press their weight. Not that Dad cares. He only listens to himself. Andrew says Dad's his own man, something he thinks long and hard about. One day Ken wants to feel like his own man, too. But not if that means calling his kids words like Bonehead and Moron all because he can't skate like his brother. Andrew says not to let the old man get to him, that he's hard on him, too. Ken can't remember one single time his dad was mean to his brother. He even gets to eat steak and potatoes three times a week. Sometimes Andrew sneaks him pieces when the old man's not looking. Mom tells him in private that the family can't afford to buy red meat, not on a mill workers salary. "Now, if your dad was foreman, well, that's different." His mom's chatty and sweet, always joking around. When Dad talks, they nod along or laugh if he's telling a joke, even if it's not funny. Ken's not sure about his future, if he's got that something special that his older brother has. Andrew tells him not to worry. "Not everyone learns at the same speed. You'll find your way." He wants to believe him. He really does.

The rain hits the roof in slow steady knocks. His mom has her back to him at the kitchen sink. On the counter is his breakfast—wheat toast, bacon, two fried eggs. She turns hearing his hello and pulls off her yellow rubber gloves in the dress Kimberly got her last Christmas.

"If it isn't my Band Aid Boy."

She calls him that sometimes. As a kid he was always breaking arms and collarbones, getting stitched up in the ER from the stupid shit he did. He sits at the table his father built after his girlfriend got pregnant and they had to rush the wedding so townsfolk wouldn't gossip too much.

"You hear me come in?"

"Lord no," she says. "I sleep like a baby these days."

She walks up with his breakfast plate in one hand, the other a mug of coffee. His mom's shrunk. Like she was left in a dryer a little too long. In contrast, Ken feels titanic. Like he looms large.

"How long has he been here?"

Mentioning her live-in boyfriend has her Norwegian cheeks blazing red. "What with the fire, what could we do."

"Fire?" Ken sips the coffee. It's shit Folgers. Twenty years in the big city and he's a java snob like the liberals he loves to make fun of.

"Left a pan on the stove," she says, sitting down. "The fire department was called. Nothing burned, a little smoke is all. But they wanted him out."

Ken cuts into an egg so the yolk runs then slurps it up with a fork. Hungrier than he thought, he tears off a hunk of toast. She watches him eat with smiling eyes.

"How the boys?" she says.

"Brandon's back home. He got in a scuffle with his boss."

"At the pizza joint? No police involved, I hope."

"Nope," he says, lapping up yolk with bread. "But it cost him his job."

"Like father, like son," she says, clucking her tongue. "He needs a woman, someone headstrong, someone who can push back."

Ken thinks the comment is a dig on his marriage. His mom and Kimberly are cordial. They play fun on account of him and the boys. But friction exists.

"I'd be happy if he'd pay rent."

"It's hard on young people these days. I see them at church. All they do is play on those phones. They're not happy. When you and Andrew were kids you were outdoors. You got into good trouble."

He grins eating the bacon. He saved it for last. "Good trouble?"

"I'm frightened for them. I'm frightened for their future."

Dimley walks into the kitchen and lays his chin on Ken's thigh. He rubs his dog under the neck. "Bet you got to pee, huh, boy?"

"Sven took him out," his mom says. "How's our star athlete?"

"Jeremy made a decision. We need to respect that."

"He called the other day. I can't believe he lives in that city. I heard from a very reliable source that black men in Minneapolis drive around looking for white people to gun down."

"Minneapolis is safe, Mom. The only thing Jeremy needs to worry about is the water."

Her eyes grow big. "Did they find lead like in Flint?"

"Oh, it's much worse. The water in the Twin Cities is charged with liberal agendas."

She slaps the table. "Ha! Like that Bernie Sanders character!"

Her laugh makes him feel loved. "You got any Minute Rice?"

"Three slices of bacon, toast and eggs, and you're still hungry?"

"For Dimley, Mom."

He watches her busy herself in the kitchen, opening drawers, filling a pot with water. Rain taps the roof. She points at the upper cabinets. "Fetch me the rice." He does as she asks then leans against the counter while the water boils. Dimley lies at his feet. "Why are you here, Ken?" And he spills it out, well, minus the sordid details. He's always talked straight with his mom. They'd sit around the kitchen table late into the night, talking about school, girls, his struggles on the ice. His mom keeps moving, wooden spoon, measuring cup, salt, butter. She's not phased when he explains *the other woman* as he calls Nikki.

"Sven would call this a quandary."

"I'd appreciate if you'd keep this between us."

"Not even the prayer group?"

"Especially not those Nelly's."

The water boils. She pours the rice in the pot then moves the wooden spoon through it. "Marriage is hard work. Anyone who says differently should have their head examined."

"I wish I could take it all back."

"Give her time. She'll come around."

"Mom? Why don't you like my wife?"

She puts the lid on the pot then hands him the rice box. "Top shelf," she says. "And who says I don't like her?"

"Even the boys think so."

"Andrew once cut open a golf ball for a science project at school. Inside were hundreds of rubber bands, all tightly wound. That's your wife. Don't get me wrong. She's her own woman. I just want you to be happy."

"And Sven? He's staying?"

She bends down and pats Dimley's head. "In five minutes, you'll be good as gold, boy." His mom looks up at him. "Don't be silly. Of course he's staying. Let me know when five minutes are up. I'm watching *Fox News*."

And his little old mom waddles for the living room.

***

Ken feels a perverse freedom pulling away from the curb. He's come clean with his mom. He isn't temporarily set upon by circumstances outside his control. And in a couple hours he's playing golf with his best friend. If the weather cooperates. Though it doesn't look promising—low darting clouds fight for airspace with a thrashing rain. And what he wants more than anything is to be outdoors with the big open spaces. To have something to do, something to keep his mind occupied. Turning onto $13^{th}$ he sees a man in a long black coat walking a snow-white dog and repeats *dog food leash dog food leash* until the gimp's roped stomach is sharp in his mind. He squeezes his eyes closed and when he looks back out the windshield he's parked at Falls High. Ken has no recollection how he got here. Well, he drove. He just can't remember how he got from point A to point B like that.

The arena looks like a beached shipwreck. He hops down from the rig then hurries across the empty lot as if the space might split open and pull him in. The entrance door surprisingly clicks open— and this might be his current state of mind— like someone's expecting him. Inside is as quiet as a church and dark enough that he hangs back until his eyes adjust. Then he walks into the main hall with the huge wall of glass. He looks down at the rink and shadowy bleachers. Every time he comes here he feels the same—the pull of regret, those game situations he wished he could take back, his dad's harping. Ken was too tall. Ken had rocks for hands. Ken couldn't skate backwards if his life depended on it. There was no end to the badgering. "Why do you fart at the table? It's not funny. Does Andrew do that? Does Andrew complain about his mom's cooking? He says nothing because he's a good kid. I look at him and think—he looks like me, he's athletic like me, he makes decisions like me. But you? You're Frankenstein on skates."

The electronic scoreboard hanging from the rafters suddenly turns on. HOME TEAM 0, VISITORS 2. The clock's running down the last twenty seconds. "What the fuck?" he mutters under his breath. Ken looks around like this is a prank. Like any second now the rink manager's going to walk onto the ice and look up at the big window and start laughing his ass off. He watches transfixed—ten, nine, eight, seven, six, five, four, three, two, one—BLAAARREEEE. Then the scoreboard goes dark.

Goosebumps run down his neck. He feels something like a presence tapping him on the shoulder. Spooked, he hightails it outdoors and across the lot in a pelting rain. What the hell was that? His mind aches for something he can't put a finger on. He feels more lost than he did even last night. Why is he in International Falls? He should face his problems head on. Isn't that what he preaches to his boys? He heads out of town where the trees fall away and the sky loosens its hold on the land—past the county fair. His eyes latch onto a ride called Tunnel of Love. It's matte black with a string of cars ready to zip star-crossed lovers into the dark unknown. Ken still hasn't heard from Kimberly. *You're scaring me*, he writes. *Tell me you're okay.* Then he tosses the phone on the passenger seat. But he keeps glancing at it while he drives. Like it's a line of blow. How long before he sticks his nose over it and has himself a snort? That would clean the meat in his head, a thick juicy rail. He thinks about the old days. Ice hockey, fistfights, chasing women. And coke and booze to make the pain go away.

Worked up, he snatches the phone again. *You seen Mom?* he writes. *Talked to her last night.*

*Call her, Jeremy,* he types while driving. *Make sure she's okay.* He's coming on the golf course entrance when he clips past. A dark has taken over the sky. Crosswinds batter the truck. There's a feeling like a deluge is about to drop. Then out the window he sees this golden beam. It comes out of the gloom like something in a movie. Blinding in its light. Like divine intervention. Ken fights back a sob. It's just so beautiful. Like God's grace shining through.

Just as quickly the sky swallows shut.

The first raindrop is like a violent snap. More rain splatters the glass. Then all hell breaks loose. He can't see. Not the road from the fields from the sky. God is punishing his sorry ass. He's telling Ken he's a no good, selfish son-of-a-bitch adulterer. "Call Jeremy," he shouts into his smartphone. Mr. Talented. His youngest even looks like Andrew. And boy, can he play. Though hockey is a touchy subject right now. Kimberly warned him not to push his son. "If he wants to quit that's his decision, not ours," she said. "Three concussions in as many months? That's scary."

"Yeah, Dad?"

"Have you called her?"

"Why can't Brandon help? He lives with you."

"Will you please do me this one favor."

"Fine. By the way. What's that noise?"

"God's fucking wrath."

Again, he tosses his phone on the passenger seat and again he squints out the windshield at the gray sloshy mess. His phone rings. Thinking its Jeremy, he picks up the call. "Well?" he says.

"Well what, Ken Dog?"

Ah, Nikki Silver. He sees her the night they met in her tight jeans and busting out of a halter top. "It's over," he says over the noise.

"What?"

"It's over!"

"Then fuck you, Ken Dog!"

Nikki drops the connection. And Ken can't breathe. It's like being buried alive. In his panic he loses control of the truck. The backend swerves onto the shoulder, kicking up gravel. He thinks she might roll and jerks the wheel hard to his left. Then he slams on the brakes.

Jesus almighty. Sweat breaks across his temple. He sticks his face in the air conditioner vent and closes his eyes, taking in huge gulps of oxygen. All he sees are lies, one after the other, building like a body count, like a coming storm. He doesn't want to play golf anymore. He doesn't want to do anything.

It takes forever to catch his breath. His shirt sticks to the seatback and he's afraid to open his eyes. Then he feels something warm and bright on his face. And he blinks his eyes open. The world has changed. A brightness stings his pupils. Sunshine pours over the cornfields. The storm—if that's what that was—is gone, not a cloud in sight. He pulls up the hem of his shirt and wipes his face. He's not sure right now, about a lot of things. Sighing, Ken puts the truck in gear and drives to the golf course with two hands on the wheel.

His buddy is putting on the practice green. The moment Ken sees him he thinks to turn the truck around and park himself in the corner bar his old man used to frequent. Because Cal's going to hit him with that look. The one that says Kimberly is the best thing that's ever happened to him. And he fucked that up? No, he's got this. He can manage a few hours with the only friend he has left. He can keep his shit together for eighteen holes. So, he puts on his cleats, neglecting to tie them, grabs a crusty Twins cap, the Pings he bought from Cal a few years back, and trudges across the parking area like the damaged man he is.

Cal waits at the green's edge with his dimpled grin. He's fit like in his playing days and handsome as all get out. "If it ain't the late, great Ken Solberg." They man-hug, Cal and his putter, Ken gripping his bag like its luggage. "Shit, man. You're soaked through."

He pulls out his blade then drops the bag on the grass. "A five spot says I drain a putt in that far hole."

"You're on. And Noonan, by the fucking way."

Ken knows he'll miss standing over the ball. It's the intuitive shit we know before we know it that gets us every time. It's like the night he walked into that bar in St. Paul and saw Nikki sitting on that stool with her fake tan and white nail polish. He pulls the cocksucker wide.

"Double or nothing you miss yours."

"Shit, Solberg. Did you come all this way to hand over your hard-earned cash?" Cal taps the ball. It runs a clean noble line and disappears in the hole. "Must be my lucky day. Come on, its tee time."

They met the summer Ken's mom signed him up for tennis lessons. She thought the sport might be an activity her youngest could thrive in outside the shadow of his older brother. Off he went with a wooden racquet he found in the garage. The instructor was the pretty Carolyn Johnston, a sophomore at Falls High.

He and Cal were the best athletes in the class. There was something about the forehand that approximated a slapshot. Same went for a two-handed backhand. Though Cal was determined to hit his one-handed like the best player in the world, John McEnroe. Ken knew about the Johnston family. He'd gotten his hockey physical from Cal's dad. But he'd never said two words to Cal. Boys in town congregated around their neighborhood rinks. On top of that the Johnston's lived in a big house on Rainy Lake. To a ten-year-old that was like living in Canada.

Lesson over, Ken walked up to Cal. "You know what your sister said about practice?"

Cal wasn't tall like he was, but he had an easy sway in his shoulders. He was also sort of pretty. "Yeah, so."

"Wanna do that later?"

"Is your brother Andrew Solberg?" Ken rolled his eyes then made a grumpy nod. Everyone gushed over his brother, even this rich doctor's son. "I saw him play at Hahler. He favors his right when he skates."

"I told him the same thing."

"What time?"

"What time what?"

"Tennis, man."

"How's four."

"Cool. And be punctual. My dad says punctuality is the spice of life."

"He says what?"

They go at the first nine, down one fairway, then up another in a zippy cart. In golf terms, Ken is a grip-it-and-rip-it guy. Around the greens he has an okay touch that defies his size, but he gets his juice from coming out of his shoes off the tee. First three holes his mind is elsewhere, his game complete crap. He both wants to speak on his marriage and talk about something as benign as weather patterns. More than anything he wants reassurance that his life means something, that in cheating on his wife he hasn't squandered all that's inherently good.

Sunshine touches everything they see. Nothing is spared, not a blade of grass or a grove of pines. It's as if the storm only happened in Ken's head. Best not to think about that. Best to think about what's real—the gorgeous afternoon, playing golf with his friend. He reaches for the cooler behind the seats Cal was nice enough to remember.

"Brewski?"

"Still nursing mine."

There was a time not long ago when he could pacify his wife for some transgression on his part by greenlighting a new project around the house. But things are different now. The boys are grown men. Kimberly hangs with a new crowd. And the women at the interior design firm aren't like the ladies from the neighborhood. They drive German imports and dine at glitzy restaurants in Wayzata. They speak up for themselves and don't put up with their husband's bullshit.

Cal stops short of the fourth hole's back tees. The men walk around to where their bags are secured. "What you thinkin', big guy?"

"How far are those cattails?"

Cal digs in his bag for tees. "Two sixty or so."

Ken finally gets ahold of one. The ball soars off his driver like it's been shot into orbit. He feels whole, like he's transcended time and space. "Out drove you, Cally."

"Dial that one in the computer."

Back in the golf cart they go. They rush toward two white dots in an ocean of green. Cal has one hand on the wheel when he smacks Ken's leg. "I was thinking about your brother the other day. Remember his pep talk before we played Virginia?"

He's heard this story before. "That the year we went to State?"

"One and the same, brother. Before the third period he held forth about how we'd practiced our entire lives for that moment. The team took it in like it was Scripture."

"Even the coaches."

"Then Andrew flicked a backhander in the absolute top shelf with thirty seconds to go. He was golden, man."

The fairway is quiet underfoot, the river out of sight. Growing up, there wasn't much Andrew couldn't do. With everything—billiards, hitting a curve ball, beer pong—he was a cut above the rest. His phone shudders in his short's pockets. *She's home, hungover, watching the Tour de France.* He smiles to himself putting his phone away. "How's the department?"

Cal slows to a stop. They climb out of the cart then stand in the sunshine, hands on their hips, like general's surveying the battlefield.

"Fire chief is what I always wanted. But as head honcho you put up with a bunch of shit. Kids want three-week vacations from the get-go. They want paternity leave. We even got women firefighters."

"That's kind of hot."

"Not if you saw Madeline Dutton in her turnout trousers."

They each grab an iron then walk over to Cal's ball.

"You ever get lonely?" Ken says.

"Who says I'm not seeing someone?"

Athletes have a way of moving through their world, a way of competing that separates them from normal people. A great athlete believes whatever he's doing is the single most important next moment in his life. Jeremy owns that expression. So does Cal Johnston.

"You know her." Cal places the iron behind the ball then shifts from one shoe to the other until his balance feels even. "Or you did a long time ago."

Ken gives his friend a strange look. "Melody?"

And Cal swings. His shot, a high fade, gets lost in the sun before it plummets left to right, dead set on the flagstick. The ball rolls close to the pin.

"You okay with that?"

This hits him harder than he'd have thought. Like he knew this the whole goddamn time. "I'm happy for you."

"Well, I'm glad to hear that. The truth is, we're serious. I think Melody is the one."

He drags his iron the short distance to his ball. He's two football fields from a green shaped like a woman's hips and his heart is no longer in it. Which is stupid and pathetic and plain wrong. Why can't he be happy for his friend? Cal was the best man at his wedding, godfather to Brandon, and the first person he called after his dad passed.

Guys like Cal sort golf into rooms. Choosing the correct club is one room. Picking the target is another. Trusting your swing and blotting out the rest, still another. By contrast, Ken's room is like a galaxy far, far away. On his downswing, he sees Cal and Melody in a feverish embrace and whiffs so badly he almost falls over. Sweat rolls down his neck. The sun feels especially menacing. His next swing is fat like his face is. His shot bumps up the fairway maybe fifty yards. Because his day's off to such a smashing success, he murders a few innocent cattails with his four iron then chokes on their feathery stalks.

They play on, fifteenth, sixteenth hole, Ken's lost track. "You ever want to flee?"

Cal squats down, checking the line of his putt. "Flee?"

"Go. Start fresh. Like when you lived in California."

"Cost a fortune these days," Cal says, standing over his ball.

"I thought you loved San Diego."

Money was never a problem for Cal Johnston. It didn't hurt that his old man was a doctor. Ken went out to visit him when Cal was teaching golf in San Clemente. Cal comped the Chargers/Vikings tickets and green fees, the dinners out. At the time Ken felt locked into a life that was boarded shut. So Cal's generosity was appreciated. But as friends went, they were moving in opposite directions. He and Kimberly were saving to buy a house. They had a little runt running around in diapers. And Cal's life was like a car commercial shot in the desert—lots of sand dunes, hazy sunshine, and women with long hair whipping in the wind.

The putt's speed is good. But at the last moment the ball has a change of heart. If Cal's disappointed, it doesn't show on his face. "I liked San Diego, but my roots were here," he says, tapping the putt in the hole. "Is that why you're home, Ken? To find your roots?"

Ken's putt rolls past the hole ten feet. "That's good," Cal says, showing mercy.

The big man picks up his ball. Then he heaves it as far as he can.

"You hungry?" They're speeding toward the parking lot afterwards.

"Wish I could. My girl's got something planned," Cal says. "Hey, there she is now."

There she is. And they chase toward her at a far greater clip than he'd have imagined this morning. His friend is eyeing his girl without a line of regret on his face. It's late in the day and long thin shadows trail across the paved road. This is all too much. The times he's thought of her, Googled her, those tricks he's played on himself, basking in what wasn't quite real, stuck in time. And now she's getting realer with every heartbeat.

What will she think of him? Will she notice the twenty pounds he's put on since college? Will she see the fatigue in his bloated face? That weariness around his eyes from worry and stress? Will Melody Fillman take one look at her old boyfriend and think—*that fucking cheater.*

She leans against a compact SUV in the last slot of the last row, ten yards from the nearest car. Melody wears a hooded sweatshirt and shorts that ride high on her thighs, shorts his wife wouldn't be caught dead in, not because she can't pull off the look, but because she believes women should wear age-appropriate clothes.

Cal parks at a forty-five degree angle, stepping from the golf cart before it fully stops. "Hey, honey." He goes to her, and they kiss. Then he leans against the car. Cal's coy and a little wide eyed and for the first time all day Ken sees that he's rattled.

Her legs are brown like July and her hair feathered like in high school but without the 80s big hair thing. "So," she says looking at Cal. "Who won?"

"Ken has a lot on his mind, Mel."

He calls her Mel? And what does Cal mean? He hasn't said shit about his marriage.

"You up visiting your mom?"

His eyes rest on her for a brief second and he feels a pull in his heart. "Yeah."

"I run into her all the time. She looks great. Tell her I said hi." Melody pushes off the car then eyes Cal. "Cheryl and Tim are waiting."

"Yes, ma'am."

They're unstrapping their bags. Melody's climbing into her little truck when Ken catches a glimpse of her ass. A feeling stirs inside him, like a long clean burn. He knows this is wrong but in his present state he can't help himself. "I'm curious. Does she drive your firetruck, too?"

Cal's smile is a little too big. "I'm worried about you, man."

"What's that supposed to mean?"

"Nothing, an observation is all. Awe, shit, what do I know. Come here you, you big lug."

Something comes over Ken. His tough exterior gives way and he hugs the friend he loves like a brother as if it's the last time he'll see him on this here earth.

# GOLD BALLS

Sherman Garrity feels a strange thump in his chest. He's doing ninety miles per hour down the 405. Noise walls rise on both sides of a concrete corridor a city block wide with only a puny three-foot barrier separating north and southbound traffic. Thousands of bone-shattering steel and glass objects dart in and out of seven lanes at near-death speeds. At any moment a blown tire or driver absentmindedly texting—and *boom*, the good life is over. Another pop goes off in his cage. He's a film producer. He makes entertainment people fork over hard-earned cash for. Granted, no one goes to the movies anymore. Not with easily digestible distractions like smartphones, Netflix, and the coming presidential election at their disposal. In 2015, Hollywood is a different beast. Challenges exist. Like financing. Every picture has a budget. Every picture has a dream. And the dream takes money, organization, vision, hard work, talented actors, team chemistry, a positive can-do spirit, location scouts, caterers, drivers, post-production teams, costume designers, luck—a sound script. Sherman feels another tap in his sternum. *Jesus. Get ahold, man.*

It's the curse of the producer. What's that saying? What can go wrong will go wrong? Jonathan Lin represents a Chinese investor who wishes to remain anonymous. This unnamed person (Lin calls him Mr. Dollars & Sense) has so far deposited five of the thirty million dollars agreed to to fund the picture. But less than an hour ago Lin told him that Mr. Dollars & Sense would gladly finance the tennis flick in its entirety on one condition: the handsome protagonist loses to a Chinese player at the film's end. No problem, right? Tennis players lose all the time to Messrs. Nadal, Federer, and Djokovic. So why not a Chinese guy? Sherman had just gotten off the phone with Jonathan Lin for like the hundredth time that day. He was at his executive producer's glass contemporary in Manhattan Beach. He stood on the patio roof on a warm afternoon in July. The house was built on the hillside and had a view of the ocean's scope and bold color. Palms shot into the sky like the stalks of giant flowers. Tall slender women in tiny bikinis played volleyball down on the beach. His eyes ran the length of the coastline. Twenty miles away a beige ring floated above Malibu's desiccated brown hills. Which meant only one thing—fire.

Sherman wasn't the only person on the patio deck. The screenwriter they were interviewing sat under the umbrella. The young man was on his phone, talking with a buddy about the latest Kendrick Lamar single. "It dropped like today, bro. It's sick." He didn't understand young people, even if the kid was a probable shoo-in for the writer gig. Joshing with his bros at an interview was not cool.

His executive producer was Richard Blanco, the notorious 90s tennis star whom the film he was trying to make was about. The script was based on his bestselling memoir, *Sport*. The problem was *Sport* took itself too seriously. Richard Blanco (the character) was about as likeable as Richard Blanco (the producer). Unlikeable people might do fine in real life. But a movie protagonist needed charisma, a trusting smile. We had to care about his plight as much as we did our own problems. The working draft also lacked the lightness of dialogue that helped a film flit along merrily even as the story hit darker terrain. And the world needed laughter. We'd become a country of snarky, chatty trolls hiding behind Twitter feeds and our so-called tribes.

His phone pinged, another text from Jonathan Lin. *New development. You alone?*

He didn't trust Lin or the Chinese. He wasn't clear what he felt about Blanco, either. Sherman didn't know the ex-tour player well. But he could pretty much guarantee that Blanco wouldn't alter the story of his life to suit the Chinese. This was a player who never won a major. Nor had he overcome incredible odds like in so many biopics. Blanco came in privileged and retired the same way. What got his attention, after the sex, drugs, and rock-n-roll, was the subtext. Here was a man jam-packed with demons, something he could relate to.

Sherman was a tennis player, too. Maybe not at Blanco's level, but he wasn't far off. He'd been taught by the famed recluse, Del Evans. Del was in his seventies when he took him on for a sizable fee. The relationship didn't last long, not with Sherman's temper tantrums. What Del provided was a sound foundation. At present, he played #1 doubles for Bel Air Country Club's 5.0 team. He was proud of his sureness around the net and ability to angle volleys this way or that. Something he wasn't so proud of was his reputation for saying the phrase *Yours, man.* A crafty topspin lob outside his reach became a *Yours, man* moment for his partner, usually a twitchy young athlete who'd intercept the ball mid-flight or sprint down the arcing tumbler and send back a sky-high lob to keep the point alive. The longer a match went on the more he repeated his favorite of phrases. It was his partner's responsibility to cover for him. Sherman wouldn't accept anything less.

What did he want more than anything? The fame that had so far eluded him. In his mind, recognition by his peers, critical and box office success, would bring satisfaction, a feeling that his life meant something, that he hadn't squandered it all away; that after thirty years he'd finally done his mom proud. Then there was his father. During his career Sherman had produced two feature-length films, several shorts, and a television series for FX. Now, none of his projects were well received, but he'd finished them, hadn't he? He'd set goals and by God he followed through. But to his dad it meant nothing. And that's where *Sport* came in. He believed that greatness resided there. That Blanco's story held everything a movie needed—drama, a cool setting, a complex leading man, sex, *even love.* It was Sherman's job to bring the product to the people. He'd proved he was a good producer. Shit, had he ever *not* found the money?

His dad could help. The challenge was convincing him to invest when Locke made it clear he'd never in a million fucking years put another dollar into one of his projects. However, if *Sport* was what he thought it was, then everything between him and his father would change. After years of friction, they'd be just like him and his mom once were. They might even have an "I love you, man" moment. He was desperate. This project was his last hurrah. If it failed, not only might his producer days be over, he and his dad might never find their way.

His phone rang, waking him from his little reverie. "Yeah?"

"We're not at a crossroads, are we?" Jonathan Lin said.

"Blanco losing to a Chinese guy? Yeah, he'll fucking love that."

"Who's running the show? You or your executive producer?"

Sherman shifted his gaze to the home's panoramic floor to ceiling window wall. Inside was the ex-circuit player and his wife talking in their glossy modern kitchen. Heather Harper wore a snug little yoga outfit— white top, black bottoms. With her honey-blonde hair, sun-doused skin, and ample chest, she was the most beautiful middle-aged woman he'd ever laid eyes on (and he'd dated beautiful actresses, some famous, some not so much). Not that he was slipping down *that* wormhole. He saw his executive producer slide open the glass doors.

"I gotta run."

"We need to meet tomorrow." Something in Jonathan Lin's voice got his attention. "The restaurant is called Almond, on Abbot Kinney. And don't bring Blanco."

Then Lin aborted the call.

The tortoise shell sunglasses Sherman wore perfectly coordinated with his white dress shirt, linen slacks and suede bucks. If he was the pinnacle of style, then his business partner was the surfer guy who'd failed to grow up. Today he wore commuter shorts and a madras shirt. Gray showed at Blanco's temples and his cheeks bore worry lines, but veins popped in his biceps. For a man in his fifties, he was in tremendous shape.

They did that thing men of equanimity and power do and faced the ocean like they were looking over the spoils of their vast kingdom. The sun was big and round and blowtorch yellow. There were bands of dark water running convergent and two oil tankers near shore.

"Sporty but not rakish," Blanco said after a while. "And handsome. With great hair."

Sherman smiled. "Ah, I get it now."

"He can't look like our writer over there. You know, skateboarder emaciated. He needs to be a man of his time."

"A 90s man."

"Muscular with substantial thighs and forearms."

"And a horse's ass," Sherman said.

"Are you making fun of my booty, Garrity?" Blanco said, grinning. "Don't worry. I'll find the perfect actor to play yours truly."

He'd heard this all before. "I appreciate everything you've done. But casting isn't your job."

"The leading man needs to be a legit player. None of that CGI bullshit."

"Let's focus on our writer over there. We need him, remember?"

Blanco turned toward Sherman. His eyes didn't waver. "I want to co-produce. 50/50 on everything."

Or maybe Blanco was a big fat dick and that was all there was to say on the subject. Sherman's eyes found the water again. His mind was moving fast. If he said no, and he had every right to, Blanco might walk. So far, he'd more than held up his end. Like the tennis academy where Blanco trained as a junior. They got it for practically nothing. And when the All-England Club snubbed their noses at the idea of filming key sequences on Centre Court, Blanco found the perfect solution, an old money club in northeast London.

"How about points?"

"It's not about the money."

Sherman shrugged like it's always about money. They turned and leaned against the railing. The writer was chuckling to something he saw on his screen.

"What did Lin want?" Blanco said.

"How did you know I was talking to him?"

"Hunch."

Sherman pushed himself off the rail. "Come on. And play nice, okay?"

They sat opposite the young man under an umbrella shaped like a cloud-white sail. The kid wore a Tame Impala T-shirt and long black shorts that matched his sneakers. Blanco lectured on truths, truths about life, truths in film. Through the enormous window his wife diced vegetables at the kitchen island while talking on speaker phone. Sherman's girlfriend, the actress Ethereal Hunt, wanted to play Heather Harper in the film about her husband's life. The role called for lap dances, 90s spandex, and running the books at a gentlemen's club in Sarasota. His girlfriend was forty-two. She'd be convincing as a bosomy twenty-something in a G-string as Sherman would starring opposite her with Borg hair weaves.

His executive producer was telling the writer the scenes had to own an authentic realism, that without authenticity the film was fucked.

"He means verisimilitude," Sherman said.

"You see *Wimbledon*, screenwriter?"

"I usually catch the men's final, yeah."

"Not Wimbledon," Blanco said. "The movie with Paul what's-his-name. The guy married to Jennifer Connelly."

"Bettany?"

"What did you think of those tennis scenes?"

"In *Wimbledon*?" the writer said. "They were pretty good."

"Pretty good?" Spittle shot out of Blanco's mouth. "Pretty fucking good? Paul—"

"—Bettany?" the kid said, hesitantly.

"—Looked like he learned tennis watching a video game. That's not verisilimifuckingtude. Verisilimifuckingtude is *Bull Durham*. Kevin Costner is badass. He doesn't look like a player, he is one. You remember the batting cage scene?"

The writer wore wire-framed glasses. His dark hair ended at a widow's peak. And a pinkish hue had entered his cheeks. "I, um, well… I never actually saw the movie."

Blanco sat back in his chair like the writer said he was going to bone the lovely Heather Harper before the month was out. "You never saw *Bull Durham*?"

"I saw parts. Just not the entire film."

"Write these titles down: *Rocky, Rocky II, Major League*. Help me out, Sherman."

"*Field of Dreams.*"

Blanco smacked the table with his palm. "Field of fucking dreams."

The young man picked up his phone. "I thought I'd record our conversation. If that's okay with you."

Blanco stared at him a good five seconds. "Are you recording now?"

"Um, no. I thought I should get permission first."

"Permission fucking granted. Should I repeat the movies for your recording device, too?"

The writer's hands shook turning on the recorder. Blanco gave Sherman the smallest of smiles. "You okay, screenwriter?" he said. "Can I get you a water or something?"

"Would you mind?"

"Heather?" Blanco shouted through the thick glass. Then he pointed at the young man. "Can you bring our friend here a glass of water?"

She was cutting an onion into two halves when she set the knife on the countertop. Meanwhile, the writer had removed his glasses, which were steaming up. "I biked over from Playa Vista. I guess I haven't cooled down."

"You cycle?" Blanco gave him a quick once-over. "The boys and I are riding tomorrow, an easy sixty. You should join us." He glanced at his producer. "You and Van Doorman in?"

Sherman remembered the secret meeting with Lin. "Can't. Something came up."

Heather walked onto the patio holding a tall glass of iced water. The moment they saw her they grew silent and obeisant like men do when an attractive woman enters their sphere.

"Our screenwriter has never seen *Bull Durham*, honey."

Heather set the glass on the table then glanced at the young man. "Is my husband playing nice?"

The kid brought the cold glass to his forehead. "That's not exactly true. I've seen parts."

"I'm playing nice, right, Garrity?"

She turned her blue eyes on him. She reminded Sherman of the 70s TV actress Linda Evans, whom his father briefly dated after his mom died. "He's on his best behavior."

"Let me know if you need anything else." And she went back indoors.

"Where were we?" Blanco asked the men.

"Batting cages."

Blanco pushed back his chair then stood. "In the batting cage scene, he and Susan Sarandon are having a sexy back and forth. The audience knows he digs her and she him. But she's committed to Tim Robbins."

"She did marry the guy," the writer said.

"Save the jokes for the script," Sherman said.

"Picture Costner and Sarandon slinging one-liners back and forth while the pitching machine hurls ball after ball. You with me, screenwriter?"

"Flirty jokes, pitching machine, got it."

Blanco stood facing the writer and held a pretend bat in his hands.

"Costner chokes up like this. Sarandon says something he finds irresistible, and he turns his back on the machine. A ball screams past his head. You think Costner is fazed? Sarandon then says something flirty. Costner turns and takes the next ball into centerfield. With one fucking arm, screenwriter. That's a metaphor about them. He's going to knock them out of the park. That's good writing. That's verisimilitude."

"I saw *Royal Tennebaums*."

"Good," Blanco said. "We know about Ritchie's breakdown. We take in the Borg clothes. Luke Wilson doesn't try to oversell his tennis skills. And he's ten times the fucking player Paul whatever his name is. Anything else, Sherman?"

"Humor?"

"You read my book, right? So, you know I'm a fucking hilarious guy. Humor them and they will come."

"Hey, that's a reference to *Field of Dreams*."

"He's fucking learning. This screenwriter just might do. What's your name again?"

Back on the 405, traffic zips along like it's Sunday afternoon. A lane opens like the universe is availing itself for him alone and he throttles the accelerator down. God, he loves this car. This is the 72' 911 coupe with black leather seats, aubergine paint, and original Fuch alloy wheels. The Germans and their intuitive design. Everything inside within reach. This one's the hood knob, that one cranks the heat. The bucket seat cradles him like a reassuring hand. This was his first car, his sixteenth birthday gift. Like all firsts, the Porsche held a certain rank. Like his first gold ball. Or the first time he got laid. Or the day he realized he was alone in the world.

Sherman holds his iPhone to his lips. "Siri? Get me Van Doorman."

"Calling Van Doorman," his sexy-voiced digital secretary coos.

His trusted assistant picks up on the first ring. "Sir?"

"I want a three-way. You, me and Blanco."

"… three-way, sir?"

The anemic Toyota he's following, brakes. He downshifts then slots the sports car one lane over snugly behind an M5 hurtling down the middle lane. "Listen for subtext, the Blanco bullshit. Oh, before I forget. What are your thoughts on Locke?"

"As in securing funds for our film, sir? Speak from the heart."

"You know what my dad said last time. To him, film ended with *Rio Bravo*." Sherman feels another pull in his chest. "Just set up the conference call."

His eyes find the hills, mired like they are in a soupy haze. Los Angeles needs a bath, a long hard rain to wipe the scum off the hills. The city is in crisis-mode. Trees are dying or already dead. Everywhere the eyes roam you see the same weary bake-potato brown. The drought of the century is having a weird effect on him. He's always thirsty. He isn't sleeping well, either. It's like when he was a kid and had nightmares the big one hit and Southern California fell into the sea.

Then there are his wealthy neighbors.

The looks they give Sherman sitting high up in their limited-edition Land Cruisers and gold-plated Bentleys. As if he's the filmy haze in the hills. He can't control his dad. Locke is like the feral animal in those 80s horror-comedy's the charismatic hero naively believes he can tame. He says people his age bore him, all that griping, all those bodily complaints. He plays tennis daily. Then he works the land, mowing, weed whacking, cutting back brush. And he waters. Oh, does he irrigate the grounds. A local television station did an exposé at the height of the drought called "The Wet Prince of Bel Air." Not long after came the threatening letters, the hefty fines. His dad lived through Nixon and the Vietnam protests, the Clinton impeachments, and this nonsense called our current political malaise. He lost his wife thirty years ago in a freak accident. You think he's intimidated? Sherman's father waters the lawn too much. So fucking what? He's eighty-four years old.

Nerves over financing has him speed-dialing Ethereal. "You wouldn't believe traffic," he says. "I'm flying and its five in the afternoon."

"Why a stripper, Shermy? Why not a special needs teacher? Or a budding playwright? Why all the flashes of tits and ass?"

"Tits and ass sell. You know that."

"I'm not joking. I've read the script. It's cliché."

"We think the new writer will help."

"Listen to the word. *Strip. Her.* I can't think of a viler, more pointed word in the English language. And lap-dancing her man? How humiliating."

"Did you take your Lexapro this morning?"

"Don't patronize me, Sherman Garrity."

Ethereal's real name is Sarah Bowels. She was an eccentric child though frequently constipated. She liked playing dress up, had an imaginary friend named David Alistance, and loved *loved* Julie Andrews. She spilled all of this to him in a whirlwind conversation in the waiting room the day they met—right before he got calf implants.

"You know my hands are tied. Gil has last word on casting."

"It's your picture, Shermy. Persuade the man."

He sees her vanilla taffy hair, those luminous gray eyes, her small teeth. "I think Lin's serious."

"Does the Chinese guy beating Blanco change the story's arc?"

"Tough to say."

"Then tell Blanco to fuck off."

"I wish I had your courage."

"Shermy? Why are you going to Wisconsin?"

A clunky van changes lanes without signaling. Sherman hits the horn, drops the beast into third, then slides a further lane over. "I told you. The sailboat. And it's a real beauty." Until now, he's never involved himself with a married woman. And Kimberly is the opposite of Ethereal. She's also the doppelgänger of his first love, Juliet Day. In fact the first time he saw her he thought *oh my god, that's her, that's Juliet after all this time*. Even after he realized it was only an uncanny resemblance, he found her mature and pleasantly midwestern. They started texting. This progressed to sexting. Then Sherman flew her to the house in Aspen when her idiot husband was at a hockey tournament in Winnipeg. The moment he saw her shoot down the fall-line of an icy steep run he'd fallen hard.

Up ahead he sees a trail of brake lights glowing up Mulholland Pass. Something like hope breaks apart at the seams inside him. So much for making Bel Air in record time. Live in LA long enough and you begrudgingly accept congestion as a major force in your life. Still, he's about to put his body through a grueling workout. How fantastic is that? It's with this enthusiasm that he calls his old man. Traffic's slowing when his father picks up the line.

"Hi, Dad. How's it going?"

The pause feels excruciatingly long. "Henrique and I are working the north sector."

"Put him on."

"He wants to talk with you," his dad says. Henrique's grandparents, Esme and Carlos Quintero, have worked for the Garrity's since Sherman was a child. After Henrique's mom moved to Ensenada with her latest boyfriend, Locke took an interest in the boy, enrolling him at Harvard-Westlake then arranging tennis and piano lessons.

"Yeah, Sherman?"

"What's going on, little man?"

"We're clearing brush on the ridge. That way if a fire comes through, and the way things are going, it's not if it's going to happen, but when."

At fourteen, Henrique is a budding environmentalist. He's installed low-flow toilets in Garrity Manor's twelve bathrooms and overseen the re-insulation of the attic with R-60 batt. The family now composts and has a rain garden (if it ever rains again). The only thing Henrique can't get Locke to agree on is not watering the property so fucking much.

"Sounds like a solid plan," Sherman says. "Put him back on."

His dad makes a racket bringing the phone to his mouth. "Yes?

"Have you thought about our conversation?"

"About the money?" The Porsche and like a thousand cars come to an immediate standstill. "Let's talk in the morning."

The line goes dead. Sherman stares out the windshield with his hand resting on the gearshift. Heat vapor blurs the rows and rows of cars stalled on the pass. He's not sure how to interpret his father. He hadn't outright said no. There's that. And talking in the morning implies a negotiation, right? But what if his dad's toying with him? Tomorrow, when they talk, his dad dashes his hopes once again.

Traffic begins inching along. His phone rings. Sighing, he hits the green call button. "Yes, VD?"

"Mr. Blanco's on the line, sir."

"Two points." There's a conviction in his voice that feels powerful. "Take it or fucking leave it."

"Fine, two points," Blanco says. "Let's draw up the contract Sunday."

"I'll be in Wisconsin looking at a sailboat."

"What about our fucking movie?" Blanco says. "You know what this sounds like? Like you're meeting a piece of ass on that island of yours."

"I told you," Sherman says. "I'm buying a boat."

Blanco laughs. "Now, you're buying? Better get that story straight before you talk to your girlfriend."

"Fuck you, Blanco. And I don't *own* the island. Jesus."

\*\*\*

It's well after five when he drives down a quiet street off Bellagio and pulls behind his assistant's Jeep Rubicon. Sherman's reaching for his gear in the backseat when his phone pings. *Are we really doing this?*

He smiles, typing Kimberly back. *Packing this second. May have a little business on the island. Hope that's okay.*

*Guess I'll have to hide your phone.*

*Hide and seek? Love that game.*

*Til Sunday.* 💋

Van Doorman exits his 4x4 wearing running shorts and a heart monitor secured around his chest. He does explosive high knee jumps on the shady street. Sherman is putting his iPhone in the glove box when it rings. He winces, seeing who it is. "Yes, Ethereal?"

"Did you show him my tits?"

"You mean the Polaroid you gave me?"

"No, Shermy. I thought it best if you sat Blanco down and described my breasts using your powers of imagination."

"I'm sort of busy."

"You promised me the stripper wife."

"I never promised anything, and you know it."

She starts crying. Sherman makes eye contact with his assistant through the windshield then lifts his finger like the call might take a minute.

"Have you told him?" she says, sniffling.

"Hmm?"

"Your dad. How much the film means to you."

"...not yet."

"Go in expecting him to say yes."

He lets out a loud sigh. "I really have to go."

"Are you meeting a woman on Madeline Island?"

"I'm looking at a boat, remember? Huge cockpit, two quarter cabins—a brand-new galley."

"The bullshit level is very high, Shermy."

He fudges his thumb in a mark on the dash. "You're overthinking this. Make the tape. I'll see you later."

"I hope Madeline Island is everything you want and more. Just try not to kill yourself. In case you forgot, that's where your mommy died. By the way, I've moved out."

"Ethereal—"

She's already hung up. They've been together a couple years. From the outset, he knew what he was getting into, that she was prone to drama and unpredictability, that her happiness to some extent was predicated on if she was working and what sort of acting was called for, if she was stretching herself as an artist. Her challenging him was what initially attracted him to Ethereal. But lately, her antics only tire him out.

Sherman dresses on the street like surfers do—doors ajar. Van Doorman is shaking out his limbs like a swimmer. His latest assistant is from a long line of midwestern boys with a knack for multitasking. But also (and way more importantly) a prowess on the tennis court that borders on magnificent—*yours, man* material all the way. Sherman sets them up in apartments. He gets them teaching jobs at clubs in West LA. The best of the bunch, whom he sees like his golden boys, not only win when called upon, they can disguise their playing level until it matters most i.e. the USTA League Team National Tournament. To date, he's won seven gold balls.

"Any dirt on Jonathan Lin?" Sherman says.

Maybe his greatest doubles partner sticks half his body through the Jeep's open window and comes out holding a pocket-size spiral. Van Doorman licks a finger then shuffles through several pages. "Parsons grad, design major, worked for a startup in Newport Beach before current gig. Lives in Mid-Wilshire."

"And he's from Beijing?"

His assistant looks up from his pad. He's bronze and extremely fit with grooves in his abdomen that resemble a corrugated roof. "By way of Arcadia, maybe."

"You mean Lin is American?"

"I thought you knew that, sir."

Shoes tied, runner's tank pulled over his head, Sherman knocks out a few jumping jacks. "Then explain his ties with the Chinese?"

Van Doorman scratches his golf pencil behind his ear. Again, Sherman admires the spidery veins showing through his stomach wall. "Because he's Chinese?"

"Don't get smart with me, VD."

"I'm working on it, sir."

Sherman checks his heart monitor. "Shall we?"

"One more thing, sir. The screenwriter turned us down."

What else can go wrong today? "Did he say why?"

Van Doorman reads from his pad. "Privileged white pricks peddling a bloated script about an asshole has-been tennis pro."

"Well, that leaves us one writer short."

"I saw Gil scribbling on a napkin yesterday."

"Our director's got too much on his plate already."

Van Doorman opens his mouth as if to say something more. Instead, he drops the notepad on the driver's side bucket seat. "Ready, sir?"

They take off at a brisk pace. His assistant explains the day's workout—three-mile warmup with 8:00, 7:30 then 7:00 clips. By then they'll be in the canyons for intervals at full intensity (heart rate threshold 180), then a ten-minute cool down to the car where they'll drink electrolytes then bro-hug before Sherman dashes home for a quickie with Ethereal. Oh, right, she's left him.

"How's the weekend shaping up?"

Van Doorman is barely breathing. "The driver arrives Sunday, 0900, sir."

"And the hotel?"

"The Hewing, Minneapolis's North Loop. Reservations at Spoon & Stable. Recommended, sir. The tournament is called Aquatennial."

"Sounds like a swim meet."

"That's a good one, sir. But no. Land of 10,000 lakes. All joking aside, we're talking downtown lunch scene, sectioned off court, spectators. It's right up your alley."

The tennis bit embarrasses him. He wants Kimberly to see him good at something other than being a privileged white prick pedaling a bloated film script. They're climbing a steep hill. Sherman sees himself playing the game he loves. His running forehand when he doesn't lift his head on follow-through, those heavy serves he pounds in the corners when he feels like a champ. Van Doorman glances at his Bell & Ross 42-mm steel timepiece, a Christmas gift from his boss, before remembering his fitness watch is on the opposite wrist. "Ease up, sir."

Both men trim back their strides cresting Chantilly Road. The houses—1950s California Ranches with white picket fences and horses in the pasture—are built close to the street. He believes this part of the world is paradise.

"We almost lost Gil, sir."

Sherman shoots a harried look at his assistant. "During his lesson?"

"He collapsed."

He grimaces with a rise in the road. He'd set money aside from his own private stash. What better way for his director to learn the game's nuances then getting his hands dirty. And he almost died?

"I want you working him out four times a week. I don't need Gil dying on me until he's through directing my picture. Have him join me and Lin tomorrow. And bring him up to speed."

"Let's pick it up, sir. We need a 3:05 the last half mile to make the threshold."

And they both kick harder and sure enough the two are propelled faster down the street. They're coming on Roscomare Road. Sherman can taste metal on his tongue and his eyes are shellacked over. He sees finish lines and crowds erupting in cheer then something like hundred-dollar bills falling from the sky. He thinks about his old man. He'll need a good speech if he's to squeeze him for cash in the morning. Then he sees that photo Kimberly sent the other day. She wore a summer dress that showed off her tan legs. Those blue eyes of hers he couldn't exactly read. He's confident she's never been under the knife. What if he marries her? Doesn't he deserve a bit of domesticity like his parent's had before his mother's tragic end? He pictures Kimberly Solberg again. This gives him a surge of adrenaline. Then the men are plunging through thick rushed air, toward the brown hills, with more intervals on the horizon.

# PROVE IT ALL NIGHT

Ken stands in line at an off-sale liquor store outside Littlefork. Day four of his sequester up north and still no contact from his wife. Two nights back, he made it as far as Hibbing. Half-drunk, in no shape to go home and beg forgiveness, he turned the truck around. In a desperate move, he'd brought the boys in, but they've kept their distance, not wanting to get caught in the middle. Last time he spoke with his oldest, Brandon asked where things stood. "With that other woman?"

"She has a name, Dad."

"It was over a long time ago."

Brandon didn't respond right away. "Mom's under a different impression."

His turn in line Ken makes eye contact with the cashier. "Peppermint schnapps. And Marlboro Lights, soft pack." The cashier grabs the bottle off the shelf then scans the cigarette brands in the built-in over his head. He's around his boy's age. A tattoo inches up his neck like a black vine. More ink in green and red hues mark his arms. Ken hands him his Mastercard. "You sell lighters?"

The kid digs in his jean's pocket then moves an orange lighter like a shell game across the scratched counter. "Borrow mine. I'll be right out."

"Much obliged."

He steps outdoors with the bottle under his armpit. The light is orange and radiant and illuminates the bugs and dust particles in its path. Twilight in the northern territories. His mouth waters breaking the pack's cellophane seal. The cigarettes smell cool and bitter. They smell like taboo. He lights one and the smoke dries his throat. Then it goes to his head. Twisting the cap off, he takes a neat pull on the bottle. The thick, syrupy drink coats his teeth and tongue.

The liquor store door opens and out walks the kid with an unlit smoke between his teeth. He wears skinny jeans and sneakers that seem too big for his feet. They smoke and cars roar past and the night is warm and humid. He looks him over with a discernible eye. "You know they're permanent, right?"

"The ink?" The young man grins. "Heard that one before. I think I'll be exploring tatts for a long time, yeah."

"You know what I mean, Spicoli."

"Spi-whati?"

"I wouldn't hire a guy with tattoos like that. You'd scare the customers."

"I got a job at this here store."

"I respect that. My kids got tattoos. My point is—what's next?"

"Like tonight?" he says, lighting another cigarette. "Heading to a friend's. We're watching *Blue Mountain State*. It's a trip, man."

Ken takes a final hit then flicks his smoke at the gas pumps. "I mean with the rest of your life."

"I'm riding out the storm, man."

Ken steps off the curb, toward the F-150. *Riding out the storm.* He likes that.

"Can I ask you something? What's with your face?"

Instinctively, Ken touches where the blow happened. "Fight, a long time ago."

"That's what I figured," he says. "You're one of those bad-asses, huh?"

"Later, kid. And good luck."

"Don't need no luck when I got me a smoke and these here good looks."

"Sure thing, Spicoli."

Ken climbs back into his rig and drives off. He's speeding along when Nikki fires off four rapid texts.

*FUCK*

*YOU*

*KEN*

*DOG*

The night they drank mescal and smoked weed comes to him. The drug was strong and had him spinning. He'd stumbled outdoors at high noon and into the street her trailer sat on with its calcified siding and broken lattice. Her squat lawn. For space to breathe. For a semblance of control. To take back his life again. Because in that moment high as fuck he felt like he'd lost himself. And the world outside Nikki's singlewide had sucked him dry. Ken feared one moment bleeding into the next.

Nikki kicked open the door then spilled her drink clamoring down the steps in a tank-top that barely held her breasts. Then she stubbed her toe on a carjack lying in the grass. Her cracked nail sounded like lumber splintering in two. She hopped around with her big bouncy tits, purple running between her toes, and screaming like it was the end of times. Neighbors poked their heads out their trailers, laughing and taking screenshots. He tried urging Nikki inside. But it was like dragging a scared, wounded animal over a cliff. She pestered some lady about her four DUI's. She told some guy named Glen she'd seen bigger dicks on babies. Then she pointed her rage at him. "Do I even know you! Take your fucking hands off me, asshole!"

All Ken could think about was his beautiful wife and his beautiful boys. All he wanted was not to be high and loosed from this place for good. Glen helped him coax Nikki inside. He washed her wound then watched over her until she passed out. Surprisingly, he made it home without being pulled over by the police. He told himself—never again.

Then came the photos. She sent them every couple days. They were nasty and titillating and shameful and wrong. The pics totally turned him on. And so, he went back.

There's a price to pay for loneliness, for indulgence, for lust and greed. There is a price. And its steep.

\*\*\*

If Ken had an infatuation in middle school, it was Fleetwood Mac's Stevie Nicks. There was something about her throaty, comforting voice that had him sitting up and taking notice. He thought "Dreams" was the coolest, saddest, moodiest song ever written. Whenever the song came on the radio something changed inside him. He became more intent and subdued; more introspective. He'd see himself from the outside looking in. The big bad world and him inside it. He not only felt safe inside "Dreams" he longed for a girl like Stevie Nicks.

By then he was spending more time at Cal's house than his own. They were way into music, Cal the mellow gold Southern California sound exemplified by bands like The Eagles and Jackson Browne, and Ken bands that rocked, like AC/DC and Led Zeppelin. With listening, they had a system. If Ken played the first song, Cal got the next two. Then Ken got two, Cal one, and so on. The system worked until Ken was selecting songs like "Stairway to Heaven" and "Free Bird"—mini-overtures that clocked in at eight minutes or more that had Cal pissing in his undies mad because outside "Hotel California" (6:31), the West Coast scene didn't have the know-how or balls to record anything over five minutes in length. After much whining on Cal's part, it was agreed that they'd each get three songs in succession, none over five minutes in duration. They held that number hard. There was no going over, not even one second, or it might lead to a wrestling match that knocked over a flower arrangement that got Cal's mom all hot and bothered and hating on Ken, when half the time it was her son's fault.

People thought they were brothers. They drove to school together. They took the same classes and cheated on the same exams. They drank the same cheap-ass beer, wore their yellow-blonde hair mullet style, and dated the cutest cheerleaders on the squad, Melody Fillman and Janet Hallstrom.

Then Andrew died. And everything changed.

International Falls and hockey had a complicated romance. In 1986, he alone lured the townsfolk into Bronco Arena when the temperature outdoors was minus twenty-eight degrees Fahrenheit. With Andrew leading the way, no one lost their job or beat their spouses or died in a car crash out on highway 53. No one caught a cold or was ever sad. The town came together like America had during the great wars.

And Andrew was their hero.

And what was not to love. This was Harvard bound Andrew Solberg. He had a sturdy jawline and ready smile for the camera. He had great hair. In games the eyes naturally found #3 (an homage to I Falls own Bronko Nagurski). On the ice Andrew had that extra gear. He found space to shake staunch defenders or find a sprinting wingman breaking along the boards. And Andrew scored at will. He scored with abandon. He scored as if he and the opposing goalie had worked out a deal beforehand.

But then the town hero died.

In death, they held a parade with Bronko leading the procession of cars down Main. Shop owners and men coming off their shifts at the mill paid respect at the curb. Children and mothers wept. Thousands packed inside St. Thomas Aquinas. It was as if part of the town died alongside Andrew and the others. Ken was there the night he died. He held his brother's hand and knelt in the snow after and cried like he'd never cried before. His brother was dead and he'd always be dead and from that night forward Ken would never be the same. Death was as serene and final as the sound the horn made—that mournful blare—at the end of regulation.

The day of the funeral he threw his skate bag over his shoulder, grabbed Andrew's hockey stick, then plodded through the snow to the rink across the street. The neighbor kids scattered when he stepped onto the ice. He skated with his head down. The more he thought about his brother the harder he pushed the blades into the corners and sprinted the straightaways. Tears streaked down his face and his heart thundered in his chest. Ken felt his brother's love and for a little while all was right with his world.

In school a week later Coach Lofgren stopped him in the hall. He told him it was his team now. "I know you're hurting. But here's your chance to wrestle your demons down and be the leader you're so capable of being." Ken made a joke about for once not wanting to be late for class. Coach chuckled with tears in his eyes. Right then in the hall between classes, being the team captain, wrestling the demons down, were the farthest thing from his mind. He saw himself inside a Springsteen song. He and Melody driving off in a fiery display of love and independence. They'd drive into the sunset and get married by a judge and live in an apartment over a drugstore that had a long counter and sold cheeseburgers and a malt for a dollar and change. He'd work in a filling station where employees wore uniforms with red pinstripes. His shift over, he'd drink Coca Cola on the walk home. Melody would greet him at the door, done up pretty and nice. The apartment would be tastefully furnished, the focal point being a big soft bed. There'd be no more fucking in the backseat of cars. Ken and Melody would be legit, a real couple. He'd give up this silly dream of playing professional hockey. He'd act grown up and pay his bills on time, attend Sunday Mass, and eat dinner every night with his lovely wife. She'd get pregnant and would glow like those calendar pinup girls that hung on the wall of the mechanic shop where he changed oil and pumped gas. His boss would tell him he was the luckiest guy in the world. Ken would face his challenges with good old American perseverance and spunk. His days would fly by with sunniness and wit. Life would be one big happy ending. This was the dream in the months after Andrew died. This was the dream he repeated so he didn't fall prey to darker notions like ending his life.

*\*\**

Nightfall and not a leaf stirs. Ken idles outside his mom's home. On the car radio is the very first *King Biscuit Flower Hour*, the 1973 rebroadcast which included a young singer named Bruce Springsteen. He opens the Schnapps and has a taste. In the living room he can see his mom and Sven lit by the television screen. He dials the landline then watches her get up from her recliner to walk into the kitchen. It's strange how he feels. He's a slapshot from his childhood home but feels farther away than when he calls from the metro.

"Ken?" his mom says into the phone. "Is that you?"

He hangs up, not wanting to explain where he goes or what he does, what he thinks about his best friend dating his high school sweetheart. In no time he's cruising through town like he has every night this week. Dinner tonight is McDonalds. The girl at the pickup window is blue-eyed, Nordic, and on the chunky side. His eyes flash on her nametag.

"How's your night been so far, Krystal with a K?"

"Can't complain."

While she runs his credit card he steals another taste of nectar. Then he digs in his cup holder for loose change. Krystal is back in no time with his tidy paper bag. "Here, this is for you," he says with his arm outstretched.

"Aw, that's so nice. But we can't accept tips."

She's leaning out the drive-thru window when Ken takes hold of her wrist when that voice in his head says *drive away, just blow this fucking popsicle stand, man.* He turns her arm over. Delicate blue veins show through her pale skin. She's inked too—a star with something like a dagger shot threw it. He pours the coins in her palm then squeezes her hand shut.

"Give it to Ronnie's kids." The girl pulls her arm back inside McDonalds then rubs where he touched her. "You kids and your tats. Sorry Krystal with a K. I'm having a weird week."

Then he hits the accelerator and blasts into the night scarfing down French Fries.

An hour later he's parked outside the church with the steeple that touches the sky. Time feels spongy and stretched, like its standing still. Ken takes a nip from the bottle while eyeing the façade then pockets it and crosses the street. Attending mass was a testament to his mom. She likened Christ to eternal happiness. That and being a prodding stick to keep her boys on the straight and narrow. Last time he was inside St. Thomas was Thanksgiving holiday. The church that Saturday night was empty but for a couple dozen scattered believers. Most were old and slouched and didn't take off their coats. He'd had a powerful vision. During the Sacrament, when the priest lifted the chalice and spoke to the blood of Christ, Ken saw clear as day his mother's death. She was lying in an open casket on a sandy beach in clothes picked out for a funeral. The image was so vivid, so haunting, that he felt a great rip in his heart. He reached past Kimberly and took hold of his mom's hand with tears in his eyes.

"May I help you?"

It's the young priest who presided over mass last November. Once St. Thomas had two priests, a brother, and a couple nuns. Now only this young man saves souls.

Ken sits halfway up the pews. "I knew Father Merriweather."

The priest's face softens. He's slim, mid-thirties, with a beard like Brandon's. "I came on after Father Merriweather passed. I'm Father Austin. And you are?"

"Name's Ken."

The priest rests a hand on the pew. "Are you here to confess your sins?"

He believes in Jesus Christ being the son of God. He believes the Eucharist is Jesus's flesh and blood. But like so many things, he's lost touch with the church. His eyes find the crucifix. Jesus is plain wrong hanging in that quasi-room behind the alter and halfway cut off from the congregation. It's like viewing Jesus behind plexiglass. Or like the time he and Cal saw the Bruins play in the old Garden and having to peer around a steel column.

"Have you been to Notre Dame, Padre? Those churches in Europe smell like thousand year old dust. There's something about their size and ambition that makes you feel insignificant. But also, a believer in mankind."

The priest cocks his head. "I think I know what you mean."

Pointing at the hanging cross, Ken says, "I never got him in there. Even as a kid it perplexed me."

"Jesus has risen. He gave his life to save us."

"I mean him hanging in back. You can't even see him from some pews."

"Why is it important to see Jesus to believe?"

He feels the bottle wedged in his short's pockets. He really wants a drink.

"True belief is based on faith," the priest continues. "Not seeing is believing."

This is why people of the cloth frustrate him. Their inability to understand nuance. "The church was half full. Doesn't that bother you?"

"Being a priest isn't a popularity contest."

"I remember thinking if Jesus were *inside* the church, then maybe we wouldn't feel so lost."

"Ah, now I see. You feel lost."

He sighs, seeing the trap he's set for himself. Ken takes out the bottle. "Care for a pick me up, Padre?" The priest gives him a monumentally disappointing stare. "Suit yourself." He toasts Jesus in his sarcophagus. Then he has a taste.

"You know how this looks to me? Like you're looking for a reason not to have Christ in your life."

Ken shrugs like the man has a point. He takes a more contemplative pull on the bottle. "I've done things. Things I'm ashamed of."

"Jesus forgives those who truly repent."

"Can I ask you something else?" he says, screwing the cap in place. "Do you think you'll one day be obsolete?"

"Obsolete? How so?"

"Is there a future for organized religion?"

Now it's Father Austin whose gaze is drawn toward the crucifix. "What kind of world will it be if God's light doesn't shine through?"

"Everything dies, everything ends."

"Not God's love."


He's clear out at the Galvin line, parked a hundred yards off the road with the engine turned off. A weepy honky-tonk from some bygone era plays on the radio. The night sky is clear, the stars a milky smudge. Ken finishes the Schnapps then chucks it out the window. There's something itching inside him, something wanting out. Another song comes on, one of those yodeling twangy numbers from someone like Hank Williams. This was the stuff his old man listened to. They never reconciled, even when the end was near. What he remembers about his old man were his hands. He had stubs for fingers, fingers that didn't bleed, the fingers of builders, carpenters and plumbers. Farmer's hands. Other things he remembers … the faint smell of cigarettes and aftershave coming off him, those hard blue eyes. His old man never hugged him. He never told Ken he loved him, either. Years after he passed, his mom told him his dad was proud for him getting a full ride to UMD. Said he thought he was the toughest son-of-a-bitch he ever saw on the ice. Hearing that, even second hand, hit him hard. Ken had to clamp down his emotions so they didn't spill over. Now, sitting in the middle of nowhere, he feels boxed in, like there's no way out. He turns the ignition key over and heads back into town. Yes, the itch is back.

# EVERYBODY WANTS TO RULE THE WORLD

Sherman is splayed out face down on his king-sized bed as if he'd fallen from a great height only to meet a bloody end with an unforgiving sidewalk. The sheets smell like Ethereal—lavender and an exotic spice he can't quite place. It's daybreak at Garrity Manor. He slept terribly, worried about the almighty dollar, worried about the scorched earth, worried about his precious film. But his thoughts keep returning to his girlfriend. This is the woman who stuck up for him when his dad threatened to cut off his allowance after *Jules in LA* bombed at the box office. This is the actress who won an Emmy for her portrayal of a Waspy blueblood, who after losing her entire savings in a Ponzi scheme, robs a bank then buys sleeping bags she gifts to homeless persons the rest of her brief life. This is Ethereal Hunt, the beautiful actress with the cool gray eyes. They've been a good team, gosh, awhile now. And he's risking their relationship for a week in the Midwest with Kimberly Solberg?

Dragging himself from bed, he does what he always does when feeling blue and puts on workout clothes then reads a spec script on the treadmill. Esme has breakfast waiting on the veranda—eggs over turmeric-spiced oatmeal, avocado toast, and freshly squeezed orange juice. He showers in anticipation of his meeting later that morning. To impress Jonathan Lin, he wears a lightweight wool suit, his grandfather's IWC wristwatch, and leather oxfords. The sun shines brightly as he strides outdoors searching for his father. Sherman loves Garrity Manor, the Tudor's big, mullioned windows on the second floor with the mums overflowing the planters, the decorative half-timbering and Camelot inspired turret, the vines growing on the stucco. It's lovely and understated, old Hollywood at its best.

His mother loved mornings, too. She was a people person with stores of energy thrust upon the very few. Certain presidents maybe. People like Oprah. She still came to him in snapshots after all these years. That ratty straw hat she wore on Madeline Island. The shopping sprees they took to South Coast Plaza. Her hippy stage when her wardrobe consisted of a long-tailed shirt and bikini bottoms. Before this bohemian turn her approach was sporty Kathryn Hepburn—wide-legged pleated gabardine slacks with a nipped-in silk blouse, a string of pearls. In what felt like overnight, she became a 60s Jane Fonda, hip to jazz fusion, Paul Mazursky films, and the party favors of the period—the Pernods and Gauloises. You name it and it went down at Garrity Manor (couples fucking in guest rooms, women walking off with her jewelry). The worst were the men (to Sherman they all had gleaming tans and wore Speedos) cajoling her into joining them in the pool or cabana, where she'd walk out disheveled and rubbing her nose.

His dad didn't approve of those parties. Most weeknights after work he went straight to his study where Esme served him dinner. He'd pour himself a drink then study blueprints or survey maps for Garrity Holdings next big project. Before Bel Air, his family had grown citrus trees and raised cattle on a farm near Downey. One day they were drilling for water and hit a giant oil field. Pretty much overnight the Garritys' became oil men. His dad bought ten acres in the newly developed Bel Air. An architect designed the twenty-two room Albert Kahn styled Tudor with a tennis court and swimming pool. Back then Bel Air was an untamed place. Mountain lions roamed the hills. Stone Canyon was a community stable with bridle trails running up to the reservoir near Mulholland Drive. It was a different world.

Sherman finds his old man on the ridge where the knotted Eucalyptus stands fragrant and unmoving. Watching him tinkering with the riding lawn mower, he feels a strange affection for the man. He's been nonstop as far back as he can remember. He'd taken over the family business after his father Locke Sr., had had a debilitating stroke, buying out his brothers' share. Locke did things differently. Four acres of Garrity Manor were sold off in half acre parcels. A few years later he ventured into corporate real estate, strip malls, and industrial parks on the outskirts of Anaheim. In less than a decade there was Garrity Enterprises, Garrity Holdings and Acquisitions, and Garrity Property Management and Development. Sherman's parents were friends with Doris Day and James Garner. They partied with the Reagans. Locke threw out the first pitch at a Dodgers game. Bel Air even changed the street he grew up on to Garrity Way. That's how it felt—like life was the *Garrity way*. Then his dad walked away, the businesses sold to a Japanese firm in the mergers/acquisition game. No one in the immediate family caught wind of his thinking. He hadn't even given his only son a heads up. To be clear, in the late 80s Sherman was rather a mess of a human being. Still, it would have been nice to be asked.

He takes a moment to gather himself. His troubles are simple. He needs financing for his new film. And maybe, just maybe, a thumbs up from his old man that his life is moving in the right direction. And so he buttons his suit coat, fluffs his thinning hair, then mimics Ethereal's pre-audition routine to steady his nerves—Sherman smiles. "Hi, Dad."

Locke is bent over the riding mower. The seat is in the up position and the battery exposed. "What do you think about goats?"

"Goats?"

His dad stands upright then places his palms on his lower back and stretches his lumbar. He's got a Robert Redford cowboy vibe—denim work-shirt, jeans, and a blue bandanna tied around his neck. "Those furry daft creatures."

"I know what goats are, Dad."

"Henrique thinks they'll keep the lawn clipped without the noise and wasted fuel."

"Is this a good time to talk?"

His father takes off his wide-brimmed hat to itch his scalp. Like his executive producer, he has the hairline of his youth, something Sherman finds cruel and unfair. "I got a visit from the water inspector," Locke says. "The city is considering legal action. Henrique asked if they were suing golf courses, too. That kid cracks me up."

"We don't need that kind of publicity right now."

Hat back in place, his dad hunches over the machine again. He grabs a screwdriver from his back pocket without taking his eyes off the battery. "Because of the tennis movie?"

Sherman stares at the hillside where he and his father planted the rows of cypress after his mom passed. "Did you ever walk away from a deal?"

Locke's fussing with a couple wires. "You in trouble?"

He wants to ask about the Chinese in general and his executive producer in particular. Instead, he walks over to the ridge's edge and gazes over Garrity Manor. At the car hanger's sleek nonconformity. At Carlos fishing leaves out of the pool with an extended pole. At Henrique racing back and forth over the clay court on the gas-powered roller machine. He lets out a long, frustrated breath. "You seen Ethereal?"

"Nope."

"She's mad at me. All because I won't let her play the tennis pro's wife." Down below, the roller engine turns off. "She's in her forties, right? Yet thinks she'll be believable as a twenty-something stripper."

Nothing, not a grunt or a laugh, not even a 'That's too bad, son.' It's like talking to his tennis racquet. This is what's wrong with him and his dad—the gulf between them. "Remember those pool parties Mom used to have? I know I was only a kid, but I think she was snorting cocaine at those parties."

"Grab me the bullnose pliers." His dad points the screwdriver at the tool belt lying at the trunk of the old tree. On his way over Sherman's careful not to stir up the sandy ground. After all, he's wearing Salvatore Ferragamo's. He flips the tool belt over and searches inside.

"Those parties were payback," his dad says.

He looks over his shoulder, confused. "You were unfaithful?" He'd always seen his dad like this perfect robot of a human being, no flaws, no weaknesses, just this steady, hardworking, unfeeling person. And he cheated on Mom? "Was this a one-time thing? Or were you banging the babes every weekend?"

"Your mother was no saint." His dad snaps his fingers. "Bullnose pliers."

Sherman's head is still in a fog as he retrieves the tool and walks over. "So, the marriage was a sham?"

"No, it wasn't a sham," his dad says, snatching the pliers. "Why is everything with you drama? Your girlfriends are drama. Your movies are drama. I knew talking to you was a mistake."

His dad goes back to poking the wires.

"Will you stop that!" Sherman says. "This is important. I deserve an explanation."

"She worked at the office."

"Your secretary? That bimbo with the high voice and big tits?" Even as a boy he was aware of the female body. He remembered Caroline as short with dark eyes and wearing tight skirts. "How long?"

"A couple months."

"Did Mom know?" His dad looks up from the battery again. "Jesus. How could you?"

He was a kid when this took place, but how had he not figured this out? And if his mom and he were so close, why hadn't she told him when he was old enough to understand?

"Did you want to take up where we left off last night?" Locke finally says.

"Give me a second, okay? It's not every day you find out your father cheated on your mom with a squealy-voiced woman with big knockers." All he can think about is his mom. You mean she not only died tragically young, he made her suffer too? Sherman feels something rising within him, something ready to erupt. But then he thinks—wait a goddamn second. His father has gifted him an opportunity. Here's his way in, a reparation for past deeds. "I know my projects haven't done well, but this is the best story I've read in a long time," he says. "To do it right, and by right, I mean shoot a beautiful film, I'll need ten million. I've already raised the other twenty. Once the film opens in China and Japan that ten million will double, even triple. And you'll get your name on the big screen—Locke Garrity, producer."

"I think you know the answer."

"But Dad! I don't think you heard me. The Chinese, who I'm negotiating with…there's something fishy going on. I can't put a finger on what that is, but it's not good."

His dad drops the mower seat and sits down. "If the Chinese are anything like the Japanese, beware. If Americans think two steps ahead, Asians got the entire project in their head, start, middle and end. They're calculating bastards."

"We saw Blanco play, remember?" His dad looks up with a puzzled expression. "Hamburg, the year we skied in the Dolomites." Still nothing. "His dad was courtside in a wheelchair. He was dying and Blanco broke down."

The old man's eyebrows perk to life. "The dad had AIDS, didn't he?"

"Yes!"

"And…"

"And … it's a compelling story. Critics love that shit. Might even be Oscar material." He'd lost him somewhere in his rambling speech. Locke has popped the mower seat again and is fiddling away. "Oh my god. The adulterer is saying no to his only son. Who, for the record, has never cheated on his wife."

"Adultery only counts if a person has balls enough to get married."

"Really? You're going there? So that's it? You're saying no?" He doesn't wait for a reply. "Fine. Whatever. But don't think I'm letting you in when it gets fun. I know how much you love putting on your tux and shining in the spotlight with your '*Aw, shucks, this suit? Armani, I think'* bullshit!"

Sherman takes the slope down the hill with big pouty strides. He feels stupid for trying so hard. Why is his father so cruel? Doesn't he know how lucky he is? So many children of this wealthy nook in the hills are deadbeats, bling this and bling that, in and out of pretentious rehab centers, trust fund kids who never grow up. He's trying, isn't he? Isn't his car collection featured in the latest *Car And Driver*? And hadn't the writer called Sherman *"an innovator… not afraid to tackle projects like the twenty-month restoration of a 1964 Ford GT40 when the research and costs were considerable…"* As father's go, why is Locke such a disappointment?

He's really worked up stepping onto the gravel drive. He'll show the fucker. He didn't win seven gold balls by being a whiny quitter. Stomping toward the car garage he hears his name called out. Henrique comes running down from the clay court. In no time he's matching Sherman's gait. "What do you do all day?"

"I make movies," he says, still pissed at his dad. "You know that."

"Locke says you don't actually make the movies."

Sherman feels an anxious bite at the base of his neck. "Well, that's true. But without producers doing the little things, there's no movies as you know them."

Henrique's medium built with bowed legs and hair cut razor-short on the sides and pomaded on top like his hero, Ronaldo. "How's the problem with the Chinese?"

"Why? You have ten million you want to invest?"

He bares a mouth full of metallic orthodontia. "I wish."

They pass into the shadow cast by the garage's roofline. His anger is receding. Henrique is easy to be around. No wonder his dad likes his company.

"Wanna help me pick out a car?"

"Can I? Sweet."

At this hour in the morning the building is like a stealth bomber hiding in the trees. In designing the garage Sherman had hired the Australian firm, Hottel and Damascus, a husband/wife team whose work he'd admired on a trip to Norway's Lofoten Islands. The structure isn't tall (the roof's peak is eighteen feet high), but fans out like a long contoured corridor clad in matte-black metal siding. It's modern and tasteful and somehow fits in with the Tudor's slate roof and lush gardens. He punches in the code on his smartphone. They watch the massive doors rise.

"You agree that shock and awe is the best way to make change, right?" Henrique says.

The globe lights pop on. "Shock and awe? Who are you, George W. Bush?"

"Locke and I are destroying the golf club's sprinkler system. We need to wake the establishment up."

He's half listening, his interest piqued by the neat row of collector cars. "That's nice." Then he frowns. "What did you say?"

"Think about it. No water, no grass. No grass, no golf. No golf, *no members*. Suddenly the country club is a public green space. How cool is that?"

Sherman has little experience dealing with kids. There are no nieces or nephews. Some of his girlfriends had children, but he always felt like a third wheel. Kids disappointed him. There was never a return emotionally speaking for whatever energy he'd invested, be it playing on the jungle gym or reading Dr. Seuss while their mother got dressed for a night out. Still, this feels like a teachable moment. He puts his hands on Henrique's shoulders then bends down and looks him square in the eye. "You know I'm on your side, right? But what you're talking about is vandalism. Trust me, rich-ass people don't fuck around if you damage their shit."

The boy lowers his eyes. They're standing at the keyholder Sherman built in high school after he made the decision to make collecting cars part of his future. The box is rudimentary and painted sky-blue. Twenty-four J-shaped pegs are screwed into the base, six per row, each spaced equally apart. Presently, seventeen pegs hold keys.

"Well?"

"Prius, Sherman. Definitely the Prius."

"I need something fast. Something that shows off my wealth and prestige."

Henrique runs his eyes down the first row of sparkling cars. "The old Land Rover. That truck is sick."

"The Land Rover … hmm… millions are riding on my meeting this afternoon."

"I know. The Spider!"

The McLaren 12C Spider with the retractable hard top and turbo charged 616 horsepower with a top speed of around 204 miles per hour. "Now, you're thinking."

Grabbing the white rabbit's foot off the peg, the two start off between the sparkling sports cars, muscle cars and antiques. Henrique gets sidetracked at the Lotus Evora. They linger awhile, eyeing it, walking around it, grinning at it.

"Is this the James Bond car?"

"You're thinking of the Lotus Esprit Turbo from *For Your Eyes Only*. Though the signature model for 007 was the Aston Martin." He buffs a blemish off the side mirror. "My Lotus was launched in 2008 under the code name Project Eagle."

"How come you know so much about cars?"

Sherman shrugs. "Just do."

Henrique points at the only car covered in cloth. "Is it true you've never driven the Alfa Romeo?"

"Did my dad tell you that?"

"It was your mom's, huh? Hey, there's the Spider!"

The McLaren 12C is parked in the last slot in the second row. You can't really miss it—the glossy papaya orange paint, the teardrop shape, the way it's built low to the ground like an arachnid ready to strike. Sherman clicks the fob, and the scissor door rises like a phantom wing.

"Go on. Check it out."

Henrique twists past the steering column and put his hands on the wheel. He does that thing he did as a boy when his grandfather let him pretend drive the Rolls, touching every button and knob in reach.

"Careful. There's a driver injection button."

Another flash of braces. "Ha ha."

He'd flown to McLaren headquarters in Woking, England on a private jet. The first thing that struck him as his driver turned onto the property was the futuristic glass and steel structure fanning out over a small lake. It was like something out of an Ian Fleming novel. But it was the production line that impressed Sherman the most. Components and parts were organized by color. Eight hundred skilled workers had a hand in chassis construction, body and engine assembly, the interior work like hand-stitching the upholstery. And everything was so quiet. There wasn't a robot or machine in sight.

The boy makes low purring sounds and pretend shifts the gears.

"What exactly did you have planned?"

"With the raid?" Henrique says. "Night vision goggles, metal detectors. And hammers."

"You know how many sprinkler heads are on a golf course? I don't, but I'm guessing a lot."

Henrique pretend-turns the wheel violently then makes explosion noises. "Oh no…we're… deaadd!!"

"I'm heading to Wisconsin on Sunday. Keep an eye on Locke, okay? And no destroying golf courses. That's not cool. Now get out. I need to go take out the Chinese."


Sherman's car collection is organized by year built, country of origin, and lastly cost. Each car is carefully nestled in a slotted lane that corresponds with a number on the peg. Each car is unique in his or her own way—each has talents of its own. He owns a Mercedes Benz 300SL gullwing, a Fiat Jolly, and a Triumph Dolomite in cobalt blue. He has a white Lotus and a white Ferrari and a Porsche 365 in ivory white with the period correct luggage rack. He owns an Aston Martin DB5 (bought from his old man) and a Rolls Royce Phantom V (only 343 miles) his grandfather drove off the lot two weeks before he died of heart failure, age eighty-eight. The newest addition, a Bugatti Chiron, has 1000 horsepower, can go from 0-124 mph in less time than it takes to read a short sentence. His cars are like friends one chooses for certain situations. For example, the 72' Ford Bronco is what he drives to the beach, the Austin Healy (British Racing Green, biscuit full leather interior) what he guns up Route 1 on his way to Big Sur. Rain means the military-grade Mercedes G Class with bullet-proof glass and a front grill that can stop an Uzi. Now, it isn't cars, cars, cars, every waking hour of Sherman's day. He goes months without obsessing of cars, dreaming of cars, fantasizing about cars, seeing a car on Roxbury Drive and thinking *I need that fucker and I need it now.* When that happens he turns into another person entirely. He goes Howard Hughes antisocial. Days on end down the car-porn rabbit hole. Sherman in silk pajamas. Sherman never leaving the dark master suite. Clicking, clicking, clicking. Images so painstakingly sharp in clarity he sometimes turns away from all that beauty. Closeups of odometers with laughingly low mileage. Brand insignias so shiny and flawless he wears sunglasses. HD takes the experience to a whole new decadent level. Slow-mo panning over super pristine boss engines. Leather upholstery so amazingly restored it seems fake. Road trips down gorgeous country lanes with an elegant, scarfed woman in the passenger seat, the viewer/voyeur experience turned on its head. One moment he's the onlooker, the next he's behind the wheel, gripping the gear shaft, working the pedal, throttling through a cathedral of trees in satiny light with a beautiful woman laughing in his ear.

And all of it can be his for a mere £499,000.

Sherman makes offers. He gets into bidding wars. He sometimes finds himself leaning back in his Eames Lounge Chair thinking *Holy shit. Did I just buy a Jaguar E-Type open two seater like the one my parents tooled around in with hardly a second thought?* It's near lunacy the trust we put into the internet, into financial transactions, sight unseen. Wiring money to a bank in Munich for a BMW he's never seen in person, trusting the car as advertised. That once he pays in full, the man in charge, let's call him Otto, will hold up his end of the bargain and ship the automobile to America, have it trucked cross-country, arriving unscathed at Garrity Manor in six weeks' time, weather permitting. Such is Sherman's fixation. That's how he got the mint 3.0 CSL but also the collector Ferrari with a falsified VIN.

He owns a warehouse near the 10 freeway in Culver City for the projects that don't make the cut. His mechanic splits time between restoring rare finds that need a total rebuild and fine-tuning the collection out at Garrity Manor. The warehouse itself holds a graveyard of half-finished dreams—cars up on blocks, gutted and left to rot, like some spoiled Lord Fauntleroy's birthday presents he got bored with mid-assembly. The worst of the bunch are stacked in the warehouse corner—a John Chamberlain-like behemoth fifteen feet high. A woman artist he was sleeping with in the 2000s made him a Bruce Nauman-inspired sign that blinks on and off in splashy red neon. JUBILEE.

There's his carbon footprint he sometimes feels guilty about. Same goes for his gas-chugging, dirty-burning, maintenance-nightmare car collection he houses in a 20,000 square-foot climate-controlled, earthquake retrofitted, near atomic bomb-proof bat cave. Like Henrique said—why not drive the Prius? Hadn't George Clooney made it hip? The problem is the Prius is a snore. It has no muscle, no character, no streamlined look. The hybrid doesn't turn heads, not like the McLaren. And in these heady bubblegum days early in the 21st Century, image matters. And so, Bel Air, California's Sherman Garrity climbs into the McLaren Spider wearing driving gloves and Cartier sunglasses and goes vrooming up the drive like a movie star.

Ten minutes later he's perched atop the 405 ramp. Southbound traffic is like a fat slithering python with a rat stuck in its throat. His eyes shoot over the basin. He sees bone-white buildings and a glow coming off the hills that's easy on the eyes. Los Angeles is first light, best light, golden light, golden shores. It's the scent of orange trees on clear mornings and helicopters flying overhead like drones. It's freeways that pulse and move and deadlock, but never sleep. It's car culture and making it big and The Beach Boys and Botox and whack jobs. It's movie studios and billboards two stories high with Charlize Theron staring at you like DESIRE. It's homeless encampments, chaotic swings in the weather, and racially divided cities. It's complicated and materialistic and shiny new. And Los Angeles is possibility—where dreams come true.

The light changes green and the Spider comes to life. This car demands more than a midlife crisis with a fat wallet. It's a precision machine—ruthless in attack—with a very light foot. For an inexperienced driver this can mean a three hundred thousand dollar car getting away from you in mere seconds. Sherman's no amateur. He's been to racing school. He and his old man went to the track up in Lancaster where Steve McQueen and Paul Newman sometimes raced. The actors always made a point to say hello. Newman even gave him driving tips—focus on the apex, keep your eyes on the track, not directly in front of you, but way out where the next curve was. His fastest recorded speed is 172 miles per hour. There's nothing like going that fast. Nothing in this world at least.

Merging into traffic, his FaceTime pings. He glances at the screen. It's Ethereal and she's naked. "Hold on." He reaches across to the passenger seat and pulls his iPad from out a leather messenger bag. It doesn't take long to turn on the hotspot and bring her alive on the screen. He leans the thin computer on the sloping console. "I thought you were mad at me?"

They've done naughty stuff before, but always after dark. Broad daylight brings a giddy level of danger to the activity. In lieu of distractions—the sputtering traffic, his all-important lunch date with Jonathan Lin, Ethereal in her birthday suit—Sherman hasn't slowed down.

The actress has hold of her buttocks like they are chunks of meat. "This perky ass should be in your film." He taps the acceleration and the Spider jerks forward like a tense cramped muscle. Then his eyes grow large. For he is seconds from plowing into a car. He backs off, switches lanes—sighs. She's changed positions, her breasts thrust camera close. "These are the tits of a college girl."

Again, his right foot paws the gas pedal and again the Spider pulses to life. He's passing cars like he's in a video game. Which confuses him. How is he zooming by trucks and automobiles and motorcycles stuck in a traffic jam? *Unless.* Unless he happens to be motoring down the left shoulder all by his lonesome. He brakes hard then surges obliquely across traffic, not really checking the blind spot, until he's tight behind a semi.

When his eyes find the screen again Ethereal sits backwards on an armchair. Her hair falls over her face and he can make out the top of her breasts, that shadowy cleavage.

"When I was younger, in auditions, they'd tell me to undress. That's the way it was back then, Shermy. These disgusting men sat behind desks with stubby erections. I knew what they wanted. I did things… things I'm ashamed of. I thought you should know that." She stands and pushes the chair away. "Am I boring you?"

"Not at all. I'm sorry those things happened to you." He takes his eyes off traffic and gives her a heartfelt glance. She's next to the window with the orange groves backlit by sunlight.

"You're at Garrity Manor?"

"I spent the night."

"Where did you sleep?"

"We have eight bedrooms, Shermy."

He isn't sure he believes her. Lately, she's acted different. Some days she doesn't get out of bed until the afternoon Soaps come on. There are tirades. Auditions, if they come at all, call for nurturing mothers, bitchy business execs or crazy cougars.

"Will you look at me, Shermy? Will you look at this face. You can't tell, can you? The eyes twice, a single face lift. You want to know how old a woman is? Look at the rings around her neck. Me? I've maybe one. Everything you see is good genes and hard work. I lead a clean life. No meat, no simple sugars. I'm not perfect. There are the recreational drugs. I'm only human."

The Spider is stalled behind an American car of indeterminate color. Quartz maybe? He toys with bumping the backend.

"Shermy? Are you getting hard?"

"Like quartz," he says gritting his teeth.

"Get me the Heather Harper part and I'll pretend you aren't meeting a woman on Madeline Island."

"I'm speechless. I really am."

"And I won't say I told you so when the person ends up not being who you thought she was." Ethereal wipes away a couple tears. "You are in a deep well of hurt. You think the next fix will make the pain go away. But it won't. *She won't.* Meanwhile I'm here. And I love you, Shermy."

***

The lunch crowd trickles in. Millennials in Supreme hoodies and women with blown-out hair and high-waisted jeans. Sherman sits against the back wall facing Abbot Kinney and its street flow. Which is how he planned it—them walking into Almond and seeing him like he's king shit. Like the tennis pic is his baby, not his director's, not the ex-circuit player's, and certainly not Jonathan Lin's.

It's couple minutes past twelve when his director holds the door open for the finance intermediary. They're talking like old friends. He wonders if they came together. Is that even logistically possible? Gil Gibson lives in Baldwin Hills. He drove his older model Lexus down La Cienega then Slauson to Washington Boulevard. Jonathan Lin is from Miracle Mile, right? This time of day the smart move is Santa Monica Boulevard to Lincoln then over to—. Why is he getting worked up? He ought to be asking questions. Like why call a meeting now? And why not include Blanco? And why the fuck is Mr. Dollars & Sense stonewalling?

The Jonathan Lin snaking his way through the maze of tables is younger than he thought with dark hair parted on the side and broad shoulders. He's clean shaven but for a tuft of black whiskers under his lip. Like Sherman, his suit looks purposed for this meeting only. It's the color of burlap, double breasted. Underneath he wears a teal dress shirt. Lin called out of the blue a couple months ago saying he'd read the script. The financing had shaped up quickly. Mr. Dollars & Sense was a big player in Chinese IT with a wad of new money and looking for places to unload it. Why not American films with a crossover appeal? It was only after the first million was deposited in Shred Films bank account that Lin mentioned the anonymous benefactor. At the time Sherman couldn't care less.

He motions for the handsome young man and his director to sit down without getting up himself then sweeps a fast look at Lin's suit. "Bespoke?"

"Hong Kong. You?"

"London," Sherman says. "We've used the same house for a couple generations."

"Tailoring is a lost breed," Lin says, unbuttoning his coat.

"What are you white guys talking about?" Even in his chair, being an ex-college basketball player, Gil Gibson is a head taller than anyone else in the restaurant.

Lin puts a hand over his breast pocket, as if offended. "But Gil, I'm not white."

"Trust me, you're white."

And Jonathan Lin lets go a high-pitched giggle. He sits back in his chair, legs crossed at the knee, arm draped over the chairback, with his torso facing the table opposite, as if he's having a conversation with half the room. Nothing about him screams drinker or pill popper or worrier or insomniac. Gil Gibson, on the other hand, has the vexed look of a man nearing fifty without a film under his belt in ten years. His first feature, *Venice Drifter*, was about a young male hustler living on the streets of LA, who, in a chance encounter, falls for the daughter of a wealthy john he frequently had sex with. The film followed the young man in his search for the girl. There were many things Sherman liked about *Venice Drifter*. The picture was shot on 16 millimeter and owned the gritty realism of Altman and Pekinpah. There was the protagonist's single-minded pursuit of a woman with so many obstacles in his way. But what stayed with him long after the film ended was the air of sadness and loss pervading the storyline. Those themes, even more so than humor, are what made him fall in love with movies in the first place. With his tennis pic, he wants a similar emotional impact.

The waiter comes around with the menus. He looks like Bradley Cooper if the actor was a serious bodybuilder and had a red mop of hair. The day's specials are stated with an air of importance. Stressed like he is, Sherman hardly hears him. He orders bottled water from France, both still and charged, and for himself, the spinach salad with gorgonzola. "And twelve oysters for us to share."

"Salmon tartare," Lin says, setting the menu on the table.

"And you, sir?" the waiter asks the director.

"Tell me about your burger."

"Gil?" Sherman's voice conveys a disproval that makes him blush. He tries smiling it away. "How about the sea bass? Or a salad?"

"Tension among the team?" Lin giggles again. "That's a good sign."

"I fainted the other day," he tells Jonathan. "My doctor says I was dehydrated." Gil picks up his water glass and takes a long slurpy drink. "Hydration. Yum yum." He looks up at the waiter. "Go on. I'm listening."

The Bradley Cooper look-a-like notes the friction by raising a mock eyebrow. "Kevin lived a charmed life. He was grass-fed his entire stress-free existence. I got to meet him once. Kev was lovely, a sensitive creature. You can't go wrong."

"Make old Kev medium-rare. With the fries, please."

Collecting the menus, the waiter leaves.

Almond is loud. There's the open kitchen, a DJ spinning records, and a bartender doing the mambo with a cocktail shaker. When he was younger, Sherman and his mom used to take Sunday Brunch at the Ritz-Carleton Pasadena. They'd dress up, her in an understated dress by Halston, him in a blazer, tie and slacks. Even as a teen he was impressed by the hotel's details. The elegant quiet in the big room, the fine silver and china, even the actor from "WKRP in Cincinnati" who played Herb Tarlek would stop by the table to say hello.

At Almond the noise is such that the producer leans in. "Okay, Jonathan. Talk."

"I heard that Shinkan Sen has been cast as the femme fatale."

The producer and director exchange glances. "You know I can't comment on that," Sherman says. "Other than to say we talk to lots of actors."

Lin strokes his soul patch. "Casting Ms. Sen would be an interesting choice. She has a 150 million followers on Instagram."

"Like my girl, Beyonce," Gil says.

Only a handful of people knew the team was in preliminary talks with the gorgeous Japanese actress. So, who leaked the news?

Lin bends forward, conspiratorially. His cologne owns a bold musky ring. "What's it like sleeping with actresses?"

"It's not 1972, Jonathan," Gil says, frowning. "That shit doesn't play anymore."

"Really?" Lin picks up his napkin, unwraps the silverware, then uses the cloth to clean his fork. "Certain actresses own that star quality. They shine brighter than most. Ethereal for instance."

Sherman forces a grin. "I'm sorry, but what are you implying?"

"Yeah, be cool, man," Gil says.

"I'm fucking with you," Lin says, chuckling. "And anyway, Ethereal Hunt is old enough to be my mom."

The oysters arrive on a silver platter of ice. And just in time, too, for the tension has ratcheted up a few levels. Sherman reaches for a roughshod shell and brings it to his lips then knocks back his head. The creature slides down his throat, salty and wet.

Lin douses an oyster with tabasco. "You never answered the question."

"About?"

"Shinkan Sen."

"We might seek her out," Sherman says. "If we knew our picture had funding."

"You know how many horny-ass Asian men want to see her fucking some strapping huge American athlete? You got to think big, gentlemen. The American market is shit. But we kick ass in Seoul, Tokyo and Beijing, and Mr. Dollars & Sense might fund the next ten Shred Films."

Then he sucks down the oyster.


Lunch over, the men stand in a loose triangle on the sidewalk waiting for their cars to be pulled around. The inland marine has burned off and throws a softer edge over Abbot Kinney.

"Blanco's expendable." Lin messes with his bangs in the window reflection. "You have the script. What else do you need?"

Gil sucks on a toothpick. "The script is shit, Jonathan."

"Blanco helps with nuance." He can hear the Spider's humming throttle down a side street. "Details can make a good movie great."

"We want Blanco out," Lin says.

Sherman is tired. He's tired of battling with his girlfriend. He's tired of the money dance. He's tired, period. Blanco is a nuisance, but why push him out? Don't they all want the same thing? To make the best film possible?

Here comes his little orange drug. The sight of the glossy machine restores his energy. He decides to channel Henrique. "We need cash, Jonathan. No cash, no pre-production. No pre-production, no Shinkan Sen showing off her tits on a screen three stories high. Tell that to Mr. Dollars & Sense."

"I've had a crush on her since I don't know when."

Gil flicks his toothpick in the street. "Get us the money and you can sit in on the sex scenes."

Lin does that creepy giggle again. "What should I tell my client?"

Sherman walks over and tips the valet a fifty. "Stall him. Tell him I'm working on pushing Blanco out. Meantime, put five million into the account. Call it a good faith measure."

"He won't be happy."

Pulling up to the curb is a Prius of the same dull sky blue as the one at Garrity Manor. His smile is hard. "Nice fucking car, Lin." And Sherman ducks into his sports car and takes off like it's a motorway. *Fuck you, Jonathan Lin. And your millionaire investor. Fuck you.*

# BADLANDS

He's passing the lot behind the Viking Bar when he sees them in the streetlamp's low jaundiced light. The town's main drag is like a centripetal force pulling him closer and closer to a center that won't hold. And he so wants to take back control. Yet here he is and there is the ticking in his chest. There are two of them. They're young and sturdy like farmhands. He sees pushing and laughing between the men with a young woman in the middle. It's near closing and he knows what he's going to do. It's like he's known about this moment his entire life. He is barefoot and feels like a cat leaping to the ground. It is so easy and it is like fate. This is how you fight.

He's closing in on the big one when the guy smiles like he had a premonition his night would unfold like this. His hook to the guy's jaw has him staggering backwards. Ken moves in to finish him off but his punch only grazes the guy's cheek. The girl in distress gives him a strange, frightened look. Like he's a complete jerk-off nut job. That and he realizes he's drunker than he thought.

It's the little runt's turn. He slaps his hands together like he's the fired up sixth man coming off the bench, score tied with seconds to play, and drives a shoulder under Ken's arm, lifting him off the ground. They hurtle through the air and end up against the F-150 with the kid's forearm cinched under his throat. The little one is rock-strong and Ken has trouble breathing. Meantime his buddy is stretching out his neck and eying him like he's the bastard who fucked his little sister.

Ken bites the little guy's finger until he feels bone. The kid is up and hopping mad now. Blood stains his forearm and T-shirt. The girl is crying for them to stop and the three men circle with their hands up near their faces. Ken is barefoot and stays low and feels light on his feet. The big one comes in swinging. He ducks then goes to the ground and sweeps the guy's feet from underneath him. The little one is red in the face and a gob of spit hangs from his lip as he lowers his head and pile-drives him into the ground, knocking his breath into his spleen. Ken gets as far as his knees. But the kid's quick and swings around and gets him in a full nelson.

"Wrestler, huh, kid?" The little one tightens his grip.

"Kill the asshole," he yells at his buddy. The big one is on his feet and moving toward him with a purpose that puts the fear in him. His black boots have a steel toe. The first kick to the ribs is stiff like something broke through. The second will hurt more in the morning. Then Ken hears Cal tell someone named Matt to quit kicking his friend. The big guy gets in one more blow, a chip shot to his nose. There's a burst of light then blood everywhere and his nose echoes through his skull. Then the fight is over.

"Was that necessary, Matt?" he hears Cal say.

"He started it."

"You broke his fucking nose, man."

The girl's arm is draped over the little guy, who's inspecting his finger with his smartphone flashlight. Ken sits slumped against the truck with his face tilted toward the stars. It hurts to breathe. Out the corner of his eye he sees Cal approach the driver's side and poke his head through the opened window.

"Keys in the ignition, Mel. Meet us at the house."

So, she's here and saw the whole thing. Hmm. Well, that's something. He turns his head until he sees her. She stands by the rear bumper with her hands stuffed inside her jean's pockets. He can't read her expression with his head swishy and all.

"I can drive," he says, pinching his nose.

"What about my finger?" The runt's pulled off his shirt and wrapped it around his hand.

"We weren't doing anything, Cal," the girl says. "I mean, who is this psycho?"

"I said I can drive."

"You're fucking drunk, man." Cal's voice has an uncharacteristic edge. "Mel? The truck. Now."

She gives her boyfriend a spirited eyebrow roll then puts a bead on him. "Just like old times, huh, Solberg?"

He hasn't moved from his place against the front end. But he's smarting inside for being the wee little asshole he feels. Melody climbs into the rig and the truck coughs to life, Ken's signal to grunt himself off the ground.

"Matt? You better push off," Cal says. "Take Krause to the ER. Let me know the cost."

"I'm not paying for shit," Ken says.

"He's something, this friend of yours," Matt says.

Krause cradles his hand. "I think he severed a nerve."

Melody sticks her arm out the window, dangling car keys. She drops them in Cal's palm. "Now get," he tells her. They watch her drive off. Ken sees that a crowd lingers on the lot's edge, phones pointed their way. Then one of them rings. He hears it, the wrestling kid and his girl hear it, everyone hears it. "Oh, yeah, right," he says, pulling his phone from his short's pockets. Sirens wail somewhere far off.

"We got to go," Cal says.

He turns his back, facing away. "Kimberly?"

"What do you want?" She sounds accusatory and maybe drunk, but it could be the buzzing in Ken's head. "Do I hear sirens? What's going on?"

"Now, man," Cal says.

"I'll call you back. Okay?"

He follows Cal across the lot. His shirt is torn and bloody. Pretty much all the onlookers are filming them on their phones. "Ya'll go home now," Cal says. "The show's over."

They hustle across the street to where the SUV is parked. The sirens are louder now. His nose feels like its plugged with stingers and he can't stop playing the fight back over in his head. He'd made a pass in the truck thinking the boys were up to no good. You mean he was wrong? What he saw was different than what went down?

"Why are you barefoot, Ken?"

"Cause I'm stealth like an Indian."

Cal opens the driver's side door. "It's Native American, asshole."

"*Oh, is it?*"

He's barely climbed in the front seat when Cal burns rubber doing a U-turn. They speed through the intersection the Viking is located on. Cop lights suddenly flicker across a brick building.

"Fuck! They following?"

Cal eyes the rearview mirror. This alarmed look crosses his features. "No fucking way. Get down, Solberg. Now."

He squeezes every inch of his big body onto the floorboard best he can. Crouching like that shoots rivets of pain up his side. All he can think about is his family and his standing in the community. "I'm fucked! I'm fucking fucked!"

Cal starts laughing so hard his molars show.

Ken gets back into his seat. "Very fucking funny."

They drive toward Ranier, Cal hunched over and under the speed limit. The car interior has a pleasant floral smell. Right, this is Melody's car. He takes in the interior being as suave as he can be—the Mardi Gras beads swaying from the mirror, an old Melissa Etheridge CD, the water bottle she puts her lips on every time she drinks from it. His mind veers back to the fight and what she must think about him now.

"You going to tell me what happened?"

"Those two were up to no good."

"Matt's a firefighter. That's his kid sister. And the guy who's finger you nearly chewed off, that's her fiancé." Cal regrips the wheel. "What's going on? And no bullshit this time."

"Kimberly kicked me out."

"I knew it. You were fucking around, weren't you?"

Swarms of light fill the car interior. Then a car blows past. "Any fucking slower and we'd be going backwards."

"How about a little gratitude? I saved your sorry ass."

They drive awhile, neither saying a word. Ken knows he's done wrong but fuck if he's going to apologize to his friend because the son-of-a-bitch wants him to. He flicks down the passenger visor and inspect his nose in the mirror.

"You know what this reminds me of? That pretty boy from Hibbing who broke your nose. What was his name?"

Ken sighs then flips the visor back in place. "McClanahan."

"That motherfucker was one nice looking dude. Didn't he model in New York?"

"Are you trying to tell me you go both ways?"

"Who won that fight?"

"Fuck you."

Cal grins, staring out the windshield. "I'm joshing you, man."

"Anyone ever tell you you talk too much?"

"All the time, motherfucker. All the fucking time."

They drive up the gravel road his house sits on. Cal's place, an old lake cabin, has wood shake siding and a dead stump out front where he guts his fish. He parks next to the F-150 then turns off the engine. The two friends sit there a moment not talking, just being, the way old friends can.

"Home at last," Cal says, staring out the windshield.

"Andrew's favorite song on his all-time favorite album."

"You lost me, Ken."

"Steely Dan, *Aja*."

"Now that's one great album," Cal says, opening the door. "Now, let's go fix that nose."

"Hey Cal?" Ken says. "Thanks, man."

"You'd do the same for me, brother."

He follows his friend up the porch steps and into the house. Cal walks around the room turning on lights. The space is new and spacious and pleasantly lit with recessed lights and a décor his wife might call country-chic.

"You've been a busy beaver."

"This?" Cal eyes the room, half-bewildered himself. "All we did was blow out a wall and put in new counters and paint and shit."

"That photograph of sunflowers," Ken says. "That's sepia, right?"

"Fuck you, Solberg. You want me to set that nose or what?"

A minute later he sits on a barstool. There's a half drunk Coors Light on the counter. Cal crouches down to eye level with his hands resting on Ken's nose.

"Get it over with already."

"I would if you'd quit moving."

Ken eyes the floor with an uneasy sensation in anticipation of the next few seconds. He notices Cal's leather boots with the round toe. "Those are slick. Where'd you get those?"

Cal snaps his nose into place. "Mall of America."

"Fuck me, that hurt."

The pain in his sinus cavity is ice-cold sharp and contains a clarity that's sobering. He drinks the rest of the beer like its water. Meanwhile,

Cal has donned a *Key West is the Best* apron. Diced ham, onions and green peppers are sizzling in a cast-iron pan. He's cracking eggs in a bowl when the bedroom door opens and Mable trots out followed by Melody wearing one of Cal's T-shirts that lands mid-thigh.

Mable comes up and sniffs his hand. "Hey, girl," he says, petting her neck.

"Looks straight, huh, Mel?"

She gets in real close smelling of lotion and toothpaste. Then she sets her brown eyes on his. Her hair is pulled back with an elastic band. And she is the older version of the woman Ken used to know and love.

"Still gorgeous?" he says, feeling stupid with his smashed nose.

"Hey, honey? You did good." She walks across the room and takes up residence on the leather couch.

"There's a twelve-pack on the side porch," Cal says. "Mel? You thirsty?"

"Nope."

"How about one of my world-famous Denver omelets?"

"I'm fine."

"This is why Mel is the finest catch in Koochiching County."

"Cal?" Melody says, reaching for a laptop sitting on the coffee table. "Sometimes you don't know when to shut up."

His smile is big and showy. "Ken was just saying the same thing."

Ken opens the porch refrigerator with his thoughts upside down. Standing among the fish nets and old lures hanging from the wood slats his heart is humming, which is wrong on so many levels. Isn't he trying to mend what's left of his marriage? Soon he's back on the stool and asking questions so he's not found out. And they don't disappoint. They gush and cackle and gush some more. They finish each other's sentences. They even tell him about the time Cal drove down to the state college Melody attended in southern Minnesota. He takes this more personally than he has a right to. It hurts almost as much as his face does. Them in college, a couple years after Ken and Melody broke up, fucking behind everyone's back.

Another skillet is on the stove, a cut of butter in it, when his phone rings. Ken slips from the stool then starts for the back deck he helped Cal build when he bought the place ten years back.

"Don't be too long," Cal says swirling eggs with a fork. "Food's up shortly."

From the deck, the water in the moon's glow is black and shifting. Lights from Fort Frances flicker in the darkness. Ken cradles the phone to his ear and concentrates best he can. But his head thrums too much to argue a position one way or the other.

"Are you even listening?" Kimberly says. "This is what I'm talking about. You are no longer here for me, emotionally."

"Can we talk tomorrow? You wouldn't believe the day I've had."

"I have a better idea. Why don't you move in permanently with your mom? You can call on that old girlfriend of yours, Melanie, or whatever her name is."

And his wife of twenty-three years hangs up on him.

The omelet is linen thin and folded into a half-moon with the perfect amount of salt to satisfy the tongue. He scarfs it down, secretly wanting another. Cal's at the cooktop, a couple bites in, when his phone vibrates on the counter. His gaze falls on Ken before picking up the call.

"Hey, Josh. Yeah, I was there. Andrew Solberg's brother." Cal cuts a section of egg with his fork. "How's his finger? Well, that's a relief. I told Krause we got him covered. I owe you, man."

Call over, he places the iPhone next to his plate. "That was the police chief. Krause's finger is fine. But it's going to cost you. That bill is on you."

"And no charges?"

"They're good kids," Cal says, forking another wedge of egg. His eyes brighten. "This calls for a celebration. Mel? Put some music on, darling. I got my tunes hooked up to the surround sound. Wait until you hear the bass, brother. It makes the water ripple."

They listen to Elvis Costello's live version of "Alison" and "Around the World in a Day." When "Brown Eyed Girl" comes on Cal croons

Melody from across the room. Worse, he unties his apron with the suggestiveness of a Chippendale dancer then boogies his way to the couch to ask his girl to dance.

"Ibuprofen?" Ken yells over the music.

Cal twirls his girl. "Bathroom."

He takes a piss with one hand bracing the wall. It's been that sort of day. Shit, it's been that sort of year. The finality behind Jeremy's decision to forgo the NHL draft, the heartbreak he felt for his eldest after losing his job and moving back home, and the precise moment he went deep with Nikki Silver.


Two in the morning comes on like a big yawn. Ken hasn't left the safety of the stool. In one direction is Cal tidying up the kitchen. In the other lies the first woman he fell hard for. Her legs are crossed at the ankle and the laptop's opened on her stomach.

"You still sing?"

Melody closes the computer then sets it on the table. Her hand finds the dog lying below the couch. "I'm rehearsing with a band."

It's like dreaming. Is he really sitting across from Melody Fillman after all this time? "What do you call yourselves?"

"Sweet talk."

"That's nice."

She swings her legs to the floor. "I'm heading to bed."

"Be right in," Cal says.

Her shirt catches on the couch. Before she can pull it down he gets a glimpse of her panties. They're red and cut high. Melody does this naughty head shake, her eyes slightly amused. Then she and the dog disappear behind the bedroom door.

"I'm hitting the hay."

"The blanket on the couch enough?" Cal says.

"Yeah, it's fine."

The place Ken rests his head smells like Melody. This sustains him until he passes out. She comes to him near dawn. He lies on the couch, covered in rags. She is hushed kisses and fevered words. She tells him things that has his heart swimming. The rush nearly carries him away. At one point she stops him, worried Cal can hear. Then Melody opens her mouth on his. And he feels himself falling into an old familiar place. "This is not a sex poem," she whispers. Then she's combing out her long dark hair, hair that stretches clear across the room and through the bedroom door. They hear a heavy thud. Melody sits upright, her ears pointy like an alert dog. Then she clamps her hand over Ken's mouth and thrusts him deep into the seat cushion. It's like being held underwater. Then the wrestler kid is squeezing the shit out of his neck and pushing him further down. He wakes, gulping for air.

He's thirsty like a river and drinks from the kitchen tap. Then he drives home in the dark before dawn.

Dimley greets him at the door with his tail wagging. Seeing his old friend chokes Ken up. He gets down on one knee and buries his head in his furry neck. Isn't that the beauty of dogs? No matter who you are or what stupid shit you've done they love you unconditionally. He decides to ride the night out to its cheery end. They set out with the chirping birds and trees hooded in the coming dawn. Ken is in a strange place. He can't quite picture his wife. And Melody is tucked inside him, buried under all his other shit. He wonders what life would have been like if they'd married. If Andrew hadn't died. One thing's for sure. The sight of her in nothing but an old T-shirt did something to his insides. He wanted to bite her ass. He wanted to press his mouth where it didn't belong.

"I need to clean up my life, Dimley."

The dog is sniffing a creosote pole when his eyes find Ken's. His tail sways back and forth like a fish swimming against a current. In that moment he loves his dog and fears the day he'll die and the hole he'll forever feel in his heart. His thoughts are interrupted by the day's first light fanning across the sky. Its blush in color and so faint its near indistinguishable from the black. More emotions sway through him. He's serious about changing his ways. He's a fat fuck who drinks too much. He hasn't done right to the people he cares about most. Then and there he decides to start over. He'll curtail his drinking. He'll get on a training program like he puts his players through. He'll measure out his food portions like Kimberly does. And he'll read poetry, not James Wright, he's too dark, he's too tightly bound to his past. But poets who perpetuate the moral and spiritual experience of illumination.

He'll be more like Andrew.

Across the street a storm door slams. Out walks an old woman with a robe cinched high on her waist. She doesn't see Ken until she bends down to pick up her newspaper. "That dog should be leashed," she says, and not kindly.

He's still lit by the fire to do good. "Sorry, Ma'am. I thought it being so early and all."

Dawn stretches across the sky. The sun's emergence touches the remotest corners of the street. Nothing is spared. Especially not his ruptured nose and torn, bloodied shirt. The woman takes in his lumpish body and how he shrinks even as he's trying to let God's light in. She hurries indoors.

What happened outside the Viking Bar was unfortunate and sad. It won't happen again. That's what he wishes he'd said before the woman rushed inside. His wounds will heal. The kid's finger will heal. We all heal in time. Isn't that what he learned tonight? We all eventually heal?

# PMCP

What was Sherman thinking? Playing a tennis tournament the weekend he meets Kimberly Solberg in Minneapolis? He knows from experience how critical the night before a big game is. He has his code. Lead a monk-like existence, drink plenty of fluids, eat free-range chicken with herbed pasta, take a hot shower, do some Vinyasa, then off to beddy-bye with a 19th Century philosophical tome he can't remember the title of. And that's the point. Keep distractions to a minimum, temptation at arm's length. And here poses the snag. If only he and Van Doorman were playing for a coveted gold ball. At least then his Mother Teresa behavior makes sense.

But that isn't the case at all. Hoisting up the Aquatennial trophy won't thwart his chances with Kimberly. Then why honor his celibacy?

She's taking a sauna on the rooftop deck. Any moment now she'll walk through the door. There'll be showers, a little bubbly. *Fuck.* Sherman must be strong. He must listen to that voice in his head, the one telling him that, for once, he should start a relationship the right way. In Aspen, they'd gotten naked on the last night. Kimberly took control of the situation. Her marriage was probably doomed but sex was not the answer. She offered to get him off. He told her their first time should be for the right reason. And he meant what he said. Which brought him back to tonight. Doesn't his PMCP seem a tad self-centered?

He's alone in the Hewing third floor suite in a damp swimsuit. He came downstairs feigning work, his anxiety getting the better of him. His abstinence went back fifteen years and the night he'd been invited to Hugh's lair before his inaugural 5.0 team finals. Like any heterosexual male versed in the *Playboy* vernacular, Sherman was damn curious what went on at those soirees in the hills. Was it one big hazy fuckfest? Did bunny-wearing Playmates past and present make you a martini and light your smoke? And what went down in the famed grotto?

The Playboy Mansion wasn't exactly Spring Break in Fort Lauderdale without the beer bongs and sullied accommodations. It was more like a treasure hunt. And the booty? A frosted birthday cake with your name on it. The guest simply made a wish, blew out the candles, and the cake was his. But that night while talking up two buxom young women from Oklahoma and Arkansas respectively, he had one of those saliva-swallowing moments of truth. What was he doing at Hugh Hefner's mansion the night before the biggest match of his career? And did he not win his first gold ball the next day? Did he not play like a man blessed by Zeus himself? How can he break with custom now?

Things are going splendidly. They had a wonderful afternoon touring the lakes by bike (him on a cumbersome ride-share, Kimberly sporting a carbon-forked Cannondale). Minneapolis in the summertime is the best urban spot in the land. It's not too hot and it's not too humid. Every bend in the trail opens to glass-blue lakes filled with Minnesotans of all kinds, out in full swing—sailing, paddle-boarding, walking dogs. At the end of this idyllic afternoon, they'd met Van Doorman in the boisterous Hewing lobby. There, his assistant gave Kimberly a steel Kryptonite bike lock and suggestions where she might secure her road bike for the night. Once she was out of sight Van Doorman brought his boss up to speed. The Madeline Island crew were busy preparing for his arrival. His vacation home was being aired out, the refrigerator stocked, and the clay court rolled and brushed. Steve-O, Sherman's righthand man up north, had test-drove the 78' Grand Wagoneer to Spooner and back.

"And our competition tomorrow?"

"Very beatable, sir."

He pumped a fist. "How was Ken Dog's?"

They'd appropriated the nickname after reading an email exchange between Solberg and his part time lover that Kimberly had screen-shotted Sherman.

"No sign of him or his truck," his assistant said. "The eldest Solberg, the tatted Brandon, handed over his mom's luggage. Big dude, sir."

"Is he a problem?"

"He gave me a visual pat down, but that was expected. He said he believed you a decent man. He said, and I quote, 'Don't give me a reason to think otherwise," end quote, which sounds like a threat, but I can assure you his intentions are noble."

"Anything else?"

Van Doorman turned on his phone then showed him a photo of a Cape Cod styled home with cream siding, black shutters, and a garage with the big door open. "Zoom in on the garage, sir."

He noted a fishing boat, two snowmobiles, and a 4-wheeler. "Ken Dog's got lots of toys. So?"

"The gun rack, sir. It's missing a shotgun or rifle."

"That could mean anything," Sherman said handing back the phone.

"In my experience with Americans and guns, sir, is they stack them one after the other, never skipping a space, that way they know when one's missing."

"You're saying he's armed and dangerous?"

"We can't be too cautious, sir."

His eyes darted over the uproarious happy-hour crowd. He saw no such person he'd describe as a bitter, over-the-hill hockey player with vengeance on his mind. "Any word from the vixen?"

The Hewing entrance door swung open. Walking toward them was Kimberly in bike shorts and a cyclist jersey.

"Nikki Silver? She was tight-lipped until I slipped her a few Andrew Jacksons. He's up north. Personally, I think she's still keen on old Ken Dog."

Just then she rounded the corner. "That will be all, Van Doorman."

His assistant gave Kimberly a polite bow then put on his sunglasses and exited the lobby.

"How does a swim sound?"

"Divine," she said.

He glanced out the hotel's front window. His assistant stood on the sidewalk like the Secret Service, eying every passerby. As if his sole responsibility was protecting Sherman Garrity at all costs. This warm feeling came over him that bordered on the avuncular.

Then he and Kimberly waited at the stainless-steel elevators in silence.


The hotel suite, nearing eight in the evening, is awash in brittle orange light. Sherman stands at the window gripping his smartphone. Down on Washington Avenue a motorcade of Segway's pass over an iron-clad bridge. In the distance, sandwiched between two warehouses, he spies Target Field's glossy logo. He checks the Blancpain, wondering what is keeping Kimberly. Thinking he might catch his father before his afternoon nap, he dials his number.

"Yes?"

"You and Henrique blow anything up yet?"

"We're having difficulty finding dynamite," his dad says. "Did you know night vision goggles cost $5000?"

"Tell me you're joking, Dad."

"About the cost? I wish."

"Blowing up a golf course is domestic terrorism."

There's a pause on the line. "When you were little, you thought Jaws was alive and well. You wouldn't swim in the pool."

"Jesus, Dad."

"You okay, Sherman? You sound stressed."

He is, isn't he? When he should be singing in the streets. How long has he fantasized having sex with Kimberly Solberg? And now the moment is at hand and he's pissing and moaning? Shivering in his swim trunks, Sherman's struck with an idea. His father is a sucker for shapely, extroverted women half his age. Maybe Kimberly can help convince Locke to throw a few million the picture's way. "Dad? Why don't you join me at the Hideaway. Think about it, okay? Gotta run, goodbye." And Sherman hangs up before he can reply.

He goes back to what he does best—pacing back and forth— no closer to figuring out the celibacy issue, when Blanco calls. "I'm sort of busy," he says into the phone.

"Alexander Field."

"Pardon?"

"That's his name, Alexander Field. He's from Santa Cruz. He acted in high school."

"And he's a player?"

"D3, yeah. I think he's the one. Boyd is doing a reading with him tomorrow."

"Have you thought about our situation?"

"With Lin? He's bluffing. You, Gil and me need to stick together on this."

Sherman lets out a monumental sigh.

"Dad still tight wadding us?"

"Looks that way"

"Want me to talk to him?"

Not a bad idea, he thinks. "I want to do this on my own."

"Hey, how's your lady friend?"

"How many times do I have to tell you. I'm *buying* a boat."

Another call comes in, one that has Sherman sighing and pacing some more. With his luck Kimberly will walk through the door the moment he says hello.

"I'm at the center," Ethereal whispers.

"Intravenous vitamin therapy? IDL peel?"

"Directional non-force chiropractic."

"Ah, Guru Livingston."

"He's on sabbatical in Mumbai."

"Guru Stephanie?"

"Haven't you heard? She's in ICU. Botched Botox. I heard her face looks like a mudslide."

"Poor thing."

There's a lull that has him thinking fondly about the past. When they were good there was this easy rapport between them. "Hey, you're not getting your tits done, are you?"

"No!"

"Tit job or no tit job, you're not getting the part."

"You don't have to be a dick, Shermy."

"I'm sorry. That came out wrong."

"This profession sucks. I go anywhere else, Manhattan even, and I'm a hot fucking tamale. But LA? I'm like the walking dead. All because I'm thirty-four."

"Forty-two."

"Are you really alone this weekend?"

The dreaded door clicks open. He holds his breath as Kimberly slips inside, her face flush from the sauna. She comes to him without a word and puts her arms around his neck. She smells a strange toxin of chlorine, salty skin, and tequila. They kiss. And the mood heats up like it had in the Elk Mountains. The towel around her waist falls to the floor. She presses her hips into his erection. It all feels so good and right. Then Sherman thinks—what about tomorrow? Is it time to let the code go?

Kimberly meets his heated gaze. They go at it a second time. The top half of her suit is now around her waist and he teethes her nipples. Then reality slams him over the head again. He sees that scene in *Raging Bull* when DeNiro resists the captivating Cathy Moriarty by pouring icy water down his boxer shorts.

"I can't."

She's concentrating on undoing his swimsuit's tie. "Hmm?"

"I need to say something."

She's pressing her nail into a pesky knot. "What? Did the actress have a hissy fit when you broke up with her?" She finally undoes the knot and there goes his shorts, a wet plop on the plank floor. Then he's yanking them up and breaking across the room like a man with lots on his mind. He parks himself at the window and tries acting cool, not easy with the stiff penis.

"It's about tomorrow. And please, whatever you do, don't judge me. I'm embarrassed as it is."

Her instincts are to cover her breasts. "I don't understand."

"I can't have sex tonight."

Up come the shoulder straps. Then she sinks to the floor.

"Did I just blow it?"

"I don't know," she says. "I guess I'm confused."

"It's my pre-match celibacy policy."

He can see the words formulating on her brow. Then her expression goes leery, then a little afraid. He sits with her on the floor. Finally, Kimberly lays her head in his lap. And they're silent as the orange slowly turns over and night gathers and the skyscrapers blink on.

# STREETS OF FIRE

Ken wakes stiff as a jammed finger. He stumbles into the bathroom and pisses in the bowl. Then he makes his way to the sink. He's afraid to look in the mirror. What does his face look like? That Red Savoy meat pie he and Jeremy split the day they moved him into the apartment on Bryant? Nah, not that bad. What the fuck was he thinking? Fighting at his age? He rustles through the medicine cabinet, swallowing 1000 milligrams ibuprofen with a bottle of cough syrup. He can hear the grownups talking above the TV din. How is he going to explain his face to his mom? Better lie low, he thinks. He opens the door tiptoe quiet.

Sven stands in the hall. His eyes widen with alarm. "What happened to you?"

"This?" He tries laughing it off. Which hurts his face and his ribs. It even hurts his knuckles. "Cut myself shaving."

"With a cleaver?"

"That's a good one, Sven."

"Your mom's making fried egg and ham sandwiches." Sven hesitates like there's more. "Mind if I take Dimley on a few errands? I might get him a leash and dog food. If that's okay."

"Yeah, sure. And thanks."

Lying down again, his head is full throttle. Like a stampede of ball-peen hammers coming at him on all fronts. He takes a fist to his skull until he sees stars. Then he feels sick and runs for the bathroom. Just in time too.

His mom is waiting when he walks out. She gets a good look at his face. "Oh, Lord."

"I slipped on Cal's deck."

"And fell on your nose?"

He barges past her and heads outdoors for fresh air. The bright stops him blind. It's one of those stunningly gorgeous Minnesota summer days, warm but not blazingly so, a broad blue sky, and bright, very bright. He digs through his console looking for his sunglasses. Then he lights a cancer stick to kill the puke taste. Dizzy, he rests against his truck. He sees his mom walk past the window. She deserves an explanation. He can't tell the truth—that he nearly bit a man's finger off because he wasn't thinking straight. But he must tell her something. He's supposed to be cleaning up his life, remember?

He's leaning against the truck when he hears a car door shut. Then a man's walking up the drive in a satin bomber jacket. "You the hockey player, Ken Solberg?"

There's something off about the man. Like he's a dweller in secrets. He doesn't even seem fazed by his face. "Yeah. So?"

The guy slips a hand inside his jacket and pulls out a manila envelope. "You've been served."

"You're fucking kidding."

The man places the envelope under the truck's wipers then trots down the drive to his piece of crap sedan and speeds off.

Divorce papers? This panic hits him. Last night when the big guy with the steel-toed boots was coming on like a beast in the night wasn't fear. This is what fear is. When the life you know splits open and swallows you whole. His mom opens the storm door to tell him breakfast is ready. He hardly hears her, tearing the envelope open. The letter is written on thick paper with four important sounding surnames on the heading. It's from Kimberly and her woman lawyer alright. Ken skims the letter's contents then charges indoors. His mom is wiping down the counter when he thrusts the letter in her face.

"She wants a divorce."

"Who does?"

"Who do you think? I screw up one time and she gets some fancy bitch lawyer?"

His mom dries her hands on her apron then sits at the table and reads in her methodical old lady way. He doesn't know what to fixate on. He sees the sandwich cut into neat triangles and stuffs an entire wedge in his mouth. Then he grabs a beer from the refrigerator.

"Look when it's dated," he says, swallowing. "It was written before she knew about that woman."

"Well, I'll be."

Ken chugs half the beer. "Is that all you can say?"

"You mean you didn't see this coming?"

"No, Mom. I didn't." He snatches the letter from her hands. "I was expecting a little more support."

Into the backyard he goes. He walks up to the aluminum shed and punches the wall. The noise is so trembling loud that a flock of birds scatter from the big tree. He hits it a second time. Then his heart starts fluttering. Then its banging in rapid clips. Physically, Ken is not what he once was. Throw in cigs, weed, junk food, poor sleeping habits, alcohol, well shit, he's living on borrowed time. Or that's what he thinks with his chest on fire.

"You okay?" his mom yells through the kitchen window.

He waves her off while taking in huge cuts of oxygen. His heart pounds and there's a dull pressure in his head. The drumming slowly recedes. Ken sits slumped under the black maple with a sour odor coming off him. So, his wife wants a divorce. Fine, he can play the field. Really, isn't divorce for the best? Then why does he want to scream his lungs out?

He gets out his phone and texts Brandon if he knew he was being served. *No. Honest to God. You want to talk?* He then dials Kimberly's number. He deserves an explanation, right? Okay, maybe not. Scared, he terminates the call. *Got your letter,* he writes her. *Can we talk.* Then he stares at the screen expecting his wife to write straight back. When that doesn't happen, he calls her closest confidant. "Did you know, Jeremy?"

"You and Mom's marriage isn't my business."

"But her confiding in you is?"

"Maybe this is a good thing, Dad. You're not the happiest guy."

"Wow, Jeremy. Thanks for the insight? "

"Mom warned me you'd act like this."

Then Ken does something he's always nagging his boys about when they don't get their way. He drops the call. Then he trudges around the house and gets into his truck needing cigarettes and a Mountain Dew. The tires squeal backing down the drive. He's accelerating past the house when he realizes he forgot his wallet. "Fucking A, Solberg. Get your shit together, man."

The call comes through when the sun is high and perfectly round. Ken sits at the throne of the maple like a mad king. He tells himself to remain calm. He will hear his wife out. And no matter what he won't point blame. "Thanks for calling me back."

"I'm done." She sounds weary and half-mad herself. "I'm tired and I'm done."

"I didn't mean for this."

"What do you want?"

He pulls at tufts of grass between his legs. "I thought we could talk this out."

"That's what Sherman said you'd do."

"Sherman? I thought your lawyer was a woman?"

"Sherman is a friend, okay?"

Ken gets up from murdering the grass. "Was Sherman who you were meeting the other night?"

"If you're asking if Sherman and I had intercourse the other night, the answer is no."

"Have you had intercourse with this Sherman guy in the past?"

"He's a friend from Los Angeles. And that's all I'm going to say."

*Los Angeles?* Ken's head is whirring. "Are you fucking this guy?"

"I'm hanging up."

"Why was the letter dated June 28th?"

"This has been a long time coming."

"*You are* fucking this guy," he says, raising his voice. "Okay, prove it. What's his last name?"

"This is ridiculous," she says. "You are ridiculous."

"You think it's easy being married to you?"

"Why am I talking to you? Go back to that bitch-whore. You deserve each other."

"Fuck you."

"No, Ken. FUCK YOU."

He goes to hang up but his wife beats him to it. Bees hum. The day is perfect and gold. Like love can be. Or sex. Or a great song. If he weren't so furious, he'd cry. Then he does what any half-baked, hungover, bitter middle aged man does after his wife insinuates sex with another guy. He Googles the man. *Sherman Los Angeles not a lawyer* produces 37,800 results in .79 seconds. He scans the first page data like a man of this most tech-savvy age—with dubious self-interest. The only name that catches his eye, the only person who somehow makes sense, is a man named Sherman

Garrity. How did he come up with this person over the tens of thousands of entries? Sometimes a husband must go with his gut.

*Sherman Garrity? The movie mogul?*

*He's twice the man you are.*

"You mean I fingered the asshole on the first try?" Ken high fives the tree. "Nice, Solberg. Nice."

Garrity's bio reads like any left leaning celebrity living on the west coast. Homes in Bel Air, Manhattan, Aspen and Madeline Island, Wisconsin. Philanthropic efforts in post-earthquake Haiti. Film producer, rare car collector, expert skier. He's won seven gold balls, whatever the fuck that means. There's a photograph of him outside some movie premier with the red carpet and paparazzi. He isn't movie star handsome, but the guy isn't bad looking, either. He owns a jaw that exudes the panache associated with money and entitlement. Twice the man he is? In what way? His moral fiber? The size of his dick? Or is Kimberly talking about what everyone talks about these days—the scope of Garrity's assets?

But wait. Just when he's about to jump in his truck and drive into a concrete wall at a hundred miles an hour he comes upon an article in the *Island Gazette*, La Pointe, Wisconsin, about a high society woman named Hannah Garrity who drowned in a boating accident off Lake Superior. Garrity was seventeen when he lost his mother. Ken throws a vacant stare across the lawn. No one deserves to lose a parent as a teenager, not even the fucker who's doing his wife.

He chucks his phone. He throws it as far as he can. It arcs across the sky like a silver lure spinning toward a clear blue lake. The phone lands in the neighbor's yard where it deflects off a birdbath. He storms over, cussing under his breath then grabs the phone and sees the screen's shattered.

"Of course it is!"

"Ken?" His mom stands at the property's edge with her hands twisted in a mess. "I think you should come inside. The neighbors are getting nervous."

And he cuts across the grass holding his smashed phone.

\*\*\*

When old enough he drove every two-bit gravel road he could find. Some nights as far as Ely before he turned the station wagon around and drove home. Those narcotic late nights, the high beams illuminating the stark fields, the forlorn trees dark against the midnight sky, Springsteen on the stereo. Ken lost himself on those roads. He thought about school and hockey, about his troubled home life, the future of a family devastated by loss, and his pain threatened to carry him away.

One night in early spring his car idled outside Melody's house. Spring wasn't a pretty season in north country. Snow flurries one day, the next a harsh cold rain. She climbed into the car wearing his letter jacket, which fell to her thighs, the sleeve cuffs folded twice over. Melody scooted over in the seat, smelling like shampoo. "What? No kiss?"

Melody stuck out her tongue. She was prone to silly faces. Her not taking herself too seriously was one of the things he loved about her. She gave him a peck on the lips. He waited, expecting something softer and wetter, a tease for what was to come later, but she was already facing forward and staring out the windshield as the sky grew black.

He put the car into gear. "Where to?"

On weekends they drove the outskirts of town, searching for far-flung places the cops and farmers didn't know about. There, with the motor running and radio on, the windows steamed and their bodies ached for what once was. But tonight, Melody was quieter than her usual self.

"Is something wrong?"

They were coming on the dirt road west of town that led to an island of aspen surrounded by farmland. Ken drove up the lane, put the car in park, and turned off the headlamps. He fiddled with the stereo until he heard their song. The moment the music began, his girlfriend started undressing.

"Back seat?"

The only bright spot in his life hadn't said a word since they left her house. And that was fine. They spoke the language of love and the language of love held no words. To them love was the tender way they looked at each other, how they made each other feel groping in the dark. Love was how they forgot, for a little while at least.

She lifted her hips in the air then slid her underwear down her pale legs until they ended up on the floorboard. Then she lay on top of him and put him inside her. This was how it always was, Melody on top, Melody in charge, Melody guided Ken to release. Then Melody holding him afterwards, stroking his hair, telling him 'hush now, it's okay, let it out, let it all out.'

Tonight, though, he heard her. It was dark inside the car and she was moving on top of him, but he heard a sound like crying. "Melody?" She rolled off and turned away. "Did I hurt you? Are you okay?"

"I can't do this anymore."

"What do you mean?"

"You're suffocating me. This stuff, what we do—it's sick," she said with tears streaming down her face. "It's over, Ken. We're over."

The words terrorized him. Andrew had been dead three months. "You can't do this. We love each other." He could feel a panic coming on. "It's gotten better. I'm better! Because of you!" She was faced away and putting on her bra. He could feel her moving past them, moving on. "Please, Melody. I beg you! Please!"

***

He listens to the meandering free verse poetry off *The Wild, The Innocent & the E-Street Shuffle* with Melody Fillman on the brain. She's all around him, in his heart and in his imagination, in everything he sees and smells. The bog willows and birch trees, the bright tamaracks. Ken slows at the long driveway of the home she and Tom Kincaid built on the lake. The one with the Home For Sale sign out front. He turns back onto 11 heading east toward Sha Sha Resort where he and Andrew used to cliff dive and drink beers and dream about the life they'd have when they grew up. Ken's caught up to a little Audi with expensive rims. A sleek bike sits upright on the roof. It gets him thinking about Sherman Garrity. Like maybe he should drive across this great country of ours and meet the man in person. They must have met the weekend Kimberly and her girlfriends vacationed at Madeline Island. Did that mean she'd been seeing the guy since last summer? Was she in love with him?

He checks oncoming traffic then pulls alongside the sports car. The driver is exactly how Ken pictures him. Think hipster eyewear or Whole Foods or Feel the Bern bumper stickers. He passes the Audi then maneuvers back into the right lane. And he slows down. He and Cal used to fuck with guys like this. They'd drive to Duluth and end up in the neighborhood where the rich doctors lived in those sweet mansions. They'd bait their spoiled sons into making chase. So he's not surprised when the hipster tucks in real tight. Then it happens—the Audi shoots to pass but Ken cuts it off. It takes only a few seconds for the Audi to glue itself back to the Ford's rear bumper. He loses sight of everything but the bike's handlebars. And he hammers the brakes hard. A long high screech follows before the driver gets the Audi under control. This time he lets the Audi rip past. What the hipster doesn't know is an eighteen-wheeler hauling fresh-cut timber is barreling down from the other direction. The sports car just sneaks by and is out of sight in no time.

Bored, he does a U-turn and heads back into town. Ten minutes later he's pulling up to Cal's place to drop off the check as promised. Parked next to the house is the white SUV, but no pickup. He's about to turn around when he spies Melody sunbathing on the back deck. He sits there engrossed in the past, seeing them clear as day, riding in that old station wagon under a bleached out sky.

Ken wakes from his stupor to find Melody sitting forward in her chair like she has the right mind to go indoors and slide the deadbolt in place. He climbs down from his rig, tramps across the grass while checking his pockets for cigarettes. Mable greets him at the deck steps, not that he sees her. He's still running his hands over his front and back pockets looking for his smokes.

"What are you doing?"

He stops with the pat down. "You mean my coming over?"

"With your hands. You look like Cal giving signals to his Little League team."

Ken muffles a laugh. "Left my cigarettes in the truck."

Because of the glare, Melody puts a hand over her eyes. "You still smoke?"

His pulse quickens hustling across the lawn. He's being summoned by the first woman to break his heart. On his way back he wonders what this might look like to an outsider, say someone like Cal. Better not linger too long, he thinks.

The gentlemen in him lights hers first. Melody blows out a line of smoke.

"He'd skin me alive if he saw me smoking."

"I won't tell if you don't," he says, shuffling across the deck then leaning against the rail. He catches her staring at him while he lights his cigarette. "What?"

"Your face."

His eyes drop to the deck boards. But then he sneaks another look. Her breasts are fuller and she's thicker around the waist. But she's still a fine woman.

She catches him eyeing her. "What are you doing in town? And I want a straight answer."

He wants to speak on lost time, what we have to show for it, what's slipped away. He wants to say a person's life is like a flash of light in the sky. We're here, we do our thing, and then we get lost to time and space.

"I got served today. I'm getting divorced."

She hugs her knees staring at the lit end of the cigarette. "I'm sorry."

"How was yours?"

She brushes the cherry end against the deck then drops the remains through a space in the boards. "In the end we clawed for things that didn't matter a whole lot. Just stuff we'd collected along the way."

He thinks he lost her when he spoke on his marriage problems and flicks his cigarette into the grass then walks over and sits on her chair's end. Melody still squeezes her arms around her knees.

"I don't have anyone to talk to."

"What about Cal?"

"You know how it is. Guys talk sports. We brag about how far we drive the ball off the tee. But the important stuff?" His voice trails off. How many times has he dreamt about this moment, them together, no distractions. Should he tell her he never completely let her go?

They hear the truck before they see him. Crushed gravel never sounded so desperate or cruel. The three of them scatter—Mable leaping off the deck and trotted across the lawn, Ken back to the safety of the deck rail, and Melody rocking back and forth in an even tighter ball.

It doesn't take Cal long to cut across the grass. "Mel," he says. "Go put some clothes on."

"Don't tell me what to do."

"We were just talking."

"And you." Cal's on the deck now and pointing a finger at Ken. "I don't want to hear nothing from you." Melody is stretched out on the lounge like a bronze princess. "Did he tell you how he fucked up his marriage?"

"He got served, Cal."

"Jesus. I don't believe you two."

"I've got an idea." She rises from the chair and puts her hands on her hips. "Why don't you two fight over little old me, last man standing wins. Whoopty-fucking-do, right?" She goes to the sliding glass door and jerks it open. "Aren't you coming, Mable?" She and the dog disappear inside.

The men stare at the empty lounge chair as if they're no good as a team without her lively presence to distract them. Then Cal runs his hands through his hair. "I fucked that up, huh?"

"You're good at jumping to conclusions," Ken says lighting another cigarette.

"Don't start with me."

Cal joins him at the rail. They look out over the water's dreamy whirl. Cigarette perched between his lips, Ken pulls out his wallet then hands him the blank check. Cal doesn't bother looking at it. He just folds it in half then puts it in his pocket.

"Kimberly's leaving me, man. She's not fucking around this time."

Cal doesn't look at his friend when he gives his shoulder a squeeze. "I'm sorry to hear that. And that shit," he says glancing at his smoke. "That shit is nasty. I once tasted it on Mel's breath. I nearly vomited."

"Remind me that next time you want to kiss me."

"Hardy har har, motherfucker."

"Well, I better be pressing on. "

The friends don't hug. They hardly glance at each other. Ken is halfway across the lawn when he stops. This is his best friend. "This is stupid, Cal."

"Call me tomorrow, okay?"

He backs out the driveway, sending up dust and rock. A mile east of Rainer he sees a buck standing in the cool of the pines. Ken pulls over and kills the engine. Crickets sing in the slough of thistle and pondweed. High above an eagle floats a thermal. The buck, full chested with a mottled hindquarter and a rack in the early nub stages, hasn't moved. He's so majestic Ken's moved to tears. He brings his arms up to eye level like he's holding a rifle.

"Pow. You're dead, gorgeous."

\*\*\*

That night he takes a bath. He can't remember the last time he soaked in a tub. Watching it fill with water he wonders if it's acceptable for a man his age to draw a bath. Even the words *draw a bath* sound wrong. He's a hockey player. He uses his fists like James Wright did words. Did the poet draw a bath when he struggled to put words on the page?

Tonight is about detoxification. It's about Ken coming clean.

He undresses quickly. There are things men of a certain age don't like to see, one being the sad mishappen outline of their former selves. Man, he's let himself go. Ken is a manatee. He is a candy bar's thick creamy exterior and gooey nougat insides. In the mirror over the sink he inspects his face. He decides he likes the whiskers. He'll grow a beard, the gray-speckled lumberjack in a checked flannel shirt. He'll take down trees with a hatchet then build a rustic cabin with his bare hands. What he can't imagine in this Norseman's fantasy is a woman. Well, maybe his wife, if he makes a huge transformation.

Falling asleep later he feels restored—like a new man. Like the sour bitter taste in his liver is flushed clean. Alcohol is his Achilles heel. If he wasn't loaded the other night, he doesn't get in a fight, which means he doesn't slobber over Melody in a bikini or get Cal fuming mad. When's the last time they argued? They were kindred spirits. They sang to the same beat—loud bars, those pre-parties cranking *Joshua Tree*, the night they broke a beer bottle and cut their wrists, blood brothers forever. What was he thinking? Him and Melody after all these years? He'll call Cal in the morning. Then he'll start down the path that leads to enlightenment.

Ken's asleep when he hears a faint soothing *ping*... then another *ping*... and he stirs awake. Then he's groping the floor for his lifeline to the world. 218 area code. *Sorry about today.*

Midnight, and his head is cloudy. *Melody?*

*He feels terrible. He loves you, Ken.*

Wedging a pillow under his arm, he sits up, drowsy but also wide awake. His first thought is why is she contacting him at this hour in the night. But then—is there still something between them? To him, she's like a train signal's faint red glow pulsating across some dark landscape. This beacon he's drawn to. Is it the same for her? *I feel bad, too.* The second he hits send, doubt creeps in. He berates himself for being so gullible. This is Cal's woman. He calls her *Mel* for Christ's sake. And Ken's meddling in that? Three minutes pass. If he wasn't completely convinced she was fucking with him before, he's absolutely sure now. Or Cal's on the other end—orchestrating this whole thing to prove what everyone has long suspected—Ken has no allegiance to anyone but himself.

Then another lovely ping. *Sorry, Mable had to pee... Got any more of those cigarettes.*

He smiles into the bright screen. *Be right over.* His mind veers backward in time. His face is now dead serious. *You ever think about that night?*

*Sometimes.*

*Me, too.*

Ken wakes to another bright morning up north. He lies there a bit, listening for his mom and Sven, but the house is quiet. He rereads the text exchange from last night, and he's surprised about the strong feelings moving through his big self. Best to keep busy, he thinks, and rolls out of bed then collects his dirty clothes. The last thing he needs right now is to further complicate his life by falling for his high school girlfriend. On the way to the laundry, he hears church bells. Ah, Sunday morning. That explains why no one's around. He's separating whites from colors when he thinks about Melody again. Is this about something that never played out? Is she the reason he's up north? Does everything lead to her? Adding detergent to the laundry tub, he has a thought. The idea is so far-fetched it puts a grin on his face. He closes the lid then steps outdoors for a smoke. No, she won't fall for it. She's too smart. But what if she does?

Ken gets out his iPhone and starts typing Cal a message. He apologizes for yesterday, says he understands why Cal got upset, that he'd have reacted the same way. *I'm happy for you. Get a drink tonight?*

*Can't,* Cal writes back. *Work.*

*Rain check, then.*

Slipping the phone back in his pocket, he thinks—this might just work.


It's six in the evening when he parks next to the curb of his childhood home. Ken grabs the shopping bags then heads up the drive under an orange sun. He finds his mom and Sven in the backyard drinking beers under the maple tree.

"Your laundry's on the bed," she says, spying the bags. "You go to the mall in Bemidji?"

"I wish you'd told me," Sven says. "Footlocker's got shoelaces I like."

Ken digs in a Herberger's bag and pulls out a suede leather jacket with a zipped front and big lazy collar. "Got you this, Mom. It's Ivanka Trump's brand. Try it on."

Smiling curiously, she rises from her chair and walks over. He helps her first get one arm through a sleeve, then the another.

"It's beautiful."

"That's 100% genuine suede."

"It's so soft," she says walking over to Sven. "What do you think?"

"Well, I'll be," he says, caressing the fabric. "It's real nice, Betty."

"You look ten years younger, Mom."

"Is it too fancy for church?"

"God will love you in that coat."

"What else you got there?" she says.

"You'll see."


His energy is high loading the equipment in the flatbed. Then he takes a long shower and gets dressed. He even sniffs the new boots before lacing them up. His mom and Sven are watching the Twins on TV when he strolls in with his new paisley shirt untucked and opened at the collar.

"For a second I thought you were Andrew," she says.

Ken smiles in a coy, reluctant hero sort of way. Then he's padding outdoors with no words to convey his sense of purpose in what he's about to do. The sunset this afternoon is the biggest, boldest he's even seen. It's a sign. He's on the right path—he's moving toward the light.

Pulling away from the curb he glances in the rearview mirror. And Ken sees his father's face. The red stain brought on by drinking and rage, the reticence and dry sense of humor. The way his dad perked up when the boy's brought a pretty girl around. They were too alike with their secret lives and violent propensities. *I am different,* he says to himself. *I am a better man.* And something like optimism flows through his bloodstream.

The first of two detours takes him past the fire department. Once he sees what he was hoping to see he drives to the cemetery. He hops down from the cab with the wildflowers he picked by the side of the road. Kneeling in the grass next to their headstones, he prays for Andrew and his dad, that in death they found peace. Then Ken scatters the flowers between the graves, climbs back in his truck, and heads to Rainy Lake. But the driveway and what it represents comes on too fast and he motors past. Two passes later he finds his courage and pulls up the long drive with the *Island View Realty For Sale* sign where Tom Kincaid and Melody

Fillman once lived in the big prairie-style house with the wraparound porch. Two cars are parked out front—her cute little SUV and a flashy blue pickup with exhausts extending from the cab like silver horns.

Twenty yards from the porch he hops down from the cab and gets to work, pulling the stereo out and stringing speaker wire along the ground. He fires up the generator then wastes no time lining up the needle, side four, track three. After cranking the volume, he sits on the truck's roof with his shiny boots dangling over the windshield.

She appears in the doorway, just the outline of her figure behind the screen. Then she walks onto the porch. It's like a movie. The decorated war hero returns home and is reunited with the great love of his life. The music feels realer now that he sees her cutting across the lawn in a plain white T-shirt and jeans. Her arms are clasped over her chest and the day's light holds on by a thread.

"What in God's name are you up to?"

He's surprised by her tone. "This was our song, remember?"

They played it endlessly. The nights they drove out in the boonies looking for a place to kiss and snuggle and fog the windows.

"Are you drunk?"

"On life maybe. On you."

"You should leave."

"Man, I love this song. Listen to that solo, Melody. Clarence Clemons was the bomb."

"Tom Jr. wanted to call the cops. I said, 'He's an old friend. He means no harm.' But Ken? You're worrying me."

He is everywhere. He is truth and he is light. Smiling, he eases off the roof then dusts his knees hoping she notices the boots. He holds out his hand. "Dance with me."

She grins in her old way. "You're crazy."

Hope floods his big frame. It's the part in the song when the music turns big and spacy. He sees them as they once were—bound to something bigger than themselves. "Come on, let's dance." He senses her reluctancy. "… come on… dance…"

She takes his hand and they slow dance. Ken sings in her ear and she is everything and more. Melody pulls back far enough to look at him. "You're a fool, you know that?"

An impulse to kiss Melody has him leaning toward her. She pulls back like she sees something in him she long suspected is true. And this makes her wary and disappointed and sad.

"Just go," she says. Movement on the porch gets his attention. He sees Tom Jr. holding a shotgun low by his side. "Go home. Go work things out with your wife."

She starts for the house. And she doesn't stop until she steps on the porch and has a word with her son. Then they go inside. Ken feels something happening to him. Like he's splitting apart. Like the whole goddamn world is disintegrating, him with it. He kicks a hole in the cheap speakers then snaps the record in half. Then he loads the equipment in the flatbed and drives off.

At the highway entrance, next to wetlands with high reeds, Ken brakes hard. He's sobbing something sick and stumbles from the cab in a frantic stupor. Cars rattle past and everything is blurred and crashing down. *The night comes to him in jumbles, in pieces that don't fit. There was Gleeson's cabin and a starry night, a frost overtaking the windshield. Snow piled high on the sides of the road and above him the midnight sky was milky white and alive.*

He reaches behind the seat. The Glock feels both light and heavy in his hand. He pops out the magazine. It's loaded alright. *She was there and so was Andrew and the rest.* He sticks the barrel in his mouth. His breathing is thick and his thoughts bigger than this score of land. Bigger than Springsteen. He's going to do it. He's going to end it all right here, right now. Tears soak his cheeks. The gun is so far down his throat he gags. He thinks about the mess he's made. Those deeds he can't take back. His eyes find the dark veil overtaking the sky. This day and this night, this end, this imperfect world. *The door on the left. Every time he opens that door he's seventeen. Him and his big fucking mouth.* Tears slip down his cheek and taste like saltlicks and gunshot and the buck from yesterday and his eyes are wide open and he will enter death like he lived life and God have mercy on his soul.

Regripping the handle, he gives the heaven's a last mighty glare—*there it is again the bedroom door and him*—and squeezes his eyes shut—*he was supposed to die, not Andrew, not the town hero.* And his phone rings. Really? With him squatting behind the truck with the Glock down his throat? The ringing finally stops. Ken spits out a loogie then wipes his eyes with his shirtsleeve. Then he gets back in position, legs spread, his death stance. This time he holds the gun with both hands. He's doing this. He fucking is. This is about liberating pain. This is about peace and eternal rest. This is about Andrew and that night. He should have done this a long time ago. His fingers find the trigger. And his phone goes off again.

Ken staggers backward in the failing light. He feels in slow motion. Like something is hitting him from all sides. Then he's moving for the door and yanking it open. He seizes the phone with the shattered screen. "What, Brandon?"

"Oh, sorry. Butt dial."

"TWICE! FUCKING TWICE!"

"Dad? What's going on?"

And he drops to his knees and lays his forehead on the ground and when he pulls back his eyes are stunned open. The gun has slippped from his fingers and lays underfoot. All that courage, if that's what that was, rushes from him like blood from a gut-shot wound.

"You're scaring the shit out of me, Dad."

"Jesus God Almighty."

"Don't do it, Dad. Please. I beg you. Whatever you're thinking, please don't."

He slumps against the door and heaves out enormous breaths of air. Brandon starts crying. "Jesus, Dad. I'm calling Mom."

"No, wait. I'm catching my breath. I'm okay."

"You're freaking me out!"

Ken lets go a long tired sigh that makes his entire body shudder. "I'm okay now."

"You sure?"

And it's like it always is with the soothing sound crickets make and the faint click of wind in the reeds, only different. "Hey, where is that mother of yours anyway?"

"Mom? She's um, she's away."

"Away? Like on a ride?"

"I don't know. Jesus, Dad. Are you sure you're okay?"

"Where's she gone?"

"You should call her. She'd like to hear from you. She'd like to hear your voice."

"Where is she?"

"Up north."

"Minnesota?"

"Yeah, no wait. Wisconsin somewhere."

Ken bends down and reaches for the Glock. He wipes it clean with his fancy shirt.

"Really? Wisconsin?"

"Why don't you come home, Dad. Jeremy and I miss you. We can get drunk and listen to Springsteen, like old times."

"I love you and your brother more than anything else in the world. You remember that."

He puts the gun away for safekeeping then climbs into the F-150. Then he's turning onto the highway back to his mom's place to retrieve his gear and his dog.

PART TWO

*"Shake it, shake it, Sugaree*
*I'll meet you at the Jubilee*
*And if that Jubilee don't come*
*Baby, I'll meet you on the run"*
**–The Grateful Dead**

# IN BETWEEN DAYS

She calls him Sherman-ocity. Like he's winged Hermes. Like the speed of his being, the way he spins through life, is something she wants in her life, too. They've been going on two days now in the north woods with the crisp-blue lake and the sky that goes on forever. Sherman-ocity. That was him that first night in the Hewing. He was like the hero of his own movie. Once they'd made up, once they'd had a good tearful laugh (him anyway), once Kimberly forgave him for his PMCP, he'd been outstanding, full of gusto and stamina, aiming to please. But the best part, what resonates in his chest even now, is how he played the next day. Sherman was the hero of that story, too. He and Van Doorman lit those midwestern boys up. The Aquatennial match took an hour, max. He'd been *Sherman-ocityyyyyy*.

They sit on the screened-in porch drinking vodka tonics on the evening of day two. His shoulders are sunburnt and itch under his shirt. They'd taken the Chris-Craft to the sea caves then lunched on a secluded island where they'd made love on a mat of grass. When they were done exhausting themselves Kimberly entered the water and cleaned herself. She was giddy and embarrassed, and he felt a strong stirring inside him. Like he'd made the correct decision in letting Ethereal go. Though at times the past nearly overwhelms him. The first time Juliet appeared they were in the sauna. When she manifested in his brain's circuitry later that night (they were making love by a roaring fire) he clamped his eyes shut and his body must have seized up because next thing he knew Kimberly had taken his face in her hands. "Sherman? Are you okay?"

Tonight she wears his hunter-green flannel and lies on a wicker couch three generations old. She reminds him of his mother, especially those summer nights they'd spend at the Hideaway crouched over puzzle pieces while his dad drank scotch and poured over maps of shipwrecks in Lake Superior. He's telling Kimberly how he stumbled onto the script. That if he hadn't been picking Henrique up from his tennis lesson, he wouldn't have run into the HBO exec whose son was in the same class. When the woman heard about his tennis background, she said the studio had passed on the script that morning. He'd called Blanco on the way home.

"And he turned out to be a real asshole."

Bugs bump into the porch screen. The last of the day's light is being siphoned off the sky.

"Have you told him how frustrated you are?"

He drains his cocktail then leans in. He's drunker than he thought. "You don't talk to Blanco. You get lectured. He auditions women for the stripper wife using a tape measure. I'm talking bust, hips, waist. It's sick."

"So, Blanco's a pig. But the question to ask yourself is this: can the Chinese be trusted?"

Sherman eyes the new woman in his life in the sconce's trembling light. He likes this back and forth. Unlike Ethereal, she has no skin in the game. He can trust her. He can tell her about a deal without it turning into her own personal drama. Why does everything go back to trust? He'd trusted his mom not dying before he graduated high school. He'd even trusted Juliet. And look where that got him. Endless nights cruising the freeways in Los Angeles like a character out of a Bret Easton Ellis novel.

"Be right back," he says. "Nature calls." He undoes the porch latch, steps into the dewy grass, then enters the dark trees with Juliet on the brain. They'd grown up together. Their moms played in the Tuesday morning tennis drill. They sat next to each other in kindergarten class at Roscomare Elementary. Juliet was there the year his mom died. She'd even visited the Hideaway. But she wasn't the one. As a teenager, if Sherman felt life passing through him like a fierce wind, then Juliet was a tree. A tree he was frantically holding onto. And now Kimberly is Juliet? Or is it the other way around? Does it matter? The truth is, he doesn't trust himself. Or he trusts he'll do the wrong thing. That he'll mess everything up—his love life, the film, the shit with his dad.

He urinates on the bark of an old tree. He has no idea what kind. No, *what species*. Where is his head? One too many vodkas, that's where. He peers at the stars through the leaf cover. God, he loves it here, swatting a mosquito buzzing near his ear. He might not know an oak from a beech, but he can spot pine shoots and maples with their distinct leaf pattern. His text sounds in all that hushed fragrant air. With his free hand, he reaches inside his short's pocket. *Stalling tactics won't work,* Jonathan Lin writes. *Either drop Blanco or we're out.* Where is that middle finger emoji when you need it? He begins knocking out a sarcastic reply using his thumb when he accidentally drops the phone. "Fuck me!"

"Sherman?" he hears Kimberly yell from the porch.

"Nothing!"

He pulls hard on his pecker, pinching the flow, then gropes the ground with his other hand until he finds his smartphone. He finishes peeing, wipes the phone's mess off on his shorts, then walks back to the house. He finds her sitting on a Turkish rug in the living room and flipping through his mom's record collection.

"You know who that was? Jonathan Lin. He wants a decision on Blanco. And I can't get my team on the same page."

She looks up holding *What's Going On*. "Why don't you bring them here?"

"The Hideaway?"

"Madeline Island is neutral territory. You know this place. You'll have the upper hand."

"You mean Blanco, Gil Gibson and Jonathan Lin? Here? With us?"

"Schmooze them, take them golfing. When they're relaxed and seeing no one's the enemy, the four of you figure out a plan."

"What about us? It means me working more."

"I think it sounds exciting. I've never met any Hollywood people other than you."

Sherman tries to wipe the gargantuan smile off his face, not wanting her to see how excited he is. "Holy shit, Kimberly. You're on."

\*\*\*

He tries not to eavesdrop.

Okay, that's not exactly true. It's hard not to hear Kimberly's voice trailing down the lawn. She's on the porch talking on the phone with her youngest boy. Sherman sits in the sun with the tennis script in his lap. It's the last day they'll have the Hideaway to themselves. If the lake home sounds like a ruined castle, it's not. The two-story house sits on a rise high above the water and is built in the manner of the family Tudor in Bel Air. The second story windows look down a grassy slope through ankle-thin trees a few football fields from the lake. Inside smells like time worn fires, the floors creak, and the split-face granite hearth was collected from a nearby field. The only renovation he'd overseen was the kitchen, the centerpiece being a slate-blue industrial stove with a griddle and double oven for those outlandish parties he thought he'd throw, though years passed and those ideas got to feel like the dreams of a naïve young man Sherman scarcely remembered anymore. Kimberly breathes new life in the old place. She doesn't make the bed in the morning, she tucks in the quilt and creases the sides. She freshens Mason jars with wildflowers. She even cleaned out the fireplace and stacked a teepee of kindling as if waiting for her good knight's return.

He still hopes his dad will visit. He pictures him scraping windowpanes or chopping wood and stacking it against the outbuilding. He sees his dad swimming first thing every morning. He was a strong swimmer. At fifteen he swam to Bayfield over a $10 bet in a drysuit he'd seen illustrated in *Life Magazine*. This was his dad the adventurer, him at his finest, the Locke Garrity Sherman always aspired to be.

His thoughts are interrupted by Kimberly's voice, which has taken on a more somber tone. Her boys have been tracking Ken Dog via Mastercard charges: Cenex, Virginia, Minnesota; Cabela's Duluth; an auto repair shop in Superior. If Sherman's following the conversation correctly it sounds like he withdrew money from an ATM in Brule yesterday. This has him sitting forward in his chair. Brule is sixty miles away. Why is Ken Dog in the great north woods? Is it a coincidence? Should he be worried?

"He's nice," he hears her say. "Can you let me enjoy myself and leave it at that?" He's surprised how much her words mean. Then her voice brightens. She says swimming in Lake Superior is like plunging into an icy bath. She's one of the good parents. He and his dad never spent an hour on the phone chatting. They've never talked through their problems. How does she do that—be that rock, that person her kids can depend on? The call ends then he hears the screen door bang shut. Sherman pretends interest in the script, looking up when Kimberly walks over.

"Well? How did it go?"

She sits in the adjacent Adirondack chair and lets out a sigh. "My husband left his mom's a few days ago. I guess he was acting strange."

"Strange? You don't think… he wouldn't it…"

"Hurt himself?" Kimberly's blue eyes find the tall pines swaying in the breeze.

"Maybe he ran off with his high school sweetheart."

She doesn't laugh. "Not calling his boys? That's not like him."

They lounge in the late morning sun, one wearing riding bibs and a Castelli jersey, the other barefoot and swatting horseflies off his shaved legs. Why had he brought up suicide? They were in a pretty good place considering the guests arrived tomorrow. Food and beverages were enroute from all points on a compass: sushi-grade tuna from Seattle, free-range meats and cheeses from Spring Valley, Wisconsin, $4000 worth of wines from a liquor store in Minneapolis named Haskell's. Steve-O, proprietor of Larson Motors, and his son Dylan had staked out lines for a music stage and bar. His oldest daughter was driving back from Duluth with three kegs of Bent Paddle. Her younger sister, the beauty with the long legs and big penetrating eyes, was on a Walmart run in Ashland. They'd erected yurts and ordered a fancy port-a-potty after the island's inn sold out for the weekend. They'd even hired a band. But what elevates his blood pressure the most is the secret guest list. Shinkan Sen, the ravishing actress playing the femme fatale, is flying in with her personal assistant. So is Heather Harper and her thirteen-year-old boy, Bjorn. Even the actor playing Richard Blanco in the movie about his life is staying at the house. It's enough for another heart palpitation.

"Sherman?" she says. "Is the tennis player's wife as beautiful in person as she is in photographs?"

"Heather? You'll love her. She's real, like you are. So many people in my orbit aren't."

"She runs a yoga studio?"

"And she's a mom. I think Blanco said she rides."

Kimberly sets her hand on his upper thigh. "Can we get her a gravel bike? Please?"

"I'll see what I can do."

They sit awhile, him marking up the text, her stretched out in the sun.

"I didn't tell you everything," she says. She mentions the troubling phone call Brandon received. "He was scared."

"Your husband will show up," he says, trying to reassure her. "You'll see."

She lifts herself up from the chair in one swelled move. Her eyes find the lake through the trees. "Wanna join me for a swim?"

"Let me finish reading this scene."

He waits until Kimberly goes into the house to change into her swimsuit to Google Solberg on his phone. He finds a highlight film someone put together of his fights set to "Welcome To The Jungle." Solberg didn't play hockey like everyone else. He skated slow and menacing. And where most players reacted to the puck, his role as punisher was seeking out the opponent and laying out bone crushing hits or slashing players in the face with his stick. It was like he dared a player to enter his zone. The fights were relentless and savage and plain sick. After watching the footage one thing is clear—Ken Solberg is not a guy you wanted to fuck with.

The porch door slams and out comes Kimberly in a one-piece swimsuit with her goggles and a towel thrown over her shoulder. He watches her walk across the grass. "Ready?"

"You don't think he's on his way here, do you?"

"My husband?" She bends over, her blues eyes swarming his. "How would he know we're on Madeline Island, silly?"

"I don't know. Would he?"

"He goes off grid all the time. Forget about him, okay? Now, are you coming for a swim or not?"

"I thought I'd check in with my dad. You want to say hello?" FaceTime is already dialing through when she smiles like she's onto him.

"You're using me, Sherman Garrity, to get your dad to pony up."

"Well, he can afford it."

"Afford what?" he hears his dad say.

When he looks at the phone screen Locke's weathered face appears. "Oh, hi Dad!"

Kimberly walks behind Sherman and places her hands on his shoulders. She bends down so the camera picks up her face. "Hi, Mr. Garrity."

Right away, his face brightens. "Who's this gorgeous woman?"

"Say hi to Kimberly."

"Now I understand why you took off for Madeline like that."

"I like your dad," she says, smiling. "It was nice meeting you."

"Nice meeting you, young lady."

She kisses Sherman's forehead then starts down the footpath that leads to the water, her goggles swinging from her wrist. She's not thin like Ethereal. She doesn't fret in the mirror. She's not concerned with what he thinks about this or that outfit. These things please him. She pleases him.

"Now, that's the woman for you," he hears his dad say.

"You think so?" Sherman says, thrilled with the comment. "Any thoughts on visiting?"

There's a long gruff pause like Locke is seriously thinking about it. "Let me sleep on it."

No sooner has he hung up when Steve-O and Dylan come around the house with lumber boards balancing on their broad shoulders. The twins follow with their straw-yellow hair and farm dresses. They each hold dolls, one cradling hers, the other dragging it by the arm. Sherman pushes himself up off the chair then walks over to where they've dropped the boards. Dylan's already heading around the house for another load. The two men gaze at the big lawn.

"Going to be a real barn buster, huh?" Steve-O says.

He's known his handyman since they were kids and Steve-O's father ran Larson Motors. "I got these movie people coming in. I'm not sure they'll get Madeline."

"You'll have them eating out of your hand, Sherman. And Bob Marley's playing?"

"You're coming, right?"

"Hell, yeah. Joanie and the twins are dancing machines."


A few minutes later Sherman's heading down the hill with a beach towel. He can hear Steve-O's little girls high excited voices and the faint rustle of wind in the trees. His phone rings. "Yes, VD?"

"I found a white truck with Minnesota plates, sir."

He stops in the cool of the trees. "Why are you whispering? Where are you?"

"Near your place, some old logging area."

"Is anyone inside?"

"Approaching as we speak, sir."

"Don't get yourself killed, Van Doorman." He can see the lake. It's rippling like a flag and is very bright. "Well?"

"All clear, sir. Engine's cold, doors locked."

"You think it's him?"

"Photo'd the plates, sir. I'll reach out to my guy at the DMV."

Sherman crosses the long planked footpath installed over the fragile grass ecosystem. He can see Kimberly swimming freestyle where the big drop-off is. Her limbs methodically break the surface and she seems tiny against the big lake. Grant's Point, when he reaches the shore, is empty. This fear rises in his throat. At its deepest Lake Superior is 1,333 feet. In the summer months the water is cold enough to kill a man from hyperthermia in less than sixty minutes. When it comes to bodies of water Sherman's governed by certain rules: one) the ocean is off limits two) with freshwater lakes, if he swims, the sun must be shining and the shoreline within a stone's throw, and three) never swim alone.

The water is bracingly cold.

Then he's underwater and moving his limbs against the tide. Light reflects off the sandy bottom. A school of minnow's jerk in the undercurrent. Farther out, he can see his lover's pale legs kicking in the liquid blue. She swims toward him and pulls off her goggles, letting them hang around her neck. Her eyes are bright. "It's breathtaking," she says. He forces a smile then swivels around so he can see the shoreline. The cold presses in around him and his eyes dart here and there like those minnows in the current. A dark thought passes through him. *He's out there, watching them, plotting his revenge.* Then Kimberly is rising out of the water like some dark phantom, the look on her face this horrifying glee. Then she's pushing him underwater. He can hear her muted laughter and his eyes are squeezed shut. Sherman can't move. He's paralyzed with fright, of what lurks on the lake's bottom.

# STATE TROOPER

Ken is chasing the night again. Chasing the lightning storm out over the big lake. Chasing a woman. Chasing time. It's like how he tore through Cabella's throwing camping equipment into his cart like the end was near. It's after midnight and there isn't another soul on the highway. Lightning flickers to the north—these luminous explosions that last several heartbeats before the sky goes dark again. He's trying to beat the storm. He's being like he always is—on the run, racing time, racing himself.

Wedged between his thighs is a bottle of Wild Turkey. Tied down in back is a cooler of beer and two boxes of dry goods. Ken has fire-starter, binoculars, a knife that transforms into a screwdriver, fish scaler, reamer and saw. He has a lightweight camp stove, sleeping bag, compact shovel, survival hatchet, crossbow and a U.S. Army regulation flashlight with 4000 lumens. He's ready for the long haul—whatever it takes to claim back what he believes in his soul is rightfully his. On the FM dial is a preacher man talking low and ferocious. Talking deliverance. About a higher power and faith in the almighty one. He likes that. He briefly closes his eyes and lets the words sink in. *The almighty one.* Then he sees his mother's face clear as fucking day. This was thirty minutes after Melody Fillman sent him packing with the taste of gun metal still fresh in his mouth. He was holding his old man's shotgun across his arms the way he'd been taught when hunting in the fields. His mom was looking at him like she didn't know him. As if his face made no sense to her at all.

"Like he needs it where he's gone to."

"You're talking like a lunatic," his mom said. "If you don't talk straight, I'm calling Cal."

He turned to Sven, who looked sheepish and old. "Where you keep the shells?"

"Above the washing machine," Sven said. "What Betty? That's where he keeps them."

There was an ache in America, an undercurrent in the country's moral fabric that was tearing the people apart. The old and sequestered were scared senseless. If young people gave a shit, it was beyond him. The rest were divided into tribes. Ken believed man had to forge his own path. Man had to take life by the horns and wrestle her down. Otherwise, he'd pitch over the falls and never be seen again.

He went to say goodbye. They stood in the living room as if he was going off to war with Sven not making eye contact and his mom dabbing her nose with a Kleenex.

"Take care of yourself, Mom. I love you." He bent down to kiss her cheek, but it was awkward with him holding the shotgun and all. She was too broke up to respond. "Come on, Dimley. Time to hit the road."

The truck is charging over a small rise. High over Lake Superior the lightning plays out like war over Mount Olympus. He's replaced the preacher talk with Springsteen and the music is like a train tunneling through his head. He's doing a buck-twenty, really pushing into the folds of the night. That's when he sees him hiding behind a rocky outgrowth.

Life never goes as planned. You think you got it figured out and Satan throws a rattlesnake in your lap. There goes the bottle out the opened window. There goes Dimley hopping into the backseat. And just when Ken thinks he's scot-free he sees the flashers wick across the dark night. Reaching for the Glock in the back compartment, he hears his brother moralizing in his ear.

"Oh, shut up," he says. "If they're coming to get me, well, then I got no say in it."

Already, the trooper has closed the gap, maybe half a football field back, the flashers bold and white. Not that Ken has slowed down one iota. The Ford hurtles on like a rocket flickering through a cylinder of light. She's done this to him, made him all desperate and out of his head. Her and that big shot movie producer. Well, he'll show her.

He doesn't see them until he does.

They stand in the road, six, seven, it's hard to count with the speed and the coal-black night. They appear like a spectacle. Like spirits of the dead. Then one glances off the hood. He's chestnut-brown with brittle legs and black hoofs. Ken manages to miss the next two only because they are spaced far enough apart that he drives straight between them. Then he brakes hard. And she's lovely. Big innocent eyes, dopey ears, maybe the most beautiful creature he's ever destroyed. The deer hits the windshield, splintering the glass. She rips like an apricot you force open with a thumb. The gear in the flatbed—poor Dimley—are thrown violently forward. Even the Glock ends up beneath his stupid new boots. Yet somehow Ken holds on.

Meantime, there's a horrible reckoning of rubber on asphalt behind him. The squad car has flipped in the air then onto its side and is skidding across the road. Sparks light up the night like on the Fourth of July and the squad car makes a beeline for the ditch, her movement *Mad Max*-esque in its speed and blunt acceptance of destiny, the sudden violent end. Then it drops over an embankment so steep it swallows the squad car whole.

The truck jerks to a stop. Instinct has him jumping from the rig with his gun in his hand. He's shaking and his heart is beating mad. Over at the crash site the squad lights lap circles on the trees. Ken inspects the Ford's front end. Bits of fur and guts are caught in the grill, the windshield is cracked, but otherwise the truck is fine. He hops back in the cab and reverses the hundred yards, parking where the squad car went in. Grabbing the flashlight, he scrambles down the loose gravel, him and his Glock, and approaches the wreck from the rear. The flashlight throws a huge beam of white light on the crash. "You okay?" he yells as he moves closer. The car's flipped itself right-side up. Steam rises from the engine. There are blown tires and broken glass, this brutal look to the sides. He can see the slumped driver through the back window. He doesn't appear to be moving.

He approaches cautiously, gun drawn, passenger side. The windshield is blown out. The burst airbag lays over the steering wheel like a droopy dead flower. The man is younger than Ken and wears his hat low over his brow. He owns a ragged jawline like he'd battled acne as a kid. He walks around the car then checks his pulse. Then he squeezes his eyes shut. *Think*, he says to himself. *Fucking think, Solberg.* He looks back inside the car. There's a photo of a woman and child scotch-taped next to the police radio.

He feels himself well up inside. He's cursed, isn't he? Wherever he goes, whatever he does, Ken Solberg leaves a blaze of destruction and pain. That first night with Nikki Silver, they were in his truck and he was about to orgasm when she said, "Come on my tits." And the moment he emptied himself sweat broke across his back. He felt this powerful shame choking the life from him, eating at his soul. And now he crawl-climbs the pitch. He gets into his rig as lightning flares over Lake Superior. "I fucked up this time, Dimley. I really fucked up."

He puts twenty-five miles between him and the crash. Up near Cornucopia he looks for a turnout, a tiny hideaway near the big lake. First and foremost is replacing the windshield. Which means driving into Superior tomorrow before there's an APB out on a white pickup with damage to the front end. Up ahead is an old farm road. He turns down the single track then kills the lights. What's done is done, he thinks. He can't turn back time. He'll pray for the man. He'll pray for his boy. Blurred images flash across his brain. Gleeson's cabin, snow piled high on the sides of the road, a glassy, slightly menacing smile.

"Andrew?" he yells out in the dark of the rig. "Is that you?"

# WHEN I THINK OF YOU

Sherman wakes with a gasp. He had the dream where he's treading water, him a speck on the surface of a big body of water. There's a feeling like something is building. At first, it's just the tiniest ripple on the surface. Then he sees it coming—this wave engulfing the sky. Then he's underwater. He's flailing and panicked—he can't breathe. And that's when he wakes up.

Early morning. His lover lays next to him under a wool blanket, a bundle of dark hair and soft rhythmic breathing. He leans over and kisses her bare shoulder then slips from under the covers careful not to wake her. Then he puts on chinos and a T-shirt and heads down to the lake. His mom was an early riser. She and Dart walked every morning while Sherman slept in. In those days they drove the length of the country every June. She didn't trust her dog and cold cargo at 34,000 feet. Dart loved the island. Water was his oxygen. He'd sense the lake before they saw the blue blur. Dart would whimper and pace in the backseat. Like he was telling them this was his place. He was the blue shimmer and the clear cold water. This place was him.

Yesterday afternoon he took Kimberly to the cemetery. His thinking was that by pointing out his mom's grave he'd show his more sensitive side. She'd see the standup guy Sherman desperately wanted to be. And this would bolster her faith in him. Or that was the idea. But the moment they were sitting in the grass next her headstone the notion seemed idiotic.

"Why was she buried here? And not California?" she asked.

"The only time my dad and I agreed on anything."

Greenway Cemetery was nice as cemeteries go, off the road, protected by trees on two sides, no more than a couple hundred gravesites, none taller than his knees. His mom's headstone was flat and rectangular like a doormat.

That moment, them sitting in the shade of a tree, he saw her—her eyes the color of storm clouds, her slender legs, sunlight dancing across her face. Something must have changed in his demeanor because she picked up on it. "What?" Kimberly said.

"She and my dad ran in the same circles," Sherman said. "But they met on the slopes in Aspen."

"I love that."

"Don't underestimate the wealthy. Marriage is a business, a merger between families."

"Is that why you never married?" she joked. "Holding out for the perfect dynasty?"

He didn't want to grin, but he couldn't help it.

"And you were in high school when she died? That must have been so hard." He'd spent his college summers hiking solo in Big Bay State Park, just him and his pain, sensing her, feeling her, learning to let her go. "We don't have to talk about it."

And then he told her everything he had pieced together about the accident. Things he'd only told his therapist and Juliet.

Kimberly placed his hand between hers then cradled it. "Ken lost a brother when he was the same age," she said. "He still struggles with it."

They were coming on the property in his mom's navy-blue Grand Wagoneer with the wood paneled sides and clunky old cassette deck. They could see Steve-O's truck through the thick foliage. It felt intimate with the sunburst and pine cover, the crunching gravel under the Jeep's tires. A saw was buzzing in the distance and they heard that precise puncture sound a nail gun made. Sherman slowed to an almost halt to navigate the truck between the two pines that acted like natural gates.

"Nervous?" Kimberly said.

He was eying the side mirrors. "I can do this in my sleep."

"With the film crew coming in, silly."

He smiled. If anything, he was antsy. What if the team thought he was trying too hard. What if the ruse didn't work? He also didn't like the idea of Solberg roaming the island like a rabid dog. The voice in his head said to come clean about the truck sighting.

"The weekend will be great," she said reassuringly.

*Tell her.* He was pulling up to the lake house when he saw his assistant. Sherman parked next to the pickup then turned off the ignition. *Tell her.* "I'll be right in."

Then he watched Kimberly disappear in the house.

Van Doorman stood next to the driver's side door dressed in the 50s gym attire of Locke's generation—stone gray sweatshirt, matching sweats and off-white canvas sneakers.

"Perimeter surveillance installed, sir."

"And the DMV?"

"My man's on staycation until Monday."

"Call him again," he said, exiting the Jeep. "And make it worth his while, say $2000."

Van Doorman took several steps backward for privacy then made the call. The saw's shrill pitch soared over the house as it cut through stiff timber. Then he heard the drawn out gust as the blade ran itself dry. Sherman could tell the conversation wasn't going well.

"Offer him three. If he says no, then fuck him."

The call ended a minute later. "Sorry, sir."

"Hey, you tried. And VD? Keep an eye out, okay?"

"Sir?" Van Doorman dropped his gaze. "I think we should tell Kimberly."

"What if it's not him? Then I look like a paranoid shit."

"And if it is?"


The sky this early morning is pale red. Thick glazed clouds, clouds you never see in Los Angeles, hang over the bay like billowed sails. He digs in his pockets, thinking he'll capture the moment on his phone, only he's forgotten it. The going is slow with the sand, so he takes off his sneakers, rolls up his chinos, then walks where the cold water breaks the shore. Invariably, his thoughts return to his mom. He sees her sometimes, even after all this time. He'll be waiting at the intersection of Beverly Glen and

Sunset and there she is idling in her Alfa Romeo. Or he's alone at Garrity Manor and he swears he hears her call out his name. She was everywhere in those early years. The mannequin at Neiman Marcus and the mother cutting her boy's prawns into edible bites at Mr. Chows. She was daybreak and she was the lazy way the sun fell across the red rocks at the state park. And she was Lake Superior's cold cruel depths.

Grant's Point sits on a triangular shape of land, a couple hundred yards across, the land swelling with sand and a small scattering of trees, but mostly bare and exposed. Out in the bay the wake is choppy with competing currents. Sherman rounds the bend into direct sunlight when he spots a dog moving his way. As the animal gets closer he sees it's a bird dog with a stick in its mouth. He's wet and wagging his tail.

"Hey, boy." He waits with his hand outstretched while the dog sniffs him. "Where's your owner?" He tries grabbing the dog's collar to read his tags, but he's cautious and keeps pulling back his head. "You fetch? You wanna fetch, boy?" The dog draws in again, animated with his voice. But he won't let go of the stick. "I only want to read your tags."

He sweeps a look east, past the driftwood sculpture someone built over the summer, into the rising sun. He figures the dog came from where Old Fort Road dead-ends at the lagoon, a favorite swimming hole for locals. Just then a piercing whistle echoes across the point and the dog takes off like an amped runner when the gun goes off. Sherman puts a hand over his eyes and squints best he can. He sees the silhouette of a man on the far side of the lagoon. The man's too far away and the glare too bright to clearly make him out. He raises a hand in greeting. The man either doesn't see the gesture or has decided not to return the favor. The dog is halfway down the shoreline now. Sherman is stepping over a downed tree when he stares hard in the direction of the man. Is that Solberg? Is he on Madeline Island?

\*\*\*

He leaves for the ferry early, taking the long way into town. On North Shore Road reams of pine and birch soar left and right, broken up here and there with deep, arrow-straight drives where he catches glimpses of brittle sunlight and shoots of blue water. He gets stuck behind a beat up van with bumper stickers like *I'm Sorry For Us* and *Hike Naked. It Adds Color To Your Cheeks,* par for the course up here in God's country. The locals on Madeline Island are a strange brew, part Humboldt County, part "Bloom County," the irreverent comic strip from the 80s. Or as one of Sherman's neighbors likes to say, "The land of broken toys."

When it comes to Solberg, he's taking zero chances. Steve-O's oldest daughter Brynn placed a few calls this morning and now scouts scour the island for a white pickup driven by a man with his description. Dylan has a buddy named Keegan who's running security out front. No one's getting through. Fort Fucking Knox. Sherman hasn't told anyone else about his suspicions. Well, except his assistance. And Van Doorman is right— Kimberly has a right to know. Wouldn't he expect the same if an ex-girlfriend was going psycho on his ass? Let's say Solberg came after them with everything he had. Property was destroyed, people hurt, maybe even killed. And Sherman could prevent the rampage with one stupid phone call.

The ferry horn blows. And he puts his phone away. He has more immediate concerns. Like his fucking movie. Blanco is the dark horse this weekend. One dissenter and Jonathan Lin and all that cash might walk. Sherman can't get his head around that. It's not like the ex-tour player has options galore. This is his chance to be relevant again and he's passing on principle? And why does he want to impress him so much? Why is it tantamount Richard Blanco see him as tycoon, producer and athlete? If only Sherman had taken one road and not another. If he'd taken tennis more seriously. If his mother hadn't died. That's it, isn't it? Her tragic end. Then he wouldn't have gone dark and done all those drugs. Then he wouldn't have thought about ending this life.

On the day his mother died he was at 4-Star Tennis Academy, a summer boot camp at University of Virginia-Charlottesville. He was coming off the courts that afternoon when he saw the camp director waiting for him outside the cafeteria. Sherman could tell by the man's demeanor that this wouldn't be a friendly chat about the hitch in his serve. He took a flight out that night then rented a car in Milwaukee. By the time he boarded the ferry his father had already taken a private jet back to Los Angeles.

The police report read like something out of a Peter Benchley novel. Locke and Hannah Garrity were kayaking the north channel up by Hermit Island when a freak storm blew in. One minute it was halcyon days forever, the next the lake was dark and broke and heaving. His mom caught a wave and went over. In the time it took Locke to right his boat without capsizing himself, she was gone. His dad went in after her, but the water was too dark, too deep—*too cold*. Neither wore drysuits. Near the report's bottom, scribbled in ink, someone wrote: *Victim-no life jacket?* And nothing else. No frogmen on the scene in scuba gear, no dredging the bottom. When he confronted the detective in charge (a man named Neveaux) he said the area where his mom disappeared was three hundred feet deep. He said the police force had neither the people nor resources for a proper search. Out and back before dinner. The flippant carelessness of it all. And the most heartbreaking part? His mom drowned less than a quarter mile offshore.

Traffic in town inches along like an inefficient bureaucracy. Up ahead he sees the sheriff's sports-utility snuggled up against the curb. As the Grand Wagoneer draws close, Sherman sticks his head out the window.

"Will I see you Saturday night?"

Sheriff Dennis has gray hair, but his eyebrows and mustache are black. "With bells and whistles."

"And the wife?"

"In her mom jeans and Aaron Rodgers jersey."

Sherman almost blurts out about Solberg. But where to begin? Tell Dennis he's sleeping with this lovely woman whose husband is capable of violence? No, it's best to keep his mouth shut so he doesn't come across like that paranoid weirdo he's so worried he's become.

"With the number of people you've invited, I want a medical tent, Sherman. With a registered nurse."

"You don't think that's a little overboard?"

"You'd be surprised how many idiots pass out at outdoor music events."

The ferry guard motions for him to park by the post office. And he speeds off. The Island Queen is slowing for the harbor. Soon cars are departing like orderly ants. His voicemail prompt sounds. Which isn't out of the ordinary with the island's spotty cell coverage. It's from Shinkan Sen's American agent. Not long after the phone call he gets a text from Ethereal with a video clip attached. He makes a mental note to view the message later.

He's on hold with the agency when the men disembark. Jesus, the gear they have. He counts two duffels, three-carry-ons, golf clubs, tennis thermo bags, and a bicycle travel bag slung over Blanco's shoulder. The agency secretary comes back on the line. She says Patrice will be with him shortly. Sherman's gaze falls back on the men, halfway across the dock now. Blanco wears a loud Hawaiian shirt, the director a wrinkled blazer and jeans, and taking up the rear is Jonathan Lin in a summer suit and poppy-blue shirt. They all sport sunglasses. They all seem too cool for school.

"Mr. Garrity? I'll patch you through."

He exits the truck with the phone pressed to his ear. Seeing the men, after the long journey they've made for him, has put a grateful smile on his face. He opens the back compartment latch.

The agent comes on the line. "Sherman? Patrice here. We have a problem."

Panic seizes the back of his eyeballs. He's pointing at the trunk and roof-rack but all he hears is *we have a problem*. Luggage is stacked in the rear compartment, the rest secured on top with bungee cords. This can't happen, not now, Sherman thinks. The weekend hasn't even begun. He must woo them—wine and dine them.

"I'm putting you on speaker phone," he tells the agent.

He climbs into the Jeep then sets the phone on the center console. The men are getting in too, Blanco the front seat, Gil and Lin sitting in back. "I'm here with the team. Now, what's this problem with Shinkan Sen?"

"So, it is true," Jonathan Lin whispers.

"It's the Trey Hamasaki part," the agent says over the speaker. "We've got concerns."

Sherman stares at his executive producer before putting on a cheery face. "It's the role of a lifetime. Think *Bull Durham* meets *9 ½ Weeks* with a little *Psycho* thrown in at the end."

Blanco gives him a thumbs up.

"I thought it was a tennis pic," the agent says, confused.

"*It is a tennis pic*," Sherman emphasizes. "But it's so much more."

"I think what our man here is saying," Blanco says. "Is that Shinkan Sen will be a household name when we're through with her."

"Is that our tennis player?" She doesn't sound enthused.

Sherman lets go a nervous twitter. "My executive producer means her stock in Hollywood will go way, way up."

"It's the sex scenes," Patrice says. "They're too explicit."

"We're talking nicely lit T&A, a little suggestive fucking," Blanco says. "What's not to love?"

"Patrice? Jonathan Lin here. My group is financing this film of ours. I can assure you the investors want to protect your client as much as you do."

"My sets are safe places," Gil adds. "Your client can bring her besties or her life coach for all I care."

"Is that Gil?" the agent says. "I heard you were taking up the game. Let's do tennis at Toluca Lake soon."

"I don't think I'm in your league, Patrice."

Sherman clears his throat. "What does your client want?"

"We have a problem with full frontal."

A gasp swirls through the cabin. There are small frowns and mildly offended nods, as if the men are insulted by the insinuation.

"How much?" Sherman says

"It's not about the money."

Another audible grumble comes from the men, followed by eyerolls. Something registers inside Sherman (call it a hunch). He reaches across the seat and opens the glove box. Inside are four Montecristo Petit No.

2's. They're blunt and dark and smell like the earth. He's been saving them for the back nine but now seems the perfect moment. He snatches them up with one hand then motions for Blanco to grab the cutter and lighter.

"The old Tubo!" Gil exclaims.

"Sherman?" the agent says.

"Just a second…"

The cigars are passed around with enthusiasm. Sherman cuts the tip off his cigar, places it in his mouth, and fires the tobacco with a special non-flame lighter. "Patrice," he says, while making quick puffs. "Are you still there?"

"Yes," she says impatiently. "I'm here."

In no time, all the men are puffing away.

"In a tennis match, there's a time when a player goes down a break or two and it feels like…it feels like the world has slipped past her reach. There's nothing she can do to slow that train." He takes a moment to gaze admirably at the cigar's tip, which is lit and smoking. "This is that time, Patrice. This is that time."

"What are you talking about? Are you mad?"

The secondhand smoke is so thick the team are waving their hands in the air to move the smoke out the windows.

"Shinkan Sen is on my island."

"She's what? Where are you? Catalina?"

"She's partying with us like it's 1999 all weekend." The men have another quiet moment—this one with high-fives, mock finger explosions, and big-ass grins. "The actor playing opposite is here, too," Sherman adds. "And they're dynamite together. Think Bogie and Bacall, think Pitt and Jolie."

"Costner and Sarandon," Blanco quips.

"Yes! Costner and Sarandon! Gotta run! Ciao!" And he hangs up to a chorus of howling laughter.

Sherman gives them a quick tour of La Pointe. The Beach Club and the old grocery with the warped wood floors, the shop that rents bikes and scooters, the restaurants that come and go, that burn down too fast or wow the seasonal visitors for the summer then disappear and are never heard from again. The broken down look of Tom's bar with its white canvas mishmash of walls and roofs, the lovely ramshackle feel of the place, that if it could it'd whisper dreams and desires, true and made up love stories, drunken oaths proclaimed on tabletops late at night. Then down Old Fort Road they go. Past a glimpse of Lake Superior, which is calm and brightly spangled this afternoon. He tells them about the Ojibwe who first settled the island five hundred years ago after the Great Spirit told their people to travel west in search of where food grows on the water.

"You mean corn?" Lin says.

"Where the fuck did you grow up?" Blanco says. "Outer space? You think corn is grown on water?"

"I think Sherman means wild rice," Gil says.

They're quiet coming on the inn, smoking their cigars and gazing out the windows, the men taking in the island's simplicity and charm, a stark contrast from the city they flew in from. As they round the bend, the sailboat masts stretch above the buildings. Then the Jeep runs up and over the tiny channel bridge. "Which one's yours?" Blanco says, looking at the boats in the marina.

"Let me guess," Gil says. "The one called *Mine's Bigger.*"

Sherman's eying the Robert Trent Jones, Sr. designed golf course that fills the windshield. He has no idea what the men are talking about.

"The sailboat, Sherman."

He flicks his stogie out the window. "Oh, that. You know how stuff online is photoshopped to death? In person the boat smelled like dead fish. By the way, tee times are in an hour."

This gets the men talking like competitive people do, highfalutin-like—on handicaps, short games, length off the tee. They're heading up the hill where the houses are cut back in the trees and little sunlight penetrates the leaf cover.

"I need to piss," Blanco says, dropping his cigar out the window.

"Prostate thing? It's a bitch getting old, huh?" Gil says.

"Pull over, man."

"We're three minutes away," Sherman says.

"Now, Garrity."

At the junction of South Shore Road/Old Fort Road, not far from where Van Doorman spotted the white truck, he runs the Jeep onto the narrow shoulder. Blanco is out the door and tromping through tall grasses where a myriad of pine stand like tethered horses. Sherman hops down from his seat and joins him in the woods. They choose the biggest trunks on the opposite sides of the grove.

"Why do men instinctively piss on trees?" Sherman says. "And why put so much distance between ourselves and the next guy over? Are males hard-wired that way?"

"You really want to make this movie, don't you?"

Intrigue over Blanco's question has him cranking his head around. "And you don't?"

"I've been called asshole, jerk-off, whore. But no one's ever said I was full of shit."

"This is our chance to make the movie about your life, man. What I wouldn't give for that."

Finished with his piss, Blanco puts his dick back in his shorts. "What about my story speaks to you?"

Does he tell the truth? About making his mark in the film world? Or is Blanco talking about what spoke to him on his first read-through? The part about losing a parent at a young age, pushing through that pain, the ability to transcend grief.

"That's what I thought." Blanco starts for the Jeep.

"Will you wait a second." Sherman hasn't completely emptied his bladder when he zips up and jogs over. "I deserve a shot like this. And I know I can make good on it. We're not that different."

Blanco regards him with what feels like an eternity. "We better get back before they think we're comparing dicks or something."

Out of habit he turns on his signal turning into the drive. Security sits on the front bumper of his hatchback. If the men notice Keegan, they don't let on. Sherman's still fretting about the conversation in the woods.

Blanco was testing him, and he blew it. Why is he so afraid of speaking his truth? They're coming on the house when they hear the distinct pop of a tennis ball being struck by an athlete who knows what he's doing. Then they see Van Doorman trading groundstrokes with their leading man, Alexander Field. He slows down and puts the Jeep into park.

Blanco slaps Sherman's arm. "You son-of-a-bitch. You really did it."

"Is that our actor?" Lin says, peering out his window.

This is the first time Sherman has seen his costar in the flesh. He's tall and tennis player lanky. Then he notices the pretty Larson girl sitting courtside.

"He comes with an entourage?" Gil says dubiously.

"She's a local girl. Her father works for me."

The rally ends. They watch the shirtless, beanie-clad Alexander Field pick balls up at the net. "He's underweight."

"We'll beef him up," Blanco says.

"His hair is too short."

"It'll grow."

"He does have that something," Sherman finally says.

"But can he act?"

"The million-dollar question," Lin mutters under his breath.

They watch a few more rallies. Sherman is about to start the engine when Blanco sets a paw on his shoulder. "Wait a second. Is this the court where young Garrity learned the game?" Blanco's inflection is part Lord Vader, part smart-ass. "How nice."

It wasn't nice... it was idyllic... a court in the woods with birdsong and silty light puncturing the leaf canopy. Where a well-struck forehand held a purity you couldn't create in a stuffy tennis club. Blanco of all people should understand this. He'd played McEnroe. He held some obscure losing streak against Boris Becker. Years ago, he was a top player. Who knows how sharp his game is now?

Blanco hasn't let go his enormous grin. "I know why we're here. The island is the most real thing about you, Sherm. I love that."

If his face was warm before, now it's on fire. Ever since he'd gotten his hands on the script, he'd dreamed about giving the ex-pro a run for his money. "I thought we might hit balls before we got down to business."

"You and me, Sherm? Play tennis?"

"I played in college."

"Did you now? Where?"

"Harvey Mudd… we were nationally ranked."

"D3? Look, Sherm. I'm sure you're a fine club player. But aren't there more pressing issues at hand?"

"I'm willing to put a wager on it." *Had he just said that?*

Blanco smirks at the backseat participants. "How much are we talking?"

"How's $5000?"

"Fuck yeah, I'll play you for five grand."

"I was thinking doubles."

Sherman can't think straight. What is he doing? A few years back, yeah, he and Van Doorman beat an ex-tour guy in doubles. Fine, it was a pro-am, Van Doorman tree'd out of his mind, and the circuit guy had two bum knees. Still, they'd won. Again, the executive producer reaches across the seat and pats his arm. "You keep your money and self-respect, buddy."

If he was irritated before—now he's smoldering. His smile leaks from his eyes. "Let's make it interesting, say fifty thousand? Or is that too much, Blank?"

"For that kind of money, we better play three out of five," Blanco says. "You've played three out of five sets before, right, Sherm?"

"I like the sound of that."

"Are we talking this weekend? You and your assistant, Van Rumple or whatever his name is?" Sherman feels light-headed. And like he might puke. "Who's my partner?" Blanco continues. "Alexander Field? That wouldn't be fair."

Ah, Sherman thinks. Here is his way out.

Blanco turns and gives Gil a stare. "I guess it's you and me, Mr. Director."

Gil laughs. "Funny, man. Real funny."

"Betting is so bougie," Lin says. "Bet on something that matters, something gained, something truly lost."

"How about creative control of the film?" Gil says.

"I like the way you think," Lin says grinning.

Angling the rearview mirror down, he locks eyes with the men in back. This feels like a setup. But that can't be. There's no way the team knows he secretly fields dreams of beating Blanco at his own game. Or did they? "We haven't secured financing," he says. "I'm not betting on jack shit until Lin shows us the money."

"Don't let me get in the way of a good bet."

Again, he stares at the money guy. Why is Lin throwing him under the bus? Doesn't he know they're mates in this negotiation?

"What can't you live without, Blanco?" Gil asks.

"My kids." Then he says, "And my penis."

"Sherman cutting your penis off with a scissors?" Lin giggles. "I'd pay to see that."

Everyone cracks up. Well, Blanco not so much. In fact, something has come over his features. Like he's staring down the barrel of a gun.

"Getting cold feet about the fifty grand?" Sherman wisecracks.

"If financing falls through with the Chinese, we throw in a clause." Blanco's voice is low and flat. "There's a two-way mirror at my wife's yoga studio. It opens to the women's showers. Heather's clients include actresses, models, hot fucking moms. You win and you can tell Heather about the peephole."

"I win and I want a front seat," Sherman jokes.

"I'm serious."

"And if I lose?"

Blanco looks him over like he can read into his soul. "You have a woman here, someone you fancy. You lose and you introduce her to Ethereal Hunt... in person."

"How do you know I haven't already done that?"

"Like you said," Blanco adds. "We're not that different."

"Is it a bet?" Lin says. "Creative control? Or humiliating mea culpas?"

The ex-pro holds out his hand and Sherman begrudgingly shakes it.

Blanco gives Gil a confident look. "It's you and me, brother."

"Holy shit," Gil said.

"Holy fucking shit," Lin says.

*Yeah, holy fucking shit.*

\*\*\*

Jonathan Lin is a scratch golfer. His swing is as big as California. He plays in a methodical way, always moving, nothing wasted. Like how he consults the card in his back pocket and the way he sticks a tee behind his ear after a massive tee shot. Kudos on his outfit, too, a white knit polo with orange trim around the sleeves and stretch chinos that fit like a glove. The shirt and pants have the same logo, a stitched symbol on the chest and front pants pocket. They stand on the second tee box, a par three over wetlands. Lin's got a gap wedge in his hands.

"What brand is that?" Sherman says, eying the clothes.

"La-Ning, a Chinese company."

"Where can I pick up an outfit like that?"

"La-Ning is China's answer to Nike," Blanco says. "I wouldn't be shocked if those clothes are illegal in the States."

Lin's taking a few practice cuts when he winks at Sherman. "Let's hope the branding police aren't zeroing in on Madeline Island this weekend." Then he swings, launching another ball into the sky.

With Lin's golfing skills, he and Sherman are up three after the first nine. That's when Blanco buys the foursome a couple Heineken's each. Sure enough, they bogie the 10th and 11th holes before halving the next two. Lin blames the beer on an empty stomach. Sherman isn't so sure. The stakes aren't high, the course isn't challenging. He figures Lin is letting Blanco win. Which he only sort of has a problem with. If it helps with financing, then so be it. He has more troubling things on his mind anyway. Before golf, he'd checked in with Steve-O's progress on the stage. Then he'd gone inside to change. He was throwing a shirt over his head when he saw Shinkan Sen and her personal assistant out his window. They were talking in the drive. On his way outdoors to introduce himself he'd run into Alexander Field and the leggy Larson girl. They were sitting on the front porch. And quite close considering they just met.

"Alexander?" Sherman's smile was 100% charm. "Don't get up. Nice to finally meet you."

The young man's handshake was firm. "This place of yours is killer, man."

"Is the yurt kitted out to your satisfaction?"

"Hell, yeah."

He glanced at the Larson girl. She smiled at him with those big eyes of hers. "It's Dawn, right?"

"That's the name they gave me."

His gaze lasted an extra beat. Then he turned back to his costar. "Maybe we can hit later. And talk character."

"I pattern myself after my grandfather. He got a Purple Heart in Vietnam. Before that he studied as a Jesuit priest."

Sherman stared at Alexander Field. Was he mistaking character for *character*? "Wait? Are you fucking with me?

Alexander slapped his knee. "Got you, man. I got you good."

He regarded Dawn one more time. "See you two around." Then he stepped off the porch and trotted across the gravel drive. He again heard the saw's piercing shriek and the crisp pop from the nail gun. The actress and her assistant were peering inside the Wagoneer as if it was something rare indeed.

"Ms. Sen? Welcome to the Hideaway!"

One sweep of his eyes and he knew—here was a movie star. Shinkan Sen wasn't tall, but she had presence. There was the perfectly oval face, eyes the color of onyx, and a mouth that held all the sadness in the world. Shinkan Sen would fill up the screen.

"Hello, Mr. Garrity." She bowed her head then spoke slow and carefully. "I want to thank you for this *opp-or-tuun-ity.*"

Terror gripped Sherman. Was this a joke? "It's me who's honored, Ms. Sen. You're going to knock the Trey Hamasaki role out of the park."

Shinkan Sen looked at her assistant with an unclear expression. The woman was old with chapped lips and tangly gray hair. "Go on," the woman said. "In English."

"I do not understand," she said. "You speak too fastly."

"Too fast," the woman said, correcting her.

"*Ah, soo ne.* Too fast."

Sherman was holding his breath. "Ms. Sen? May I have a word with your assistant in private?"

He led the woman to the backyard. The men were busy building the stage steps, Steve-O measuring the risers with his tape and Dylan making pencil marks on the lumber.

"What's your name, Teach?"

"Sensei Yamaguchi."

"Okay, Sensei. Why don't you tell me what the fuck is going on?"

"What do you mean?"

He squeezed her tiny brittle arm. "Her English sucks."

Pride entered her wrinkled, squashed face. "Shinkan is making progress."

He smiled so hard his face hurt. "She needs to sound American, not cute little foreign exchange student. She's playing a sexual dynamo who eats men like they're nachos."

"You're hurting my arm."

"And you're breaking my heart."

He let go of her arm then watched her storm down the lake path. Sherman then walked around the house far enough to see the actress, who sat on the Jeep's bumper, lost on her phone. "Shinkan! So good to finally meet you!" He gave her two thumbs up. Then he put his phone to his mouth. "Siri? Get me Boyd Baker."

While the call went through, he saw Steve-O trudging toward him. He was big like Blanco. His gray shirt was sweat marked and he wore knee pads. "Can we talk?"

Siri was connecting him with his casting director. "Can you make it quick? Got a minor crisis on my hands."

"Who's Romeo?"

"The lead in our new film."

"Dawn is seventeen."

"You want me to talk with him?"

Steve-O placed a hand on his shoulder. "That would be great."

Boyd came on the line. "Sherman?"

"I need to take this," he said to Steve-O. "And don't worry. I'm on it."

The carpenter nodded then started back around the house's corner.

"When were you going to tell me?" he said into the phone.

"About?" Boyd said.

"Oh, you're good. You're really good."

"How about a hint?"

"Her English, dumb shit."

"Oh, that," Boyd said. "I didn't know, honest. Sorry, okay?"

"Sorry, okay? *Sorry, okay?* Sorry okay doesn't cut it when our fucking movie star speaks zero English."

"Like everyone else, I got swept up in her spell. She's like a Kardashian."

"She has two hundred lines," Sherman cried.

"If you're trying to make me feel like shit, it's working."

"What do you propose?"

"What about those language camps for overachieving high school students?"

"You think!" He severed the line then speed dialed Shinkan's agent. The call bounced into voicemail. "Hi, Patrice. Guess who this is? I didn't want you hanging on the money thing. How's ten million…pesos! When were you going to tell me she spoke English like a second grader? During opening credits? I should sue your ass for selling me bogus goods. You know why agents get a bad name, Patrice? Because of people like you!"

Sherman hung up perspiring, then stomped around the house. Out front he spotted Gil and Jonathan, already in their golf gear, staring into the woods. Curious, he walked over to join them. "Walking meditation," Lin whispered.

Shinkan Sen stood among the trees. She was doing this slow motion dance. One moment she was a marble statue, the next a hand opened ever so slightly. It was mesmerizing stuff. Sherman felt himself being drawn in like the others.

Gil nudged him. "Hey, check out our moneyman?"

Jonathan Lin had gone over to sit on the yurt's step. His arms were wrapped around his knees and he was rocking back and forth, his eyes shifting nervously. "She's everything I imagined."

"And I thought I had problems," Sherman said.

***

They're on the 17th hole, and it's all even. With the island's scarcity of land, many of the holes share greens. This means it's easier to hit them in regulation but also gives rise to tricky putts across massive green space. Or so it is for Blanco. To hole his putt, he stands with his back to the flag and attempts one of those imaginative, near impossible parabolic benders where you aim the opposite way of the cup and hope for the best.

Sherman and his playing partner are standing by the green when Lin nudges him. From his back pocket he takes out a 4x6 headshot of a confident young man with wavy black hair. They watch Blanco's attempt roll past the hole and into the rough.

"His name is Sean Ping," Lin says loud enough to carry across the green. He gives Sherman the photo then walks to his mark below the hole. "He was born in Australia and has impeccable English. And he's a top squash player in Hong Kong."

Gil, who's tending the flag, drops it on the slope then walks over. "Handsome kid."

Surveying his line, Lin rubs his putter blade like it's a genie bottle. "His agent is sending on-court footage. Sean Ping is our man."

Gil takes the photo over to Blanco who glances at the picture. "What next? This Chinese guy is my long lost half-brother from a one-nightstand my father had on a layover in Shanghai?"

"Quit being so dramatic," Sherman says.

Lin's putt stops a few inches from the cup. "Finish the hole," he says, tapping in. "Let me make a call."

So, the men putt out, the flag's replaced, and Jonathan Lin places the call. The 17th green grows quiet but for the knock of a woodpecker. No players wait from the fairway. It's the embittered foursome, the phone call, and the knock-knock of a bird.

"Why are you being so stubborn, Blanco?" Sherman finally says. "And you, Mr. Director? What do you think?"

"Let's see what Lin says."

"How diplomatic."

"Can we change gears a second?" Gil says. "I know this guy in Madison, a documentarian. Should I see if he's available?"

"For what?"

"Document the process. Two-person crew, nothing crazy. They could be here tonight."

"Like a companion piece," Sherman says. "Not a bad idea."

They look up to see Lin striding toward them, smooth and cagey like. "Mr. Dollars & Sense proposes we keep the ending as is. Instead, we substitute Sean Ping for the player your character mentors."

Blanco's grin is fiendish and hard. "You see what he's doing, right?"

"What?" Sherman says. "It's a workable solution."

"They start with a small change to the script, like me losing to a Chinese guy. But what they really want is something bigger, something with far greater reach."

"What is he talking about?" Lin exclaims.

The longer the conversation goes on the more Sherman wants to bash a five-iron over Blanco's head. "If you think anyone gives a fuck who you mentored in 1996, you're more messed up than I thought."

"How do we know they don't have ulterior motives?"

"Like what?"

"Like agitprop shit," Blanco says. "All I know is if the Serb is Chinese, we've created a sympathetic Chinese character."

"Oh my fucking God," Lin says.

"We do the same thing," Blanco says. "Ever see an American war movie that didn't paint us in rosy colors?"

"*Apocalypse Now*," Gil counts off. "*The Deer Hunter*... the one with Michael J. Fox..."

"A Chinese player helps with the bottom line," Lin says. "It gets people in the theatre. This is about protecting the investment. You get that, right?"

Can anything else go wrong?

\*\*\*

It's a glorious evening for a dinner party, if anything a bit cool for July. The guests are mingling on the lawn. Piping across the property is a snazzy 70s jazz number by The Crusaders. Sherman stands on the porch in a double-breasted suit made of soft Italian linen. He's overdressed, but this is his land, his party, and his people. From across the lawn he hears Kimberly's laugh. She and Heather Harper sit huddled at the firepit like besties. They had their first fight, all because he couldn't control his impulses. In this case they were getting dressed for the party when she opened the wardrobe and pulled out this polka dot thing on a hanger. One look at the pilled double-knit material was all it took.

"How about I wear that wraparound dress I wore in Minneapolis?" she'd said.

As if he didn't have enough problems. Like the budding relationship between his costar and the Larson girl. Steve-O had already read him another riot act. Sherman was mixing a drink when the handyman walked into the house in his work clothes.

"You and Joanie aren't joining us?"

"Don't change the subject."

Sherman raised a mock eyebrow. "Okay," he said slowly.

"I saw Dawn smoking a cigarette. With him."

"You didn't smoke when you were younger?"

"You said you'd take care of it."

"Steve-O... chill, buddy, okay?"

And to think he was about to bring up Kimberly's soon-to-be ex-husband. If there was a man who might flush old Ken Dog out of the woods it was Steve Larson. He'd lived in these parts his whole life. He and Sheriff Dennis trapped beaver and muskrat. They knew the island like Sherman did the lines on a tennis court.

Not long after, he sees Alexander Field break across the lawn like a young man in need of the potty. He times it so he's skipping down the porch steps as the actor exits the green plastic dome.

"Enjoying yourself?"

His actor wears a lightweight down jacket, T-shirt, and board shorts. "Oh, yeah."

"Careful with Steve-O's daughter. He's a deer hunter, you know."

"Everything's cool."

His eyes graze the coat's mustard-yellow fabric. "Call it a warning, Puff Daddy."

Sherman wanders indoors. The jazz fusion isn't working. Nothing is. There's still time. He can change minds. He can make this film work. Thing is—he wants everyone to be happy. He's not. He's like a grab bag of goodies that greedy hands are fighting over in the pitch dark. What the party needs is a lift. His mom was the perfect host. She never drank too much. She made a point to speak to everyone invited. She even made time for the staff. He's hiding out on the porch with his second Tanqueray Tonic when a server opens the screen door with an empty tray under her arm. She reminds him of a lamppost—wiry tall with a small head attached on top.

"You don't look happy," he snaps at her. "Go clean yourself up."

The comment has her on the verge of tears. Sherman hands her his pocket square. "Sorry, that came our harsh. Please don't cry."

She leans against the doorframe and wipes her eyes. "You're not letting me go, are you, Mr. Garrity? I really need this job."

"When I was your age, I lost my mother. I had every reason to cry. But you know what? I picked myself up. I wouldn't allow myself to wallow. I realized life is precious. It can be taken from you just like that." He's getting worked up. She died thirty-seven years ago. When was he going to let his mother go? "These people are important in my world. It's critical they feel the love. You know what I mean?" She nods her head, sniffling. He's taken a few twenties from his wallet and pressed them in the server's hand. "Go take a few moments and compose yourself."

Sherman's mixing another cocktail (his third but who's counting), when he happens to look out the porch screen just as Steve-O's daughter walks up from the lake all sexy and slow, followed by Alexander Field. She leans against the spine of a creamy birch in her frilled dress and red cowboy boots. His costar presses into her in a tender way. Instead of warning the couple as promised, Sherman turns his gaze on the late summer light breaking across the trees. He thinks of Juliet the summer she showed up with her bags, unannounced. He was eighteen and had driven cross-country in the 911. And he was a mess. One day he was legit tennis tour material and the next moment he was lost inside a music video of his own invention. He was experimenting, trying on new hats. Like the guy he kissed in the bathroom of some bar on Hollywood Boulevard after they'd done a line of coke. Like the night he drove to Tijuana with plans of spending the last days of his life drinking himself to death. Now, that's not to say his life was all doom and gloom. There was a new style on the streets, helped no doubt by those John Hughes inspired teen movies. Young people were wearing camel overcoats, dress shirts buttoned to the throat, and pleated slacks. The day Juliet appeared on the Hideaway's front steps he wore high-waisted Willie Wear slacks and a baggy white Comme des Garcons dress shirt.

"Hi," Juliet said, embarrassed. "I'm not intruding, am I?"

He'd arrived at Madeline Island without any pretenses. The anniversary of his mom's death was a couple weeks away. He wanted to scream when he wanted, cry when he wanted, and listen to the music he wanted. The last person in the world he expected to see was Juliet, though secretly, his heart was leaping with joy.

"How did you find me?"

"I asked this cute girl taking ferry tickets if she knew you. She wrote quite precise directions on the palm of my hand. Gee, Sherman, has she been here before?"

Prior to Juliet arriving, life at the Hideaway had been anything but clean living. He was drinking himself into a stupor every night. It started around noon, a self-congratulatory beer for making it through another day. Then he made his way to the wine cellar, grabbing a Chateau La Mission Haut-Brion 1966 like he was shopping at Gelson's. By five he was cranking *Can't Buy A Thrill* and dancing around the house in his mom's silk robe while plotting his own departure from this cruel world.

For Sherman's entire life, his mom had symbolized light. But now that light was snuffed dead. He no longer believed in the light. Because not following the light made the unimaginable possible. How did he see it going down? As close to the same exact spot where she'd vanished. He'd picked out three large stones he'd fitted into the kayak's netting. The way he envisioned it, he'd push offshore at dusk on the eve of her disappearance, then paddle to the spot off Hermit Island, where he'd open one his dad's prized Guigal Cote Rotie la ladonne 1978's, toast his mom, drink his fill, then fill his clothes with rocks and slip over the boat's side and never be seen again.

And now his plans to kill himself were in real jeopardy.

They were sitting on the dock an hour after Juliet arrived in their trendy rags, sipping ice cold Absolute in tall shot glasses. It was one of those pristine summer nights in the north country. The sky was peach, the lake a rapture of splintery light. Sherman lit a cigarette then leaned back, using his hands for support. Juliet sat several feet in front of him with her legs dangling over the dock's edge.

"Why are you here, Juliet… really… And if you say George and you are worried about my well-being, I'll puke. I will."

She looked over her shoulder. Tears filled her eyes. "We are worried, Sherman. We just love you so much and would hate if—"

Juliet burst into tears. He flicked his cigarette into the water, then scooted over and put his arm around her shoulder. Then Juliet was pushing him away and running down the dock, sobbing.

"I'm glad you're here!" he shouted after her.

Having Juliet around took some adjusting. For starters, he didn't want her thinking he was in some dark place he'd never recover from. Thus, he made a valiant effort to curtail his drinking during daylight hours. Also, he thought it important to enthuse the positive. This meant dragging Juliet out for morning runs or hikes. Still, he smelled a rat. He rang up George, who was visiting his boyfriend Michael in Brooklyn. First thing George told him was that Juliet was available.

"Ah, I knew it! You two are in cahoots!" Then Sherman said, "What do you mean, available?"

"She broke up with Tarzan Boy. You remember the Zemlicka family? They own that interior design firm in Beverly Hills. Tarzan Boy got the youngest Zemlicka pregnant."

"Really? How wonderful...I mean for the Zemlicka girl."

"Don't mention any of this to Juliet," George warned. "I promised I wouldn't say a word."

A couple days later they were lying in the sun near the house, it being too cold near the water. Juliet was reading *Oscar and Lucinda,* Sherman flipping through *Spin Magazine,* when he stopped to gaze at an advertisement. "You know this guy?" He held up the full page Calvin Klein underwear ad. Tarzan Boy aka Lance Albert was this ridiculously good looking guy from Harvard School for Boys. He had the hair and the jaw and the lips and the abs. So this was big news, them breaking up.

"We're no longer an item," Juliet said.

"Oh?"

"Don't 'oh' me. George told me he told you I broke up with the dickhead."

"Then why all the secrecy?"

Juliet blushed. "The right moment never availed itself," she said. "And you called him Tarzan Boy?"

On calm days they took out the Chris Craft or played tennis. He made her soft-boiled eggs he served with melon and Bloody Mary's. He played Juliet his mom's music. And they put a considerable dent in the wine collection. Not once did Sherman tell Juliet his true feelings. Not once did he take her in his arms when they stood up after watching another sunset and kiss her. Even the night he had an inkling that's what she wanted him to do. He was a gentleman. He said goodnight in the hall outside her bedroom while brushing his teeth. He controlled himself like the man his mom would have been proud of. One night they rented *Angel Heart*, which frightened them both. They were cleaning the kitchen afterwards, her at the sink in rubber gloves, him drying the dishes.

"Can I sleep with you tonight?" Juliet asked.

Sherman acted nonchalant placing a plate in the cupboard, but his insides were thumping. "I should warn you. I move around in my sleep."

She showed up in his bedroom five minutes later holding a pillow to her chest. She wore a T-shirt and underwear. "Remember that night in eighth grade? When we played Spin the Bottle?"

"Sort of," he said, lying. "Why?"

"Remember how I asked James Mulligan to go into the walk-in closet twice. The whole time we were in there we just talked."

"Okay…"

"I was afraid that getting involved with you would ruin our friendship." The pillow hit the floor. Then Juliet pulled the shirt over her head. "But the thing is…"

The next couple weeks were indelibly marked in his mind forever. They were a real couple, holding hands in public, making meals together, and having sex whenever the mood struck. At the same time, the one-year anniversary was coming on fast. Which meant lots more drinking on Sherman's part. And he wasn't sleeping. They'd go to bed and next thing he knew he was pacing in the living room. When Juliet tried to intervene, when she asked if his insomnia had something to do with his mom, he slammed shut like the porch door. Everything smashed into a million pieces when he found her gossiping on the phone with George.

"I know who you're talking to!"

"George and Michael want to come up. Doesn't that sound wonderful!"

"Why can't you people leave me alone!"

"We want to help. We love you."

"I DON'T WANT HELP!"

He'd finally pushed Juliet to the edge. She slammed the receiver down. "Worst decision of my life."

"Yeah, crawl back to Tarzan Boy. You deserve each other."

"You need therapy, Sherman. And you drink too much."

"At least I don't have a God complex. *I know, I'll fly halfway across the country to save poor Sherman Garrity!*" His voice was pitched high, his attempt to sound like Juliet. "*Once I sleep with him, he'll be A-okay. That's the power of my pussy.*"

She hurled the phone, cord and all, at his head.

"Missed, bitch!"

Juliet was sobbing now. "I don't think my feelings for you are as strong as they once were."

# CAUTIOUS MAN

She's like a person he once knew. Or at least he doesn't recognize this side of her. She and her blonde colluder. They're like sisters huddled in a clingy, gossipy embrace. The blonde tilts her head back and laughs at something Kimberly says. Like his wife is the bomb. No, he doesn't know this side of her at all. Jazz elevator music pipes over the lawn. Waitstaff in white oxfords collect appetizer plates and empty drink glasses. They can't see him hiding in the dense tree cover, not in the fading light. He switches trees but his eyes keep going back to his wife. She's done something to her hair, colored it maybe. She's also wearing a dress he's never seen before. An idea formulates in his mind. He sees himself slipping onto Garrity's property with his new hunting knife. No, he's rushing in with a grin on his face, the Glock blazing, making short work of these beautiful, bleeding-heart liberals. Then he's vanishing into the woods never to be seen again. Though that thinking is faulty. He's on an island with only one way off. What Ken needs is a Plan B. Like stashing a car on the mainland then renting a little outboard. Once his work is finished, he'll zip across the lake and be gone for good. His desire to harm is large. Yesterday in Bayfield he stopped for more provisions. He happened past a bar on the main drag with the door open. The TV behind the counter was reporting on the accident. "… a decorated military and family man has died. The incident is being investigated as a possible crime scene.…" Had the sheriff made the color and make of his truck? Was he a wanted man?

Ken brings the binoculars back up to his eyes again and zooms in on the producer. Is he willing to die in taking out Sherman Garrity? He's not sure, but he knows one thing. Whatever happens, it will be on his terms. It will be the opposite of the heartbreaking thing that transpired a few nights ago.

That thing eats at him like bleach.

# FREE FALLIN'

The party is finding its sea legs. Sherman starts down the hill to Sinatra's version of "Send in The Clowns" when his text chimes. He reaches inside his suit coat and pulls out his iPhone. *Well? What did you think?* What does he think of what? Then he remembers the video clips sent earlier that afternoon and presses the ▶ button. Ethereal, dressed in a see-through nightie, sits at a cocktail table with a spray-tanned woman with enormous breasts. Background noise is an 80s hair band he can't quite place and the club's lighting is low and seductive. She stares into the camera like the actress she is. "Say hello to my friend, Kitty."

Kitty meows while toying with a long coiffed bang. "Your friend told me all about you."

"Kitty knows cads like Richard Blanco," she says, talking over the strip club clamor. "The Dodgers hangout here. They throw money around like it's a game of Uno and promise dancers Ferraris and shit."

"More like gift cards at Cheesecake Factory," the stripper quips. Kitty then admires her cleavage like she's only now realized her breasts are hers. "Is it hot in here? Or is it me?"

Sherman looks up from his iPhone like he's doing something wrong. He's convinced the entire party is staring at him like he's the world's biggest perv. But no, he might as well be invisible. He gulps at his cocktail then eyes the screen again. "Kitty's been showing me moves—Backdoor Man, the Bump and Grind." Ethereal looks thoughtfully at the stripper. "I've been meaning to ask…"

"Are these real?" Kitty gets her hands underneath her hefty flesh and hoists them up for the camera. "Yes, they are."

"Really?"

"Okay, they're not."

"Would you mind?" She scoots closer. "I'm going to feel her tits, Shermy." He glances up again. Doesn't he have more important shit on his agenda? Like the film? What about the movie star from Tokyo? She's the glue that holds this flimsy picture together and she speaks English like a four-year-old. "They're firm," Ethereal says, checking for buoyancy. "But where mine are pillowy soft, these tits aren't going anywhere anytime soon."

"Oh, meow," Kitty purrs. "Me-owww!"

"See, Sherman. I got this. Tell that to your director. Or is Blanco running the show?"

And the video shuts off.

The second clip begins amateurishly out of focus, the camera shaky. Def Leppard's "Pour Some Sugar On Me" plays loud and grating. The lens finally zeroes in on an image that resembles a giant Cheeto. Ethereal sits on said Cheeto straddling a young man with a pot belly. The camera shifts perspective abruptly to the guy filming, a blotto-faced dude underneath a Cardinals ball cap.

"Waz up, Los Angeles."

Back on el Cheeto, the actress leans forward suggestively. The guy underneath her is enjoying the show when she slowly bends backwards. Arching back impressively she suddenly gets this look on her face. Like she's reached some kinetic point of no return. She tries smiling it off, but it's clear, to Sherman anyway, that Ethereal's stuck. Her hand finds the couch abruptly. She then blows a stray bang that's fallen over her face.

"Grind my bro," the camera guy says. Ethereal whips around like a dog eager to please his owner and sticks her ass up in the air. "Dental floss," the guy filming says. "Nice."

"The bump and grind," she says into the camera.

The young man, wearing chinos, tents out after a third firm pass. He turns toward his copilot with this drunk grin. "You getting this?"

"Awesome, bro. Truly epic."

"See, I'm a natural," Ethereal says, climbing off the guy.

"Angel, or whatever your name is," he says with the boner pushing through his pants. "I paid for a whole song!"

"Phone, please," she says to the camera guy.

"You heard my bro, old lady."

She gets in real close with her cleavage and pouty lips then snatches her phone from his hand.

"What the fuck, bitch!"

She turns the phone on him. "How's it feel, *bitch*!"

Then the video goes dead. Once again, Sherman's gaze shoots across the manicured lawn. And once again, no one seems to know he exists. The video disturbs him enough that he speed-dials Ethereal. "Yes?" Her voice is cautious.

"Are you okay?"

"About…?"

"The strip club? Those asshole frat boys?"

"Awe, Shermy. You're such a sweetheart," she says. "So, how's things?"

He's losing it, isn't he? His kind, meaning his and Ethereal's kind, all the people drinking cocktails on the lawn, who are they? How far will they go to get what they want? To take what they think they deserve? He drains his gin & tonic, then puts on his best face, the face of a man who's lost everything important in his life yet somehow hung on and goes to greet his guests. However, as he's approaching the men he sees that something's adrift. They're talking about China and a social credit program that Blanco read about in *The Washington Post*. Lin calls it facial recognition. He says it's nothing Apple isn't doing.

"For spitting in public?" Blanco says. "For a parking ticket? That's social policing."

Sherman steps into the circle his coproducer, director and moneyman make like an enthusiastic intruder. "Why all the grim faces, gents?"

"Type in 'how to make a bomb,'" Jonathan Lin says, his face red from the alcohol. "And see who's knocking on your door. China has 1.3 billion people. They have issues places like the United States can't comprehend."

Stories float around the studios. China isn't investing in Hollywood, not like they used to. The new players are Russia and Saudi Arabia. An oligarch might pour twenty million into a spy caper taking place in Europe, but the picture better deliver on opening weekend, or someone might get hurt. Or so went the story. Sherman knew a screenwriter who worked for a cop television series in Shanghai. The Chinese had rules every studio had to adhere to if they wanted to penetrate the film market: cops don't carry guns and they never kill citizens; villains are infiltrates from South Korea or Japan, but never China. The push was to keep the homeland as pure as possible.

Shinkan Sen happens to walk past in an orange couture thing that looks like a strait jacket. Strolling with her (and talking in slow, loud sentences) is Blanco's son, Bjorn. The two are heading toward the ping-pong table. Sherman glances at Jonathan Lin, who stares madly her way. A thought comes to him. What better way to secure financing then get the world's sexiest actress to have a weekend fling with the dashing Chinese American?

"Jonathan? You got a minute?"

He points him in the direction of the beautiful actress. "Ready?"

"Ping-pong is not my sport."

"Dude, come on. She's hanging out with a teenager. You're one cool cat in comparison."

Lin brings the crystal tumbler up to his lips, but he doesn't drink. "I don't know."

"It's like your tee shot. Just swing, man. You're a natural."

"Tee shot. Natural. Got it," he says. "Wait. What if I slice it into the trees?"

"You're overthinking this. You're a man, she's a woman, the rest is in your head."

A text comes through from Van Doorman. *Keegan is hungry. Can we arrange for food?*

He gives Jonathan a gentle push. "Go get em, Tiger."

His moneyman drains his drink. Then he's on his way.

*Does Keegan need a Frappuccino, too?*

*Ha ha, good one, sir.*

Across the lawn Jonathan Lin introduces himself to the movie star with a theatrical bow.

*You joining us for dinner?*

*Making one more loop around the island.*

Bjorn is much better than the actress. He's gallant, lobbing easy shots she can handle. Shinkan, on the other hand, is hunched over the table. Every time her paddle makes contact with the ball she makes these spirited comments in Japanese that has Bjorn and Jonathan grinning. Sherman watches the game like the nervous dad of an introverted boy at a birthday party praying his son fits in. From his jacket's interior pocket, he takes out a cigar. After it's lit he wanders over to the ladies. Wool blankets lie across their laps. Sherman unbuttons his coat and goes to sit down but changes his mind, electing to stand behind his date for the weekend.

"You never told me Heather's daughter was the third best tennis player in the country," Kimberly says, looking up at him. He remembers Elena Blanco's Instagram page he gleaned just yesterday: freshman at Stanford, part-time model, supports Bernie Sanders' candidacy. "We should introduce her to Jeremy. I think they'd hit it off."

The glow from the fire casts Heather's face in soft flattering light. His eyes catch the lipstick smudge on the rim of her champagne flute. She wears a knit dress with a mock collar. She's gorgeous, sophisticated, a head-turner. He can't help but imagine her soaping off in her yoga studio shower. "I've got an idea. Why don't we all meet in Aspen this winter."

"His place is amazing, Heather. Do you ski?"

"Probably not like you."

Glancing over his shoulder he sees Jonathan and Shinkan walk down the slope to where the new bar is located. He makes the smallest of fist pumps. Then he eyes Blanco's wife again and thinks—*what am I doing? Getting a hard-on for my executive producer's wife?* Sherman bends down and kisses Kimberly's neck. "I'm sorry about before."

She reaches for his hand and squeezes it. He's bringing the cigar up to his lips when movement in the trees gets his attention. It's shadowy dark across the lawn but he swears he saw something big—like a person—dart from one tree to another. Gripping the back of the chair, he peers harder into the darkness.

"Sherman?"

Heather's question summons him back to reality. He flicks the cigar in the grass and gives her a winning smile, a smile that's pure Hollywood muck. "Hey, where is that husband of yours? I need to run a few things by him."

"I think he was meeting Bjorn down at the lake."

He strides down the now quite dark path that leads to the water, a walk he's made so many times day and night that he knows it by heart. Only tonight, he takes the route in a frenzied state. As if his life's in danger. As if a man prone to violence and bodily harm might jump out of the shadows with a huge fucking knife or a huge fucking Dirty Harry .45 Magnum and end his life, a life he knows and loves and cherishes, and more than anything else, doesn't want to lose. He—Sherman Garrity— scion to Garrity Manor, eligible bachelor, film producer, philanthropist, dater of fine actresses, winner of seven gold balls, dead, deceased, NO MORE, all because of Kimberly Solberg's resemblance to a lover from way back in his tortured youth. It's all so ridiculous and pathetic and melodramatic and not worth it, if that means he's going to be dead before he reaches the hill's bottom. And then Sherman's out of the woods and trotting across the long planks. Blanco and his boy are at the shore of the big lake and its quite a sight now, the dark turbulent bay, violet sky, and the waves crashing the shore.

But then something else takes over. Seeing Blanco skipping stones with his son feels too private—it hits too close to home. He should head back to the party. He's invading a private moment between a boy and his dad. He's ruining the memory the boy will recall thirty years from now, when he's Sherman's age, about the wealthy man with a lovely vacation home in Wisconsin interrupting the greatest moment of his childhood and will be the basis for years of therapy and abusing drugs and alcohol and feelings of worthlessness and self-loathing that borders on suicide. Just when he's about to turn around he hears his named called out and then he's jogging up the path and he can smell the water and hear the surf and he feels self-conscious about his Italian suit and leather derbies and he's glad it's a fresh water lake and not the ocean because saltwater is not good for Italian leather and he loves his dress shoes like he loves his cars and his lifestyle and he's so glad he's alive and not dead he gets this huge smile on his face that shows his worry lines and crow's feet he's tried to hide with Botox and facelifts and he's glad the sun's slipped over the horizon so they can't see how hard he's trying.

"Who's winning?"

In Blanco's palm are three smooth stones. His son peers into his hand as if it were a treasure chest of jewels. Bjorn chooses the largest stone then side-flings it at the water. Sherman is reminded of the black and white photographs his coproducer sent him when he was a boy training at his dad's tennis academy in Florida.

"How'd you like to play your dad as a teenager in our movie, Bjorn?"

"Really?"

He watches Blanco's reaction. "I've heard worse ideas," the ex-player says, half-heartedly tossing a rock.

"Well, Bjorn? What do you think?"

"Would I be in scenes with Shinkan?"

His dad shoots a helpless look at the producer.

"Your dad knew Shinkan's character as an adult."

"Hmm," Bjorn says, processing this information.

"Sherman and I need to talk. Go see if your mom needs anything."

Bjorn side-arms his remaining stone. Then his face lights up. "Seven skips in heavy surf. That ties you, Dad."

He scrambles up the sandy rise for the footpath.

"Stay on the path," Sherman warns. They watch him trot toward the house. "He's a good kid."

"He takes after his mother."

"I envy you, man."

Blanco picks up another stone, turning it over in his hand. "Thanks for flying them up. I mean that. Now, what's on your mind?"

"Kimberly knows about the bet. It won't be long before she tells Heather."

Blanco searches his face. "You told her?"

He's always been an exceptional liar, ever since his mom died. "I did."

"I hope she finds out."

Sherman searches across the water. On the mainland, lights are blinking on. "You don't trust them, do you?"

"The Chinese?" Blanco says. "What do you think?"

"We're running out of options."

"Then sit on the picture until we figure this out."

"My father and I saw that match in Hamburg," he says. "Your dad was in a wheelchair. Who did you beat again?"

Blanco heaves a stone farther than Sherman could ever imagine. They watch it cut through the surface like a knife. "Shirokov."

"You drubbed him."

"Double bagel."

"I want to do something before my father dies. Something I'm proud of." They look back at the house, which is lit gold in the trees, though neither makes a move to go. "He's never been back here."

"Since your mother died? I was like that. I thought not visiting the cemetery was punishing my dad for dying."

"Can I get your take on something else?" He tells Blanco everything he knows about Solberg, his mysterious whereabouts and ferocious leanings. They're walking single file across the wooden planks now with Blanco leading the way. "He might be here. He might be watching our every move."

The athlete stops at the tree line. "And you're fucking his wife."

"What should I do?"

"You have a gun?"

Sherman throws his arms in the air theatrically. "No!" he says. "Why? Do you?"

"How about Van Doorman?"

"Is my assistant carrying? What do you think this place is? Dr. No's secret lair?"

"Has Kimberly talked to him? She might be able to de-escalate the situation. Then you're a fucking hero."

"So, you think the threat is serious?"

"How the fuck do I know?"

They climb the small rise in the dark. The party noise is louder. "Hey, Blank. You sure we can't call off the bet?"

"Sorry, Sherm. I'm not wired that way."

# POINT BLANK

He watches her from afar. Maybe that's how he's always been—seeing her from a distance, criticizing her from a place removed, unwilling to let her in. What he should do is march straight across the grass and up to his wife and have it out with her. Apologize, yes, but also help her see what's self-evident from where he stands—*these aren't her people*. His eyes lock in on the man standing behind his wife and smoking a cigar. Like the woman sitting below him is his property. Like he owns this island. And he sort of kinda does. He's sure they've fucked. That he's made his wife feel the way Ken once had. And that's like a knife through his heart. That's an image hard to push down. His thoughts flood with violence. He sees himself inflicting the kind of pain that causes permanent disfigurement—trauma that never goes away. He even sees himself hurting his wife. And he turns away in shame. *Hurting Kimberly?* The mother of his kids? The woman he's spent half his life with? Without realizing it, he slips deeper into the trees, haunted by his dark thoughts.

Exiting the woods a few minutes later he happens upon one of the guests and his boy on the shore and hops off trail then swings north through a cluster of brush. Ken takes cover behind a boathouse. He watches the father and son sling rocks at the water. He feels a strange kinship with the man. Here is an athlete who finds times with his boy when he could be up at the house knocking back martinis. Ken misses his boys. They've become his sounding board, his support team. What would they think seeing him like this? Spying on their mom? He's about to call it a night—to reassess his obsession—when Garrity walks up the footpath in his fancy suit. Soon the athlete's boy jogs back to the house. The movie guy seems anxious. He's brought these people to the island for a reason, but tension exists. Why?

His phone vibrates in his pants pocket. Ken has picked up Garrity's WIFI signal, *Hideaway*. Several old texts from the boys come through, as well as one from his assistant coach wondering when he'll return to Minneapolis. He clicks onto the unsecured network but there's no new information about the sheriff investigation. Out of curiosity, he googles Garrity's latest film. An article from *Variety* pops up with a picture of the athlete when he was younger. "Tennis Memoir *Sport* picked up by Shred Films." Ken scrutinizes the two men again. They've started back across the path. It occurs to him that Garrity may know he's on the island. Why else all the security? And where is the young man who follows Garrity around like a servant boy? Out searching for his whereabouts? If Garrity knows he's here (now Ken is certain of it) why hasn't he told Kimberly? She'd have tried to reach him. Or the boys would have. Which means Garrity doesn't see him as a threat. Or he feels he can handle whatever Ken throws his way. Does that mean he has weapons in that house? Is he allied with the local authorities? Right now, are they closing in?

He's careful working his way back to the house. If Garrity knows what kind of man Kimberly married, then he's watched video from back in the day. How Ken handed out justice where and when it was needed. Otherwise, he patrolled the ice like a cop on his beat. There was nothing like being the team's bad boy. Brawls happened every game. It was vicious and an adrenaline rush and addictive as shit. He got lost in the insanity of those moments. Where everything outside his immediate vision blurred. When it was just him and the other guy beating the living shit out of each other. It was like a beautiful car crash night after night.

He's got Garrity in his sights again. He wants to pulverize the man. He wants to break him slowly over several days using only his bare fists. He may have ruined his marriage. But he can make Garrity pay.

# BOYS DON'T CRY

He's sort of drunk. Not drunk-drunk. Not belligerent-drunk. Not falling over himself drunk. More like squishy brain drunk. And this is Sherman's toast. These are the words he's pained over wanting to get the message just right. He stands at the head table in his Italian suit. It's dark outdoors but for the candles and Christmas lights hanging between the tree branches. Staff fill water glasses and set out salad plates. The documentarians arrived only minutes before and are busy with their gimbles and steady-cams and boom poles. Everyone's being polite and not eating for this is Sherman's moment. And he wants to exhale deeply. The impulse is strong. He must fight back the reflex to let go a big, slow, molar-exposing yawn.

"When my great-great-great grandfather built this place I think he had a gathering such as this in mind." His gaze falls on his new girlfriend. She sits up front with a smile on her face. His eyes briefly get lost in her mouth before he clears his throat.

"Great-Great Grandfather called the place the Hideaway. And as you can see, we're hidden from the road and the lake, even our neighbors.

Here's a fun fact—when the cottage was built Great-Great Grandfather was careful not to destroy any more trees than necessary. We Garrity's were conservationists even back then."

The last comment gets a few chuckles. They're with him. Which is fine and dandy, but he's veered off course. An uneasy quiet enters his head. "Where was I?"

"You were telling us how the cabin got its namesake."

"The beautiful Kimberly Solberg, ladies and germs," he says, extending his arm toward his lover. "And yes, Great-Grandfather saw the Hideaway as a place of refuge. I don't think he'd have understood the modern world. These things." He reaches inside his suit pocket and pulls out his iPhone then holds it up like it's exhibit A in a murder trial he's presiding over. "Aren't these things awful?"

This is off script, too.

"Don't get me wrong. Smartphones are great for directions or a quick weather report. But pray God, why have we let these things take over our lives?"

He's officially lost them. The coquette in the red cowboy boots is thumb-texting on hers while her new beau spies over her shoulder. Blanco sneaks a piece of lettuce and his son stares up at the constellations in wonder. Out the corner of his eye he also sees the camerawoman inching closer. He must be careful. The toast is supposed to be a simple welcome. He purposely held off dinner until everyone was properly lubricated (for a tipsy guest is a hungry guest, another pearl of wisdom from dear old mom), but he got sidetracked with his backdoor negotiations. And the people are ravenous. He sees it in their eyes and the way they lick their lips in anticipation of the local chèvre, market vegetables, and croutons swimming in sorghum vinaigrette.

"This is sacred ground. Every morning we see such wonder. Weather patterns developing off the coast, those strange prehistoric looking birds with the huge wingspans." He sees his moneyman lean over and whisper in the movie star's ear. "I think our finance guy has gotten over his fears."

Jonathan Lin holds up his wine glass. "To Sherman."

Everyone lifts a glass. "To Sherman!"

"The Hideaway's held strong in storms and brutally cold winters. It's done okay in tough times, too." Here, his voice shakes a little. His gaze falls on the house and the memories the building stirs up. Tears cloud his vision. This isn't part of the speech, either. Why isn't he keeping it together? Is this the trait of a strong leader? No wonder he's having a difficult time getting the production team onboard.

"I'm not usually like this," he says, wiping his eyes. Kimberly blows him a kiss. "I'm grateful you're here. My great-great grandfather...shit all my relatives dead and alive...they're grateful. My hope is you come away feeling Madeline Island is a special place. I sure think it is."

He lifts his drink. And they rise from their chairs and cheer. This takes him by surprise. No one has ever given him a standing ovation.

"I almost forgot! Bon Appetit!"

# SHE'S THE ONE

He wanders like an animal, foraging, not rushing, feeding off land and air. He daydreams. He's a big daydreamer. He likes being lost in his head. He'll wander into a glen, see heron, quaking aspen, a shift in the winds, and his mind is elsewhere in the best possible sense. If only the boys were here. If only he could share in the pink color the cliffs give off at dusk or take in the turquoise tint of the water. Walking among the trees Ken feels safe, looked after, at home with his dog and his thoughts. He is nature. He is nothing and he is all things.

His camp is situated in the island's heart. There are two ways in. The official entrance is a narrow lane offset by two yellow No Trespassing signs. The other is an abandoned lumber road that looks as if it led to nowhere. About a quarter mile in is a meadow with a dried-up pond and stacks of thick-cut pine ready for delivery. His needs are simple. Breakfast is cold—boiled eggs or granola, dinners on the portable stove. Anything he can boil with little odor. A clump of Jack Pines is where he has his morning bowel movement. There's nothing like a shit in the woods to start your day. Ken isn't worried about being found out. Every morning he breaks down camp then parks the truck at the condos or the marina. Plus, his face is healed. He goes everywhere by foot. Walking is easy on the island with the knee-high ferns and pine saplings, the cool smell of the woods. Rich people don't peer into the thicket from their kitchen window with suspicion. Rich people aren't mistrustful. It's different with the locals. When he comes upon an old fishing shack, he moves like a deer, careful where he steps, wary of dogs and electric fences.

Garrity's property, situated on a point high above the water, is more to Ken's liking than he'd care to admit. True, it speaks of money with its slate roof, big windows, and tennis court. But it also feels real and looked after. He's yet to see his wife in broad daylight. She's all he thinks about. And not just her sharing a bed with Garrity. Out on the trail he remembers everything. Like when they first met. She was pretty the way you step outdoors on a bright morning in January and the snow blinds you while warming your face. Back then she had burnt-dark hair and wore Levi's with holes in both knees and chunky sweaters that smelled of perfume. Her eyes were the color the lakes gave off a few days before they froze for the winter. She was regular height and sometimes went on her tiptoes while eyeing him comic-warily before giving Ken a kiss. As if she didn't quite trust his big strong self. She could handle the puck okay, having grown up with brothers who played hockey. The first time they skated was on the pond at Lake of the Isles. That was the day he fell in love with her. With her pigtails under a knit stocking cap and her frame dwarfed under a UMD sweatshirt. They were playing one-on-one on a sun-filled afternoon. The ice was cleared of snow and maybe fifty skaters were on the narrow inlet. They'd been dating a couple weeks. Already he felt a kinship with her. They were compatible and passionate lovers, able to spend whole days together and not get bored or need a break. He'd drive down from Duluth on his day off. They'd make love in her dorm on the Minneapolis College of Art and Design campus then talk into the night. He told her things, deeply painful things… about his brother and his fraught relationship with his dad.

On the ice that day her cheeks were pink and her mouth set with determination as she tried steering a puck past his huge skates. He let her score. Which pissed Kimberly off. She told him to play her straight up, no fooling around. "And wipe that grin off your face, Ken Solberg." And she went at him again, this time faking right then switching the puck over on her left side. She got the space she wanted but pushed the puck wide. "Damn it all to hell," she muttered. And Ken laughed. He laughed like a man without a care in the world. He laughed like a man in love. He loved everything about her. She would save him. She'd pull him up from the darkness. Here was the woman he'd been searching for. He couldn't take his eyes off her. Her eyes and that body—her soul. The way she looked at him and saw him for who he was. For the man she believed he could be. And he loved her for that with everything he had.

\*\*\*

God hasn't been in his life in a long time. When he was a boy, he never questioned his faith. In college, he saw God like an eagle soaring some thermal and not too interested with the way humans had fucked things up. Then one day God became a lonesome conceit or a poem too tricky for his own good. And Ken put him in his pocket for safekeeping. But lately, he feels the divine rushing through his bloodstream. Something about waking every morning at sunbreak—all that earthly silence—has him thinking only a benevolent God created a natural wonder like Madeline Island. There are miles of pristine shoreline. Plenty of space for a man to wash his privates and shampoo his hair without getting weird stares. Lake Superior is one clean lake. It's probably drinkable (Dimley laps it up like Ken did alcohol), though he's cut his consumption way back. Out here, he doesn't need drink. He's fine with the woods and walking trails, the critters and solitude. He tries his best to live off the land. He knows what plants are edible and how to set a trap to lure big game in. There's a Springsteen tune for his new condition, he just doesn't know the title yet. He'll know it when he hears it. He'll hear the song, turn to Dimley and say—*that song is me*. Until then, he'll carry on with his eyes wide open. He'll hike and be cunning like the wolf. When it's time to act, he'll be sober and steady-handed, crystal-clear with his intentions.

He's in a new place. He feels things, deeply charged things. Like the symmetry in nature. Take the perfectly formed maple leaf with its pointed leaf blades and toothed edges. Proof there is order in the universe. Proof there is beauty in all things. Proof he's healing. Proof he's letting go.

Out on his own, on the hard, well-traveled paths, he makes promises with himself. Like going cold turkey. Like being happy for Kimberly. Like admitting he brought this shit-show on himself. In those moments an energy pulses through him more powerful than booze or weed or sex. He realizes he's taking control of his life. He's love, not violence. He's wisdom, not ego. No more fistfights and wasted hours. No more fucking around. He'll attack the day like it's his last. His boys will see him for the father he's always wanted to be. Choosing light, not darkness. Choosing to laugh stuff off, to let things go. This way of thinking is easier on the Apostle Islands. Here the light inside him burns strong. But it isn't like he's turned into Saint Luke overnight. Take the other morning. He was coming on camp after his morning defecation and who does he see but Garrity's young assistant riding a mountain bike through the woods. He pushed Dimley into the high grass, laid on top of his dog, stroking his neck, soothing him with 'hush now' and 'there, there, boy' until the kid was out of sight. Then Ken was moving through camp with a purpose that was antithetical to his recent transformations. That raw power was back. And it was strong.

# THE LOST JOURNALS
# OF SHERMAN GARRITY, 1983-1988

April, 1983

George, Juliet and I saw *The Outsiders* for the fifth time! The movie is everywhere... Plaza Westwood, Warner Center, Glendale, Sherman Oaks Galleria... I really related to Ponyboy. There's something about the character that speaks to me, though, at thirteen I'm hard pressed to explain what that thing is... I may also be in love with Diane Lane... she's just so wonderful and pretty. If things don't work out with Juliet, I may need to call on Diane... har har har...

But back to the film. It so inspired me I decided to start a journal like Ponyboy does. And just so you know this is not a diary. I'm not explaining my feelings on the page for all to see. Or confessing my mad desires in the pursuit of love. I just want to see what happens if I write stuff down... so anyway... here goes.

May, 1983

For the first time EVER, Juliet held my hand at the roller skating rink. The song was Asia's "Heat of the Moment," the disco ball turned. Though something is bothering me. Juliet's palm was damp. Does this mean she likes me? Or the opposite? I asked Mom what she thought about the wet hand/dry hand argument, but she was too busy with her pool party with Dad in Palm Desert playing golf.

At the party, Gita Dhar, who mom says is a very free spirit, lost her top during a wrestling game in the pool between the men (the Speedos) versus the women (the bikinis). Gita has HUGE BOOBS.

Lastly, and most importantly, Wren had a party where we played Spin the Bottle. And Juliet chose me! Kissing her was like the best moment of my life. Her lips tasted like the cherry lip gloss she wears way too much in my opinion... unless we're kissing then her lips are slippery and soft and taste amazing. Another something happened at Wren's... Juliet again won five minutes in the walk-in closet and this time she chose James Mulligan. They were in there a really long time and when they walked out to cheers, no less, James lifted his arms in the air like he had conquered Egypt or something.

What was wrong with how I kissed? I consulted George on the matter. He was as confused as I was. He did offer one suggestion, practicing kissing on my forearm. I think I'm finally getting the hang of it. I close my eyes, part my lips, and dream my arm is Juliet's lips. Oh, the things we do for love!

New Year's Day, 1984

Got braces last month... they really suck. I look like Jaws from those James Bond movies. Juliet looked at my mouth and made the same face she made the night we watched *Meatballs* and Fink won the frankfurter eating contest.

What else... let's see...

I still have nightmares about earthquakes where our house falls into the ocean... Mom and I won the Mother/Son tournament at the club, beating the Rothmans, 8-2. We're going to Aspen over the break... one big happy skiing family... if I sound sarcastic it's because Mom and Dad fight all the time... over the stupidest stuff... like him not putting the newspaper in the recycling pile or her having wine with every meal.

New Year Resolutions: get a better second serve, learn to drive (Gramps promises to let me practice around the circular drive as long as he's passenger), be the sort of loving son who brings the 'rents' together, ask Juliet to go steady.

March, 1984

She said no. Can you believe it? What's wrong with us being boyfriend and girlfriend? We're practically family. I'm not even wearing the orthodontic head gear to school anymore. George thinks Juliet is a lesbian. But he thinks everyone is gay or lesbian. I'm starting to think George might be gay. Here's why: one) he's into watching men's ice skating on TV two) he has a poster of Rob Lowe in his room, the one where he's got like a rock-hard jaw and is lifting the hem of his tanktop so you can see his stomach, three) whenever we're at a party and couples start partnering up, George always disappears, four) lately he's wearing an earring in his left ear and everyone knows what that means. Juliet asked him the gay or not gay thing.

"Maybe," he said. "No, definitely not!" Then George changed the subject.

May, 1984

So here's the latest with Juliet… I'm acting like I'm totally over her… I even started dating her best friend, Moira Stafford, whose father is like head of Warner Brothers or something. She's got a movie theatre in her house, a popcorn machine, and recliners. She's not pretty like Juliet is, but Moira's cute, which I'm hoping will make Juliet see me in a more attractive light.

On the upside I've seen the following movies at her house… *Valley Girl*, *Risky Business* (awesome), *Mr. Mom* (super funny), *Flashdance*, *Rumble Fish*, *Max Dugan Returns*, *E.T. the Extra-Terrestrial*, *48 HRS* (love Eddie Murphy), *The Outsiders* (again), *Meaning of Life* (hilarious) *Tootsie* (overrated, slow), *Tron*, *Joysticks*, *Blue Thunder*.

June, 1984

George is onto me. He says go for it. "What do you have to lose. It's only Juliet?" But that's it. I have everything to lose. I also feel like shaking George and saying, "What about you? You're not exactly shouting from the rooftops about your fondness for boys. Other than me, Juliet, and the guy in the Missing Persons T-shirt you held hands with at the Michael Jackson concert, who knows your little secret?"

June, 1984

Bel Air CC had a team match last weekend. I'm the best 14& Under, hands down, but like Abrams, Hammer and Murdock are older and stronger. But then Coach Don says Abrams is in Massachusetts checking out schools, Hammer's got a sprained knee, and Murdock... no one knows where Murdock is. Suddenly, I'm playing #1 singles. If that's not enough pressure, I find out the kid I'm playing is not only my age, he's the best fourteen-year-old in the United States!!

In warmups, I remember what Del Evans used to say... figure out the guy's strengths and weaknesses then formulate a plan. Believe me, this guy was solid on everything. So we spin racquets to see who serves first. And I shit you not when I say I came out like a ballbuster. I don't know what came over me, but I couldn't miss. I go up 3-0 (we're playing an 8-game pro set). Well, then the gravity of the moment like overtakes me. I don't win another game. Still, the first three games against the best our

country has to offer? There's hope for me yet.

June, 1984, continued...

At Madeline with the parents...Moira and me are history with a capital H... all because she intercepted the note George passed me in PE where I checked off the yes box about who looked better in gym clothes, Juliet or Moira. I was over her anyway. It's my favorite time of year SUMMER in my favorite place MADELINE ISLAND with my two favorite people MOM AND DAD. It's strange but Madeline is the one place where they get along. They swim together, they kayak, they sit on the porch at the end of the day drinking cocktails. If we only lived in Madeline Island year-round, I'd have the world's happiest parents.

July, 1984

Mom turns 43 today. That's so old! Though she doesn't look a day older than thirty-five. She calls herself a bohemian, a word I had to look up the meaning of. So a bohemian is a person who's socially unconventional AND likes the arts… well there you go, Mom. Anyone who likes being barefoot, smoking pot, and dancing when she cooks is a bohemian in my books. Happy birthday, Mom!

March, 1985
Juliet's style is Girl Next Door. Unlike most wannabes at Sherman Oaks Mall, meaning the New Wavers or Punks, she's into Esprit and Benetton. She smells nice. Not sure what perfume she wears (make mental note to look on her dresser next time I'm over), nothing splashy, nothing hitting you over the head with its olfactory power. Juliet has a huge smile… she smiles at just about everything… even me.

March, 1985, continued…
There's a new tennis pro at the club named Tom. He's taller than Dad, not much older than me, good looking, but not in an intimidating way. He plays more like Edberg than Lendl, which I can appreciate, hits a cleaner ball than Coach Don, so our rally's last a long time. He says I'll be ready for sectionals… fingers crossed.

April, 1985
For a teaching pro, Tom's pretty smart. He actually reads books. And get this, he saw Prince last year, Purple Rain tour, like tenth row, main stage. He and his buds camped out for tickets. "This dude showed up with a gun," he tells me. "We let him in. I mean, what's more important, "Let's Go Crazy" or my life, man?"

April, 1985, continued…
Tom says I need to throw my toss farther out in the court and "go get it." He says the only thing stopping me from being the player I can be is me. He's always saying stuff like that. When it comes out of his mouth I admit nodding along like we drink the same Kool-Aid. But then in matches I feel the old me taking over. I seize up on short balls instead of ripping winners I'm very capable of hitting. I miss first serves like they went out of fashion years ago. In no time at all I'm calling myself bozo or dickwad and truly hating on myself and tennis and life in

general. Why am I driven for such excellence? Fuck.

May, 1985

Tom wants me to slow down. He wants deep breaths between points, fiddling with my strings, visualizing... now that's a word he uses a lot. I tell him I can visualize all I want, but I can't visualize what the other guy is going to do. "I'm not a mind reader." He laughs, says try it and we'll discuss next lesson. Yeah, Tom's pretty cool.

May, 1985, continued...

So, okay, here's the thing: I'm a goal-oriented guy. Mom says I get my motivation from Dad, which is cool, I guess, though for the most part he's kind of checked out. Goal-wise, there's three things on the near horizon: passing my driving test in June, reaching round 32 or better in this year's sectionals, and growing more experienced with the opposite sex... second or third base is optimum, but hitting a homerun would be very choice.

I've got my eyes on a couple girls now that Juliet is dating Lance, which is still hard to believe. I mean he's ridiculously handsome. The day he brought his portfolio to school I admit his modeling pictures were killer. He'll probably make the cover of GQ. But really, Juliet? In class he's always staring out the window like some retard or making eyes with her, which makes me want to vomit. And I thought Juliet had a good head on her shoulders.

June, 1985

Holy shit! Tom's a genius. Was it just last week when I broke all my racquets and tried to run cars off the 101 after losing first round in a warmup tourney in Northridge? Today at sectionals I tried my best to do what Tom said, you know, visualize and stay upbeat, even when I did stupid stuff like double fault to lose the first set. And lo and fucking behold! It worked!

New Years Day, 1986

It's been a while, huh? I guess that's because life got a lot more serious. We're all studying for SATs like mad. Everyone talks about schools they want to attend. George is shooting for Berkeley, where his old man got his law degree. Juliet wants someplace small and elite out East. Which really rubs me the wrong way when there are so many choice colleges right here in LA!

Tennis has gone from bad to worse. Tom says that in every serious endeavor there comes a time of reckoning. I guess this is that fucking time. Thus, I'm doubling down: 200 serves a day, weights, video analysis, mass protein consumption. I'm going to lick this reckoning or else.

It's not much better on the home front. Dad's like a ghost. Even when he's around he's got this look on his face like he'd rather be somewhere else. Mom's gone off the deep end. She wears this huge crystal necklace she thinks emits strange powers. She's got an astrologer who deals in perpetual motion machines. And her psychic tells her a break is coming though the woman didn't offer up any more details than that.

And you know how I ran the Range Rover off that steep embankment up in Benedict Canyon and Dad lost his lunch over it? Well, it gets worse. The other night George and I are at a party in Sherman Oaks when this super-hot girl from Japan asks if we'd drive her to Encino where there was another party she wanted to crash. I was driving the 911, which meant George scrunched in the backseat so lovely Megumi could copilot. We were listening to *This Year's Model* and zooming down the 101 when Megumi set her hand on my thigh then checked out my wrist.

"Is that a good brand?"

I shrugged like probably. "Ask my dad."

She then took my wrist in her hand and eyed the watch closer. "Is Patek Philippe like a Rolex?"

Let me stop here and say Megumi was so fucking hot she was smoking. She had like a Madonna peroxide shag and wore this black cocktail dress, the back completely exposed but for a couple strands of string keeping it from falling down.

Her hand had found my thigh again. "Can I wear it?" I'm like why not. I thought if this gets me remotely naked (or more) with Megumi, then I'm in.

The party was raging like she said. Some house in the hills, closer to Calabasas than Encino, indoor/outdoor pool, live band, hundreds of kids—a rager. She got us beers then said we should blow off George, which I was more than happy to do. We went upstairs and found a bedroom that wasn't locked.

Inside was this awesome glow-in-the dark aquarium with angel fish and eels and shit. We started making out. And it was unbelievable. Megumi let me feel her tits. I was thinking this is it, I'm losing my virginity tonight to the hottest chick in the valley. About a half hour into our make-out session we came up for air. Megumi volunteered to get us refills downstairs. I went looking for George to fill in the dirty details, but he was AWOL. I'm sure you guessed where this is going. Megumi returned with refills. We started kissing again. And the door burst open. In walked this big dude in Hobie shorts and Vans. He was like "What the fuck, Jane."

"Jane?"

Jane or Megumi or whatever her name was, was pulling up her dress in a way that made me think this wasn't the first time she'd been busted.

"Wait," I said. "Is this it?"

"You mean the last time you'll ever see me? Probably."

"Oh, well, okay. Oh, can I have my dad's watch back?"

"Sure thing, Sherman." She unclasped it but instead of handing it over, Megumi tossed the watch in the aquarium.

"What the fuck!" I ran over and stuck my whole arm in the water, pulling it out. "My father will kill me! It's not waterproof!"

May, 1986
Tom has these sayings... trust thyself... see yourself as thou truly are. He uses this lame British accent when he makes these pronouncements. I'm like, you're so not funny, dude. Yeah, he's improved my game. But I'm thinking Tom has even bigger issues than me.

May, 1986, continued...
Juliet reminds me of Mom. She's always in a good mood even

when I'm being a complete dick. We play tennis at the club. Like Mom, Juliet hits one good backhand then wants to order a cherry Coke and hang out by the pool. I'm realizing she doesn't have my drive.

There are very few things I'm serious about and tennis is one of them. My goal is a scholarship to USC or UCLA, though I'm not ripping up the So. Cal's rankings (current boy's 16 & Under- #24). Not bad, but a long way from Los Angeles' own Richard Blanco. The one time I saw him working out at Riviera Club Juliet happened to be tagging along. Her eyes turned especially blue when she laid eyes on him with his little headband and even littler shorts. He's got seriously cool hair to go along with a seriously cool name and he's handsome in an All-American Boy Next Door sort of way. But if I liked guys, and trust me I don't, but if I did, I'd go for a Matt Dillon type. He's just way cool and not so caught up in his looks. I'm just saying.

May, 1986, continued...

Full confession: Juliet gets my insides revved up big time. Sometimes when I'm around her I can't think straight. I stare at her like she's the statue of David, which I'm checking out in person if it ever comes to LACMA. Of course she busts me and my gonzo stare and immediately thinks she has lettuce between her teeth. I snap out of it really fast, but I'm totally embarrassed and end up pretending I'm cooler than Sting, when I feel the complete opposite. Should I tell her how I feel and possible scare her away forever?

June, 1986

It happened. I guess it had to with her being so hot and all. They went all the way. Well, that was according to George, whom I admit seems privy to the more intimate details of Juliet's life now that Sir Lancelot is in the picture. It really hurts knowing she's "damaged goods," and at the hands of him of all people.

The other night the three Amigos were hanging out at George's swimming pool. Juliet was wearing this tight striped

French blouse that really showed off her figure. I kept sneaking looks at her tits. Her body was making me CRAZY. We were getting drunk on gin and tonics George had pilfered from his parent's wet bar. Juliet went to the loo. And George punched me in the arm, and not soft, either.

"Could you be more obvious?"

I made a face like I didn't care if my lust for Juliet was that transparent. "She's beautiful and the woman of my dreams, even if she's damaged goods," I said.

George being George passed out first. I almost told Juliet that Lance was a dickwad. But I held my tongue, and drunk as I was, that was a miracle in itself. We were having such a grand time. With us, there's never a dull moment or like a weird lull. Our conversations flow like a perfect river.

I'm coming to terms with the idea of contentment. As in being content Juliet and I are friends and nothing more. I think they call that maturity. I better sign off now… Ciao, Bella.

July, 1985
Lance is idiot #1. Yes, he's the latest The Gap model; yes, he's got thick long hair, smoldering blue eyes and kissable lips (that's what Juliet says); and yes, he's buds with Judd Nelson. But the guy can't tie his shoes and talk at the same time. And having a halfway intelligent conversation with Tarzan Boy? The other day he asked me what I was reading.

"It's not Updike's best novel," I said, showing him the cover. "But it's not throwaway material, either."

He whipped his hair back as he's prone to do about a thousand times a day. He said, and I shit you not, "So, it's non-fiction, then?" How does Juliet go out with such a putz?

February, 1987
It's official. I fired Tom's ass. It was maybe the hardest thing I've ever had to do. I cried. He cried. We both cried. Just joking. But like come on, Tom! My game is in serious free-fall. And he says Rome wasn't built in a day? Oh, really Tom? There's a news flash.

More news on the Juliet/Lance saga. She came

back from the week in Merida with his family looking as lovely as an Aperol Spritz. I went straight home and punched a hole in my closet door. Which put my tennis on permanent hold with a broken wrist. Why does life suck so much?

July, 1987, continued…
I'm starting to think I only dreamt playing Spin the Bottle with Juliet. Also, I sort of wish we weren't friends. That way, I could act like a dick and get away with it, like so many guys do. She might even see me in the same light as Tarzan Boy.

July, 1987, continued…
An abridged version of Mom and my conversation at Angeli Caffe after seeing *Room with a View*. Imagine a half-eaten pizza and picked over penne arrabbiata on the table.

"Mom? Do you think there's something wrong with me?"

"Of course not."

"Is love just bullshit?"

She threw her head back and laughed. "Is this about a girl?"

"Sort of…"

She waited, fingering the stem of her wine glass.

"I see all these movies, Mom. Like the one we just saw about the Riviera."

"Florence, dear."

"Whatever. My point is this—is it all bunk?"

She smiled then sipped her wine. "Love is an amazing thing, Sherman."

"And if the other person doesn't feel that same amazement? What then?"

She reached across the table and squeezed my hand. "You're going to find someone, Sherman. You'll see."

July, 1987, continued…
Another recent conversation transcribed to the best of my ability, July 9th, 1986, Juliet's swimming pool, 9:56PM.

Juliet: Are you gay, George.

George: I think so.

Juliet: That's so great!

Sherman: We're really happy for you, George.

Juliet: Are you going to tell your parents?

George. Not in this lifetime.

Sherman: I think that's wise, George. Remember how your

parents took the news about you choosing BU over Berkeley?

George: They're not in a good place, spiritually.

Juliet: We love and support you, George.

Sherman. Yeah...

George: I don't know what I'd do without you both.


July, 1987, continued...
Leave for 4-Star Tennis Academy, Charlottesville, Virginia, in two weeks. Afterwards, I fly up to Madeline Island to spend a few days with Mom and Dad. I'm a little nervous, branching out on my own like this. I've never gone to a camp without George or Juliet tagging along. Mom says I'll do great. I take great solace in those words.

August, 1987, continued...
Mom is dead. The 4-Star tennis director told me. I think I'm in shock because I feel nothing.

August, 1987, continued...
Mom is gone, like dead, like I'll never see her ever again. I feel very alone right now.

August, 1987, continued...
Mom is dead, a drowning at sea. I'm not satisfied with the police investigation. What do you mean, you can't find the body? It's in the goddamn lake, you assholes.

August, 1987, continued...
Mom is dead. I think I've been drunk seventeen straight days. Like all day long.

August, 1987, continued...
Mom is dead.

September, 1987
Back in Los Angeles. I'm not doing so well. Panic attacks, times when I can't stop sobbing. I won't lie to you. I've thought about ending my life. I don't mean I've sat around the pool with George or Juliet discussing why life would be better off without me in it. Just that I've seen things, dark soulless things. In English the other day I was explaining to the class why Jay Gatsby was THE TRAGIC FIGURE of American literature. In my mind's eye, I saw myself punching the window then

sticking a sharp piece of glass into my carotid artery.

Juliet's a constant presence. We don't talk about what happened so much as she's just there, in my room while we study, spending the night in the guest room, riding with me to and from school. I'm not sure I'd still be here without her.

November, 1987

WHY? NOW THAT'S A WORD I THINK A LOT ABOUT THESE DAYS. AS IN WHY HER? AS IN WHY NOT HIM? AS IN WHY TAKE THE ONLY THING IN MY LIFE THAT WAS FULL OF LIGHT? AS IN WHY, GOD? WHY PUNISH ME? DID I DO SOMETHING WRONG? DID I WRONG YOU? WHY DO I BELIEVE IN YOU ANYWAY? IT'S NOT LIKE YOU'VE BEEN THERE FOR ME BEFORE. YOU KNOW WHAT? I DON'T LIKE YOU ANYMORE. SO THERE.

November, 1987

It's difficult right now. Existing in a house with a dad whose idea of grieving is pretending nothing's wrong. I wish he'd talk to me. I wish he'd tell me he understands my pain. I wish he'd be a dad for once and not shirk from his dad duties. My therapist says give it time. She says the emotions I'm feeling are normal. She says she'd be more worried if I was angry. Guess what? I'm fucking angry.

December, 1987

A typical conversation between father and son around Christmas time.

Him: Will you ever learn, Sherman? First you total a car, then you charge $150,000 on a credit card?

Me: You know what's sad? I lost two parents the day Mom drowned. The only difference is you're not dead yet.

Him: You know what I'm going to do?

Me. I'm waiting, Locke.

Him: I'm taking your allowance away for two whole months.

Me: Fine by me. I make more cashola dealing coke anyway.

Him: Is this about your mother? Because I can't bring her back. I know it's hard,

Sherman. But she's not coming back.

Me. What? Is Daddy going to cry?

Him: You ungrateful little...
SLAP SOUND.

Me: Great, Locke. Just great.

What a year 1987 is turning into.

December, 1987, continued...
Call it a truce. Dad invited Juliet and me to Palette's opening night. We ate tofu soup, spicy shrimp wrapped in clear paper, and Beijing duck prepared by six of the best chefs in the world. Dad flirted with Jacqueline Bisset, who wore this crazy furry animal around her neck. She's the most beautiful older woman I've ever laid eyes on. I tried flirting with her myself, my lame attempt to spark a little jealousy from Juliet. But alas, she didn't take the bait.

Dudley Moore entertained everyone on the piano. He's amazing. It was one of those nights when I really missed Mom. She used to take me to all these society parties when I was a kid. Places like Ma Maison or the Biltmore. Picture Mom in elegant Oscar de la renta or Bill Blass. Then picture me, a tiny lad in black tie. She'd introduce me to Robert Altman as her "little man." I once sat on Farah Fawcett's lap while she and Lee Majors argued about what she ordered for dinner. Mom danced with all the charming men, from Tom Selleck to Ryan O'Neil. I loved being her little man.

January, 1988
I find Dad looking through the *Interview* with Michael J. Fox on the cover. He's ogling a full-page ad promoting the new Belinda Carlisle album, *Heaven On Earth*, when I snatch it from his hands. Dad sticks his tongue out. "God, you're so juvenile!" I scream.

Speaking of juvenile, I was snooping around his room the other day looking for cash. I find an old *Playboy* with Bo Derek on the cover. Spoiler alert... she's kind of hot. Anyway, how juvenile, huh?

April, 1988
My dream to play pro tennis is over. It was pure dribble, pure fantasy, denial city. I naively

thought that being an international tennis star would allow me leverage so to speak… to exist above normal society: think competition, notoriety, cash payouts, and chicks even hotter than Juliet, begging me to make love to them. Boy, was I wrong.

May, 1988
George sent me a postcard from Boston U. He met a guy named Michael. He says he's interesting and smart. He says he can't wait to see me over summer break, that so much has changed in his life for the better.

June, 1988
New goals: not fight so much with dad, do less drugs, smile more, be less sarcastic, take my car collection to the next level, ask Juliet to marry me. Okay— that last item about marriage, I stole that from *The Graduate*… watched it the first time since mom died. It was her favorite movie.

July, 1988
Today is Mom's birthday. Dad left for work early, no mention of what day it is or if we were doing anything special later. Business as fucking usual. Maybe he's over her. Maybe there comes a time in a man's life when he moves on, when he thinks, goddamn it, the woman I devoted my life to is gone and there's nothing I can do about it.

I'll probably drive to the ocean in the Alfa Romeo, listen to *Sound of Silence, Heart Like A Wheel,* The Crusaders *Greatest Hits, Sleeping Gypsy,* and smoke some doobie wah.

Miss you Mom! Love you! Be well wherever you are! X0XOXO!!!!

July, 1988, continued…
It's strange… Mom not here. The lake spooks me. Usually, I live in the lake, even swimming at night. The past week I've gone in to cool off twice, and never past the dock. What's wrong with me? What am I afraid of? Am I that far gone?

July, 1988, continued…
I didn't tell anyone I was coming, not Dad, not George or Juliet. I didn't even call Steve-O ahead of time to open the place up. I came

incognito, cross-country, just like me and mom used to do.

A year later the Hideaway smells lifeless, even eerie (if eerie has a smell). When I left last year, I forgot to empty the refrigerator. Now it smells like something has died in there. Steve-O had it hauled away. He brought me a cooler to store food until the new one arrived.

July, 1988, continued…

Mom's bathroom reminds me of those carefully rendered scenes in movies indicating someone's left town in a rush… a toothbrush standing in a Mason jar, the cap off a tube of Crest, a makeup mirror fine dusted with fingerprints… her fingerprints I realize. Plus her hydrators and oils, this marble roller she used to run over her face to increase blood flow.

Standing there with all her personal items I suddenly get shivers down my neck. Somewhere I'd heard the heebie-jeebies like that means your in the presence of a spirit or ghost or what have you. "Mom?" I shout. "Is that you?"

July, 1988, continued…

I keep her albums and ashtrays and cookbooks, the glacier glasses she bought in the Andes, one floppy hat, and her silk robe that still smells like her. The rest I pack up then take to Salvation Army in Ashland.

I feel lighter afterwards. I feel strangely closer to Mom. I realize the Hideaway is really mine now. I can do what I want with it: sell it, burn it down, turn it into a brothel, make it a hangout for party people like me.

Steve-O drops off the new refrigerator. Afterwards, we walk the property. I want a dock that can withstand ice sheets and huge arctic winds. I want a new shake roof. I also think the court needs a facelift.

"I'm thinking clay."

"Whatever you want, Sherman."

As much as I feel the pull of mom's shadow, I realize I have to start thinking about myself more.

July, 1988

Week two I finally get into the groove… I even call Dad so he won't be worried.

Then Juliet shows up…

August, 1988, continued…
George and Michael are here, staying in my old bedroom. They met at BU. Michael is pre-med, a vegetarian, and a highly ranked squash player in New England. We get along grand.

Michael took one look around the Hideaway and said, "Oh my God. This is so Nantucket I could puke!"

At night we watch films by Godard and Kurosawa Michael pulls out of his bookbag like someone else does a John Irving novel. He's into the underground music scene… Fugazi, Jane's Addiction, Galaxie 500. He and George saw the Robert Mapplethorpe retrospective in Boston. "It was raw and honest, like nothing I'd ever seen before… truly affecting. It changed my life."

Being around Michael is like feeling you've woken up from a deep sleep that's lasted your whole life. He makes me want to get out more, be curious. Live.

We stay clear of conversations about me and Juliet, where she's at, what she's

up to. My insides feel carved out. Like an essential part of me is missing and may never return. Love stinks, as the song goes.

August, 1988, continued…
Juliet wrote me on Bates College stationary, where she'll attend this fall. She says she and Eve sat next to Michelle Pfeiffer and her agent at The Ivy. She says the actress is even more beautiful in person. She's done Ecstasy a couple times since she's been home. A part of her wants to do the drug with me. But she's wary, too. Because E is like the most beautiful feeling in the world, like a love train that never stops. Thus, she's not sure she can control herself around me.

She ends the letter by saying Madeline was something both of us needed. Yet it wasn't reality. She misses me terribly, but believes we should be friends, not lovers.

August, 1988, continued…
I watch them when they're not looking. They're sweet on each other. This has a weird effect on me. I can't help thinking about

me and Juliet, what could have been.

Sometimes I get scared thinking about George, his future life. AIDS is fucking scary. I just want him to be safe. I'm so happy he's found Michael. He deserves a good guy, and Michael fits that bill.

August, 1988, continued…
Having the lovebirds around beckons another question… am I destined to be a bachelor the rest of my life? Don't get me wrong. I'm not jealous. I just wonder why things don't work out for moi? If Paul Simon is to be trusted than I am an island living on an island and dreaming of falling for an island girl. Or am I rock?

I make a pact with myself this morning. No more feeling sorry for myself, taking more risks, making something of my life.

August, 1988, continued…
Michael wants to kayak to one of the islands. We find out to rent a tandem sea kayak (George isn't fit enough to paddle the two miles over open water on his own) we must take a class on the mainland. Stockton is the closest island that's not Basswood or Hermit (I made it clear I'm not interested in either of those places) … so Stockton it is.

Full disclosure: I'm really scared to do the crossing.

August, 1988, continued…
On the day of the class, we're fitted for drysuits. We must perform maneuvers in the water (think worse case scenarios). George is so nervous his teeth chatter even before we get in the water.

After we get home dread or something equivalent starts filling me up like gallons and gallons of lake water. But I can do this. I need to do this. Right?

August, 1988, continued…
Michael pays close attention to the weather reports. We need a calm day.

August, 1988, continued…
The night before the crossing, the three of us drink wine down by the water. Michael looks over an aerial map we'll take with us. It's waterproof and shows the

water depths in lettering so small you have to peer closely to read the measurements.

"How long do you think it will take us?" Michael asks me.

"A couple hours."

"You nervous?" George is looking at me. "For the record, I'm petrified."

"I'm heartbroken about what happened to your mom, Sherman," Michael says. "She sounds like an amazing woman. But the odds of you leaving this world in the exact manner your mother did, well, it's quite remote."

George socks me in the arm. "He makes a valid point."

August, 1988, continued...
Today, Michael, George and I kayaked to Stockton Island. We brought lunch prepared by the Inn and a small cooler of beers. It was a perfect day for a crossing. The lake was flat and blue, the sun bright. About halfway across we rode these big rollers. They weren't scary, more like being swept along by the hand of a benevolent giant. There was one point when I felt this emotion so powerful that

tears blurred my vision. The only thing missing was Juliet.

August, 1988, continued...
George and Michael left today. I drove them to Minneapolis in the 911, which was a little tight, but we managed. It was like old times with George scrunched in back! The drive back to Madeline was uneventful. Michael gave me two cassettes, "A gift for your splendid hospitality," he'd said. Morrissey's *Viva Hate* and The Sugarcubes *Life's Too Good.*

Once back on the island, I called Juliet. We talked for two hours. It was good to clear the air. I told her I wasn't going to kill myself after all.

She laughed. "Well, that's good news!"

The anniversary came and went without consequence. It rained most of the day. I sat on the back porch in a fisherman sweater and jeans, smoking cigarettes, and thinking. That itch I sometimes get, to move on, to not overdo my stay, kicked in. It was time to leave anyway. School started in ten days.

I packed that night then left on the first ferry in the morning. I didn't call Steve-O until I'd reached Fargo.

"Close up the Hideaway for the year," I told him. "Thanks, my friend."

Then I drove west, into the sunset.

# CHINESE PROXY II

Sherman stands next to the stage nursing his hangover with a Bloody Mary. It's noon and the band's doing a soundcheck in heavy winds. Dylan is stage-right, hammering the last shingles on the tiki bar, which in hindsight is sitting too close to the stage, though there's nothing he can do about it now. He gets out his smartphone and checks the Doppler app again. A storm inches toward the island with touch down estimated around the time Marley hits the stage.

On the outside he is a picture of calm. He wears a crisp Thom Browne polo and matching shorts. He has a Russell Simmons snapback perched on his head. He's even wearing $600 Prada flipflops. Inside he's another story. There's his executive producer doing his best to sabotage talks with the Chinese. There's maybe an unhinged husband on the prowl. And a couple hundred strangers are storming the Hideaway later tonight. If only Ethereal were here. A little Adderall and Sauvignon Blanc and she's a mightier multitasker than even Van Doorman. He puts the call in when that voice in his head says it's a bad idea. The backup singers are repeating "No *woman, no cry*," when Ethereal picks up the line.

He turns his back to the loud music. "Hi."

"What's that noise?"

"The Bob Marley cover band. That's why I called."

"Because of some shitty band?"

"But I thought... after our conversation last night..."

"I don't have all day."

He tries thinking of a better way of saying what he wants to say without actually saying what it is he needs to say. "I brought the team in, only we're at a stalemate," he finally says. "Thought I'd get your input, is all."

She says nothing. She's quiet like she's never quiet.

"You still there?"

"You flew the team in?"

He tries chuckling it off. "Shinkan Sen is here. You should see her. She's a wow."

"A *wow?*" Her sarcasm is thicker than usual. "Did you call to rub it in?"

"Rub it in? What are you talking about?"

"Who got the Heather Harper part? And if you say Charlize, I'll scream. I'll fucking scream, Shermy."

"I need your help. That's why I called."

"Oh my god. This is about funding your stupid picture, isn't it?"

She severs the line.

The band is now playing a rousing version of Whitney Houston's "How Will I Know." Also, at some point during the phone call, one of the video crew is standing next to him. She and her glide cam. He smiles like the relaxed man he's not then turns his attention back on the stage. This was his music: "How Will I Know," "Beat It," "Girls Just Want To Have Fun," "Hungry Like The Wolf." This was the music he played after his mother died. He'd sing his lungs out in the shower with tears in his eyes. Because Whitney Houston (like Madonna and Janet Jackson) breathed the positive. Because Sherman refused to let the dark extinguish his mother. Because a person had a choice. And he chose the light. To lean the other way was too dangerous. He'd been there. He'd gone all goth with the eyeliner and black lipstick, the designer street drugs, the dreams of killing himself. And one day he woke up and thought enough was enough.

"And I thought I paid for a Bob Marley cover band," he jokes.

The woman pauses in filming to glance his way. She's in her twenties and has a small round face, a face made smaller by her big round glasses. "Whitney Houston's daughter died last night. Weird how."

She's dressed like a person accustomed to long shoots on her feet—
T-shirt, khaki shorts, hiking boots.

"What do you mean?"

"You know how Whitney Houston died in a bathtub from an
apparent overdose?" He hadn't but plays along as if he did. "Her
daughter's death was eerily similar."

They tune back into the song. For him "How Will I Know" takes on
a life he hadn't thought about before. "What was her name?"

"Bobbi."

"Like her dad. That's so sad."

There's another long stretch of silence between them.

"They're pretty good, huh?" he says after a while.

The camerawoman's attention is still on the viewfinder. "Honestly?"

"I'm a big boy," he says. "Lay it on me."

She's concentrating her energies on the two singers synchronized
dance moves, which include a hand clap, head shake and dropped
shoulder, all to the beat. "Your generation tires me. Instead of striving for
real change—and you've got the energy and know-how to do it—you
cling to the past. Your cocaine days and MTV. Your Berlin wall. Talk
about sad."

Sherman smiles best he can considering his headache. This is just like
Millennials or whatever this generation is called. They have all the answers.
Well, try leading for once. Try negotiating with Chinese interlocuters in
bespoke suits or pro athletes with egos the size of Lake Superior. He
drains what's left of his morning chaser. Then his phone rings. "Need to
take this," he says, walking for the back porch. "Van Doorman?" The
young woman follows with her lens pointed at him. "Can you hold a
second?"

"We lost Lin, sir."

Sherman stops in his tracks. "What do you mean?"

"He's left the island."

He sweeps a gaze behind him. "This is private," he says to the girl.
"Thank you." He starts for the house again. "Now, what did you say,
VD?"

"One of our scouts saw a well-dressed Asian man board the express ferry to Ashland."

"He's bailing?"

"Want me to follow in the Chris-Craft, sir?"

He presses the phone into his skull and tries to think. "Sit tight. Let me mull this over." Lin is gone? That makes perfect sense. They treated him like an errant schoolboy. What next? Solberg in the trees taking the team out one by one like a sniper? Again, Sherman feels the camera's intruding gaze. "Don't you have anything better to do?"

"This is my job, Mr. Garrity."

"As your boss I'm telling you to shoo off," he says. "Seriously."

"The contract stipulates shooting all weekend long. I'm sure you read the fine print. We've the freedom to move in and about the events surrounding that time frame as long as we don't infringe on anyone's privacy."

He's getting tired of the pushback. "Like I said, this is private."

She smiles. She has Ethereal's small teeth. "I guess someone didn't read the fine print."

His head pounds harder. His thoughts are of flight—as in running the opposite direction. But then he remembers the conversation with his assistant. Soon he's trotting through the woods to Lin's yurt and hoping the girl loses interest. Only she's moving with him like they're filming a scene in an action movie.

He knocks on Lin's door then tries the knob. He can't believe it. After all the work he's done, the Chinese are lost to them? Unless… unless Lin and Blanco cut some backdoor deal while he soaked his head this morning with vodka and tomato juice. No, that doesn't make sense. It's his script. He alone has control. Then why does he feel played?

*Hitting balls soon*, he types frantically into his phone. *You in, Jonathan?*

The woman is walking stride for stride with him when they see Gil in the backyard with a couple scripts under his arm. "You seen Lin?"

His director stares at the woman. "Who's this?"

"This was your idea," Sherman says.

"Ah, documenting the process."

"Have you fucking seen him?"

"You okay, Sherman? You seem stressed."

He feels his nostrils flare. "I'm fine."

"I want to read through a few scenes between our actors. Can you wake up our pretty boy?"

He takes a shortcut through the kitchen with the camera girl hot on his trail. That Springsteen song about a freight train running through the narrator's head plays on the house speaker system. The chef makes an omelet in a copper pan. When she realizes she's being filmed she does a couple theatrical egg flips then throws a match in an oiled pan that throws up a violent eruption of blue. The camerawoman gets the footage though it's hard to read if she's impressed or not.

Skittish, Sherman grabs a mug from the cupboard. Then he gets his phone out again. *How did it go with our movie star last night, Jonathan?!!* 😳 He sends the text then reaches for the French Press. In walks Kimberly wearing a cycling jersey so pink it hurts his eyes. Her cleated shoes go clackity-clack on the stone floor.

"Any news on your husband?"

Kimberly had been up early speaking on the phone with her youngest. She sighs, reaching for a banana on the counter. "Why is she filming?"

"Document the process. Just ask Gil."

Kimberly doesn't think he's funny. "I didn't sign up for this."

He turns to the camerawoman. "See? I told you. No one likes you."

"Heather and I are taking a ride."

"Lin's disappeared," he says. Nothing registers in Kimberly's eyes. "I think the Chinese are pulling out."

"Did I ever tell you how much I hate Springsteen?"

She leaves, eating the banana. The chef follows with her plate of food. The room feels tiny and contained with only Sherman and the camerawoman inside. "Gotta hit the loo, bladder thing," he says. "Don't go anywhere. Promise?"

In the master bath he pries open the window, pops the screen out, then climbs outside. Who's waiting? "How did you know?"

"Lucky guess," she says.

"Well, come on then."

And she and her camera follow.

They reach the yurt a minute later. An odor hangs over the tent that's sweet and malodorous. Sherman eyes the camera mischievously then pinches his thumb and forefinger and brings it to his lips, pretending to inhale. Then he knocks on the door. "Alexander?" They hear rustling bedcovers and covert whispers. "Any day now."

The actor lets himself out wearing the puffy coat and swim trunks. He runs his eyes over the boy from California, the sunburnt pecs and bloodshot eyes, the lost gaze. "How high are you?"

His costar juts out his mouth, all attitude. "I thought this was vacation, Dad."

"Don't smart-ass me. You know what this opportunity means?"

"I'm going with the chi. The flow."

He rolls his eyes. "Gil wants to read lines."

"Hey, are we on film?"

"Ignore her," he says. "Did you see Lin this morning?"

The young man is giving his face a fingertip massage. "I can't feel my face, man."

Sherman is suddenly fed up with his leading actor and grabs his arm. "You're coming with me. And you in there," he yells through the canvas tent. "If your dad were here, we'd both be up shit creek without a paddle."

"Yeah, yeah, yeah," he hears Dawn mumble.

"Did you get all that?" he yells to the camera girl.

He leads his young star down the seldom used deer path with the camera woman not far behind. It's slow going with Alexander stumbling over tree roots and whining about pine needles pricking his feet. They get to the beach, which is bright with the wet stones and sunshine. Maybe twenty-five yards away is a woman building a sandcastle with her two infants, otherwise Grant's Point is empty. Out over the mainland this towering thundercloud sits like a rogue state.

"Get in," he tells his costar.

Alexander gazes at the water with his stoned pupils. "You're joking, bro."

"Dive the fuck in. Right fucking now."

His costar sticks his toes in the water. "It's cold."

"Ok, that's it." Sherman ducks under Alexander's torso and lifts him onto his shoulder.

"Don't you dare! I'm warning you!"

He walks Alexander out ten feet or so then heaves him off sideways into waist-high water. The young man comes out wide-eyed and lets go a whoop then whips his wet hair back. He's a pretty boy with the lightest blue eyes. Physically, a transformation is needed if he's to become the tortured two-hundred-pound athlete with shoulder-length hair. But they have their actor. He'll be a fine Richard Blanco.

Alexander lurches toward Sherman like he's about to return the favor. This goofy smile breaks across his face. He yanks off his down coat and gives it a hurl. "Send Dawn down."

"Look, Puff Daddy."

"Why do you keep calling me that?"

"I was once young myself. But I'm telling you, be careful, amigo."

He watches the actor swim freestyle with his head out of the water. He remembers being the young man's age. "I bet you're quite the ladies man."

The kid lets go a big-hearted smile. "Me? Nah."

Sherman, on the dock now, walks out to meet Alexander, who's swimming toward the ladder. "You know Ethereal Hunt?"

"Should I?"

"She's an actress ... won an Emmy a few years back."

Nothing registers on his face. He reaches the chrome handles, then lifts himself into the crouched backstroke position like at a race's start.

"Anyway," he says. "We're like..."

"Copacetic?" Then the young man throws himself back first into the water.

Sherman glances behind him. The camerawoman is at the dock's edge, pointing the camera their way. "Yeah, well...it's run its course."

Alexander treads water where the drop-off is. "Happens, bro."

"She's unbalanced, pills and shit," he says. "She sometimes scares me."

The young man lifts his arms above his head and stays afloat pumping his legs like scissors. "You think she might hurt herself? Heavy, bro. Very heavy."

"But hey! Enough about me. You're studying the script, right?"

Alexander drops his arms, still treading water. "Like they'll be an exam later?"

"Reading for subtext." It's clear that the kid has no idea what he's talking about. "The why's, Puff Daddy. Why did Blanco choose one path and not another? What drove him? What's said and not said. The subtext is the door inside Blanco's soul."

"Whoa. That's deep."

The producer smiles over his shoulder, but the camera girl is no longer there. She's walking past the mom and her two children with the glide cam hanging by her hip.

"Oh, that's great!" he yells after her. "I finally say something brilliant and you're counting seagulls!"

Sherman sends Steve-O a message on his phone. Then he turns to Alexander. "Spend time with Blanco. Observe him. Listen to his speech pattern, play tennis with him. Embody him. Dawn is going home. If the reading goes well, and I'm in a good mood, maybe she can join us tonight."

"But Sherman?" he whines.

"The conversation is over."

"Anyone ever tell you you're a hard-ass?"

"You're the first, Puff Daddy."

The producer heads back to the house when his phone rings. "Thanks for returning my call, Dennis." Sherman explains the situation to the sheriff, exaggerating where necessary. "Look, my girlfriend is scared. She can't sleep. She's drinking like a fish. This isn't the first time he's come after her."

"You don't know if he's on the island."

"I have my suspicions."

"Even if he is here, I can't escort him off Madeline if he's not breaking the law," the sheriff says. "This ain't Russia."

"When did you become such a Boy Scout?" He disconnects the call, wanting the last word. He's emerging from the trees anyway. Dylan and his toolbox are gone. The band hangs out on the lawn, waiting for lunch. Sitting on the stage amid the amps and electric guitars is Gil and Shinkan. The director opens and closes his mouth like a fish. "Reee----ggaarrd," Gil says.

"Weeee…gallled," the actress repeats.

Gil scoots his chair closer and peers into Shinkan's mouth like a dentist. "Tongue down. Ith soud sun ike dis. Ra ra ra…raaaaa."

"Making progress?" Sherman's smile feels pressed on.

"Let's break until Alexander's ready. And Shinkan? You got this."

He and the beauty high-five. She slips Sherman a circumspect look before pulling out her vape. Then she hops off the stage and walks toward the house. He almost asks if she knows where Jonathan Lin is but thinks the exercise will be too exhausting.

Gil has taken out his phone and thumb-scrolls. He wears a TV On The Radio T-shirt and dungarees rolled up past his bare ankles. "How did your hit-around go this morning?"

The director grins without taking his eyes off the screen. "I'm not getting in the middle of your prick fight with Blanco."

"Just remember who brought you in."

"Look, I'll shoot the best picture I can, on time, within budget."

"Do I have your support?"

They hear the screen door bang shut. Out walks Dawn in petite shorts and a midriff shirt that shows off her naval. She's eating an apple. In her other hand is the script.

"On the Serb being Chinese?" Gil frowns. "We've got bigger problems, like our movie star's English skills."

Alexander appears at the path's entrance. He squeezes water from his jacket like it's a towel. "Gentlemen," he says. They watch him walk in the opposite direction of Dawn, who's heading for an Adirondack chair near the stage, not even a glance.

"What happened to him?"

"I put the hammer down." Sherman steps onto the stage. "And that goes for you, too, missy" he yells at Steve-O's daughter, who looks up all innocent and bursting with youth. Then she takes a huge bite out of the apple.

A gust of wind nearly sends his ballcap flying. Everything feels out of control. Progress on financing is incremental at best. He isn't exactly keeping the young lovers apart. And his actress can't pronounce her R's. *But hey—the team is trying!* It doesn't take much imagination to see where this plane crash of a film is heading. His mom, if faced with a similar predicament, would insist on positivity, on channeling good. So when he sees Blanco jogging down the lawn in nothing but running shorts he thinks sunny forecast, not rain, bright eyes, not sad smiles. Even when he sees the former professional's muscular physique, Sherman doesn't compare himself. Instead, he cuts himself some much needed slack.

"Our friend here is reading the script."

Blanco hops onto the stage and runs in place. "Well?" he says, eying Dawn. "What do you think?"

Sitting in the Adirondack she is all legs and confidence. "He's kind of a prick. And the women are so cliché. Blonde stripper with a heart of gold? Asian sexpot into S&M?"

"Maybe we found our new writer," Gil jokes.

"If Blanco is so smart," she continues. "Wouldn't Heather bore him after a while?"

The men look at each other, smiling. "Shit, Dawn," Sherman says. "Maybe you should move to LA and read scripts for a living."

This enormous smile shoots across her face. "Really?"

The ex-pro drops down next to a stack of amps and bangs out military pushups. "What's the latest?"

"On Kimberly's husband?"

Gil looks up from his phone. Even Dawn glances over. Does Sherman let everyone in on their little secret? Fuck it, why not. Nothing else is going right this weekend. "We think he's on the island."

"The dude's an ex-hockey player," Blanco says pushing out his set. "Some sort of menace on the ice."

"Like some bad-ass looking for retribution?"

"We don't know what he wants, Gil."

"What's Kimberly think?"

Sherman feels a presence over his shoulder. He spins around to see the camerawoman. "Were you filming us?" Her face turns red. "That's convincing."

Blanco leaps to his feet then shakes out his arms. "Who's this?"

"I'm Tabitha."

"Tabitha is documenting the process."

"Okay," Blanco says slowly.

Another surging wind presses down the big pines. Which lends to his growing consternation. His phone rings. "Yes, VD."

"We spotted the truck on the incoming ferry, sir."

Sherman feels his pulse quicken. "Did you get a photo?"

"I'm not there."

"We need his face, Van Doorman." He glances at Blanco. "I think we got him."

Van Doorman gets back on the line. "She's transmitting, sir."

A moment later the text comes through. Attached is a blurry photograph of a jowly middle-aged guy with a ten-day old beard. Everyone, including Dawn and Tabitha, stand around Sherman and his phone.

"Is it him?"

"… maybe…"

"What's wrong with his face?"

"Is that a shadow?"

"We need a better quality pic," Sherman says into the phone.

"I'm enroute, sir."

"Don't lose him, VD."

The producer hangs up to find Tabitha circling the group with her glide cam. "Is something going down, Mr. Garrity?"

"No," he says. "Nothing's *going down*."

"I'm still unclear what we're supposed to do if we find him?" Blanco says.

"How should I know?" Sherman says. "By the way, have you seen Lin? We can't find him either."

"You're having one helluva weekend," Dawn says, tossing her apple core in the woods.

Again, they're interrupted by a phone call. "Bad news, sir."

"Don't tell me you fucking lost him."

"Already?" The irritation in Blanco's voice has Sherman feeling an association with the star athlete that borders on affection. "How?"

"How, VD?"

"She was on her bike."

"She was on her bike," he relays to the others. "Wait. Bike? How old is this scout of yours?"

"Eleven, sir."

"You mean we have a major-league psycho on our hands and you put an eleven-year-old Ranger Rick on the case?" He hangs up. "Un-fucking-believable."

"Just to be clear," Dawn says. "We have a *possible* major league psycho on our hands."

Blanco's expression is strange. He's staring in the direction of the drive when he looks at Sherman. "How many roads are on the island?"

"Four," he says. "You don't think—"

They start sprinting for the driveway, the ex-pro in jogging shoes, Sherman in his expensive flipflops, and Tabitha filming at the same time. "Where are you two going!" they hear Gil yell.

"Keys, Garrity?"

He's aware of the tight air and the atmospheric pressure, the powerful wind clipping his heels. "In the Jeep."

"Can I join you?" Tabitha says, keeping up best she can.

"Fat chance," Blanco says, "And I'm driving."

"Like hell you are."

They come around the house to find the Jeep parked in the shade of the trees. A sous chef is taking a smoking break on the front porch and Alexander's wet puffy hangs from a branch next to his yurt.

The men have pulled away from Tabitha. "But guys!" she yells, giving up.

Blanco beats Sherman to the truck. "I've seen your driving skills and I wasn't impressed."

"I'm fucking Mario Andretti, dude."

"And that's my wife out there."

Blanco hops in, turns the key over then shifts the truck into drive. Then they're hauling ass up the narrow bumpy driveway with grass growing in the middle, not slowing for the birch trees/sentry posts. "Watch those—!" The passenger side mirror clips a branch, snapping a twig off. Then they're through and coming on the exit fast. Keegan's up and getting the hell out of the way and then the Jeep skids onto the gravel road and roars toward town.

It takes a couple minutes to speed down the hill and past the golf course. Blanco slows for the channel bridge. "What kind of truck?"

"I don't know... a pickup."

"The color, Garrity. What fucking color?"

"White. I think it's white." They take the sharp turn across from the Inn at three times the legal limit. Through a slot between the buildings is the lake—cobalt blue this afternoon with white caps racing across its surface. Storms freak Sherman out. Winds whipping the water into a froth, land, sea and horizon the same dull gray.

"The speed limit's twenty," he says, not that Blanco slows down. "Take a right. And try not to kill any children, okay?"

Like it sounds, Middle Road is two-laned asphalt that cuts through the island's belly. Sherman isn't sure what direction the girls rode. He and Kimberly had done a few rides, but each time was different. Would she want a headwind halfway into the ride? Or get it out of the way at the start? Are they circumnavigating the island? Or mixing the route up for a longer trip?

"What if we see him?"

"We follow at a safe distance."

"What if he recognizes us?"

Blanco takes his eyes off the road long enough to look Sherman over. "You haven't told her, have you?"

"I couldn't find the right moment."

"Fucking man up."

"I fucked up, okay? But this could be bad. What if he's already found them? What if—"

"Would you calm the fuck down?"

The day is beginning to feel like an inventory of small deaths. Nothing too catastrophic to stop Sherman cold, but each hurdle like paper cut after paper cut. They drive the length of Middle Road. "Follow the lake," he says. "We'll take North Shore Road back into town."

"Call her."

Sherman turns on his phone. "No fucking bars, man."

Blanco grabs his phone off the armrest. "Try Heather. The code's 1-1-1-1."

"You're kidding right? You know that's the first password someone would try if they stole your phone."

"We're having this conversation now? Just dial the fucking number."

In unlocking the phone, Sherman uses big, exaggerated finger movements to go along with his big, exaggerated voice. "One. One. One. One." Then he sighs. "No signal. Where are we? The middle of fucking nowhere?"

They reach the gravel portion of North Shore Road. Up ahead a dirt cloud appears. Blanco sits straighter in his seat and Sherman feels his insides constrict. But it's not the truck and the woman's expression driving past doesn't speak to trauma or dead bodies lying by the roadside. The rest of the way into town is rolling hills, brittle sunshine and dust devils. In La Pointe, they get a glimpse of the western sky. The clouds are striated and stacked like a great pagoda in the sky.

"Which way?" Blanco says at the town center.

"Turn left."

"We already went down that road."

"Just fucking do it, okay?"

They speed out of town again. Sherman is thinking worst case scenario: Solberg making mincemeat out of the women with his truck, him forcing them into the woods for execution by firing squad. Then they see them. They ride two abreast just shy of South Shore Road. Sherman nearly cries. As they near the women Blanco pulls the truck into the opposing lane and slows.

Sherman sticks his head out the window. "Howdy, ladies."

Kimberly, riding on the outside, glances at him in her helmet and racing sunglasses. "Everything okay?"

"Just checking your times. This is a Strava segment, right?"

Heather gets a worried look on her face. "What's wrong, Richard?"

Blanco leans over the armrest and yells through the window. "Everything's fine, honey." Under his breath he says to Sherman, "Tell her, you pussy."

The producer has on a big fake smile. "We'll follow you back to the house. Think of us like your team car."

Blanco sighs then pulls the Jeep back into the right-hand lane. "I know kittens with more courage."

"I'm going to tell her."

"Sure thing, Sherm."

It's nearly five when the four ride up the rode the Hideaway is located on. Keegan, sitting on the car bumper, waves them through. Sherman lets go a weary breath. The shindig starts in two hours and he feels beat up. His phone pings.

*Spotted him, sir.*

*Ken Dog?*

*Lin. He's on his way to the beach. And he's wearing a Speedo.*

*Lovely.*

*That's one way of putting it, sir.*

Not long after, Sherman crosses the footpath. A warm wind hits him in the face. The swells he sees battering the shore are at least four feet high. In the time it takes to reach the shore, Lin is toweling off. Lying on a beach chair is a black leather man purse.

"We missed you today."

Lin puts the towel around his neck. His suit is the midnight-blue color of his hair. There's also a noticeable change in his demeanor, call it a chill.

"Shinkan digs you, man," Sherman adds. "She raved about you all afternoon."

The moment he brings up the actress's name the coldness falls away. Jonathan Lin even giggles. But then he gets serious again. "There's been a new development."

Sherman thinks about those pool parties in Bel Air. He didn't trust the men wearing Speedos. His younger self couldn't comprehend why. He only knew it involved his mom. He only knew it was wrong.

Lin walks over to the chair where he's left the satchel. It's buttery leather with a thick gold zipper. "We have what you film people call a product placement." He unzips the case and takes out a smartphone that's tall and thin.

"A smartphone? That's hilarious."

"Chinko smartphone. This is a prototype. The official launch is 2021."

Sherman can't believe what he's hearing. "It's a period film, Jonathan. It must look and feel like the era it takes place in. Smartphones weren't a thing in 1996." He stops himself. For he sees in Lin's mouth that this isn't negotiable. "That won't fly. You know that."

Lin slips the phone into the satchel, zips the case shut, then starts for the house.

He fucking knew it. Films today aren't about exceptional storytelling. They aren't about grappling with the human condition. There's no space in modern filmmaking for films simply being films and nothing more. Commerce rules the day. Superheroes and horror flicks and Disney cartoons guaranteed to make kids laugh and parents cry. It's what Lin said on the golf course—*the fucking bottom line.*

"This is bullshit. You my friend are bullshit!" he screams at Lin's backside, his strong shoulders and hip bones, his inky hair. "Tell Mr.

Dollars & Sense to fuck off. And if you think I'm tough, wait until Blanco hears about this!"

Lin is halfway across the marsh. And Sherman falls to his knees in the sand. He has tears in his eyes. This is fuck-all bad.

# SPIRITS IN THE NIGHT

His mind is all over the place. One minute he's immersed in life around an inland lake—the turtle warming its shell on a rock, the tiny bugs that sit on the water's surface as if resigned to the fate of fish food—the next he's thinking about the past. A few years back the team was in St. Cloud playing an invitational. The bus passed a sign on the outskirts of town. *Tarot cards, palm reader, seer.* Ken drove back later that month. She was a large woman with big crazy eyes. There was a dreamcatcher and a painting on the wall of an Indian Chief in full regalia sitting on a spotted horse. She lay his hand on a small round table with an embroidered cloth then spread his palm flat and touched the lines there. The woman said he was mad with desire. "The so-called good life," she called it. "Wine, women and song." She spoke about spiritual oneness. She said he sought to possess the mother in women, that his masculinity was caught up in the mother figure. "Your phallic tendencies will be your unraveling," she warned him. "In your current state the center will not hold."

Wine, women and song.

A space is opening inside him that is fine and clean and deeply knotted. Like a door that leads to a room without walls. Out in nature, sounds and color take on a tall vibrant order. He no longer is Ken Solberg, husband, father, coach. He's beginning to think he's more than the sum of his parts. But how can that be? *How am I more than the flesh and bone walking this path?* And like a flick of a switch, he's back inside his head, with his old thoughts and complaints.

Wine, women and song.

Random thoughts come to him. *Who am I? Why is the lake blue, but when cupped in my hands it's clear enough to drink? Why did her steady blue eyes calm those parts of me that wanted to lash out?* He feels like shouting, maybe he does, maybe he doesn't. Instead, he finds himself sitting on an old stump on a trail. He stares at his hands, his fleshy, veined hands. Hands that cut open men's faces. Hands that hurt people. But also, hands that once searched her face as if they were thirsty or blind. He's up now in the classic fighter pose. He ducks and bobs, rolls his shoulders, swings a few jabs. Man, he loved fighting. The tension in the air was palpable. Him and his nemesis circling, gloves off, the adrenaline pumping through his vortex. The enforcer was hockey's ultimate deterrent. The guy who kept the game from turning into bedlam. You put a hit on a great player, someone like Wayne Gretzky, and you'd pay for it. Maybe not next shift, maybe not even next game. But you'd pay.

People heard enforcer and thought monster or goon, the worst possible scum on earth. They thought sucker punches, blindside hits, sticks to the face and the back of the neck. But an enforcer was so much more. To his club, he was revered. And his loyalty to the team bordered on religious. But playing that role took hard work. The last thing Ken wanted was to let his team down. Every night was the same. Who was he fighting? What special gifts did they bring to the ice? Did they have a long reach? Were they bigger than him? More insane? And how would he react?

Maybe he'd grab the guy's shoulder pads, get him in close, then pummel the shit out of his face. Or maybe he'd mix it up—pull the guy in (and punch his face) then push him away, then pull him in (and punch his face)—until he was staring at a bruised tomato. Sometimes he let the other guy get the first punch in to get his juices going. It wasn't anarchy. Enforcers honored a code. Don't kick a downed man. Don't punch his head through the ice. Skate away once it's over.

The first few punches were key. And getting hit square in the face was never a good thing. The hardest part? Waiting. Sitting on the bench, knowing your turn was coming. There was only the fight. Pure survival mode. Kill or be killed.

\*\*\*

Florida. The trip they took to repair what was lost. For the sake of the marriage. Florida. The hotel in that placid old town with the mahogany staircase and ceiling fans, the desk clerk in a bowtie. They bought outfits, hers a summer dress of muted yellow, his seersucker and pliable. He felt outside himself in the heat and palmettos. In the hospitableness of southerners. Like a character in a play. But something happened in Florida. They got to talking again. They got back to seeing themselves as they once were.

And it bore true, a few years anyway. He was content, and content was a fine thing to be. But he was drifting again. His fixation with the past was like a disease. Why couldn't he fully commit to his wife, heart, body and soul? A river was not a straight line. It bent and moved agreeably with the land. Why couldn't Ken be more like a river?

He's so deep inside himself he's lost his way. He'd been following the trail along the sparkling lake. But now he's somewhere else. Above him are old growth Hemlocks rising five stories off the forest floor. These are trees made in America. Trees laid bare. Trees deeply furrowed and towering. The forest interior suddenly feels big and noteworthy. Like he's walking with God's disciples. Ken hasn't gone ten paces when he thinks change is afoot. The next moment he's consumed by the dead sheriff. He should be at the bottom of that ditch. He's no good and he knows it. Some nights he can't sleep. Or he jolts awake with his heart beating faster than a runaway train. He sees the squad car flipped on its side and him standing over the man with the dead eyes. Then he sees the photograph plain as day. Taped like it was on the dash. The look in the boy's eyes. Like he'd never known sorrow. Like his life up until then was melting popsicles and playing catch with his father.

He walks on.

But the trail has lost its shape. Gone are the Eastern Hemlock. In its place are scraggly black spruce and choked scrub, the murky dark. And now every way he turns is a dead-end of toppled trees and bushy quagmire. Ken knows things. If disorientated, follow a river downstream for it usually leads to civilization. Climb a tree for perspective, start a fire. No, wait. Prepare a fire with dry, combustible debris for a search-party plane. Retrace one's steps. Failing that, stay put and wait for help. He thinks about his current position and backward he goes. But it isn't easy. It's like hacking through thorny bush. He goes at it the only way he knows how, head down, mouth set, without complaint. Twice he opens his cheek on a sharp bramble and twice he shakes a fist at the sky.

Then a clearing.

It couldn't have come at a better time. Because Ken is exhausted. He needs to get his bearings back. Then he sees it—a flat spot he sprinkles with dry leaves. There he lies down, fetal position, and sucks his thumb. Soon he's at the old rink lit up at night like a Christmas tree. Him and Andrew, always him and his older brother, with their North Stars jerseys and sticks cut down to size, carving the corners, feeling the momentum in the turns, like they're going somewhere.

The world shifts.

He's in the station wagon he and Andrew share. It's night and he's driving down a desolate country road in winter. He wears the down puffy coat passed down from his older brother. Coming on old man Gleeson's cabin he sees Platt's Camaro hidden behind the big linden. So Andrew and Platt beat them to it, probably with a couple girls. Breaking into cabins is a rite of passage, what high schoolers do for kicks during the long slog of winter. And Gleeson's is perfect, newly built and hidden from the road. Pulling up to the cabin Ken feels a strange sensation. Like he's been here before. Then Melody's throwing her arms around his neck. "Be right back," she says. They are really doing it! The first time! And a diaphragm is better than a condom. Andrew says so, Andrew says you can really feel it, and if it doesn't work, if his girl gets pregnant, well, that's what his parents did, got hitched, and look how that turned out—Andrew Solberg, greatest hockey player. EVER.

"Anyone home?" he shouts.

Gleeson's cabin smells like fresh milled lumber and new paint. Warm air blasts from the furnace. And he gets that weird feeling again. Like something isn't right. He's also feeling strange, sluggish, and his head kills. Better not be coming down with the flu. Not tonight! If she asks if something's wrong, he'll pretend he's his older brother and smile like there's nothing he can't do.

Now he stands in a dark hall. A feeling like dread floods his frame. As if something lurks down there—something Ken must confront. Now he's inside the bedroom and there's the town hero, his older brother, hockey star Andrew Solberg, him and his on again/off again girlfriend, Ellen Enzler. His brother lies on the bed, asleep in his clothes except for one hilarious detail. He has one sock on and one sock off. Old Enz is slumped face first against the headboard.

"Enz can't be comfortable, huh?" He nudges his brother's shoulder. "Hey, wake up." He takes a closer look at his face. It's weird, like glazed wax. "Andrew? Is that really you?"

Man, he's tired. He slides his back down the face of the mattress and slumps on the floor. Closing his eyes feels so good. He sees them again at the old rink. God, he misses those nights. Just him and his brother putting in the hours. There's something pure and magical about those lost days. There's also a voice in his head saying, *get out, you can't stay much longer.* Then someone is trying to break through the soft putty called his brain. It's his girl and she's hysterical and punching the shit out of his arm, trying to pull him to his feet.

He dozes off again. But Melody has no quit. She's a force to reckon with. She wakes him again, screaming it's dangerous, that they must leave at once. And she gets through Ken's thick crusty skull because soon they're stumbling outdoors and sucking in the cold arctic air. He takes off running through the snow. His quads burn like those nights at the rink when they were building toward greatness. The mighty Solberg boys, destined for glory. Or Andrew was. But now he's dead and never coming back. Ken doesn't see the barbwire hidden in a snowdrift and snags his coat on a top nail. The fabric tears like paper. His mom will be so mad. But she's headstrong. She'll weather this. But Dad loves Andrew so much. If someone deserves to die, it's Ken. He's the blemish, the evil in the world. Then he's in his truck and racing down a highway with the sheriff closing in. Then he sees the Sheriff's sleeping face.

Why did he have to die? Why, God? Why?

# FUCK ALL BAD

She's in the shower. And thank God—because Sherman is a mess. A freaking smartphone? He stands in the master suite, his breathing erratic, then dumps the entirety of Kimberly's purse on the bed. Only he finds nothing deadlier than Benadryl. So he does the next best thing and tromps across the front yard and knocks on Alexander's yurt. His lead actor comes onto the landing brushing his teeth.

"Got any more weed?"

Alexander runs the bristles over his molars. "I'm clean, man. The lake baptism worked."

"For me, Puff Daddy."

The kid smiles through his toothbrush. "Talk to Dawn."

"Okay, let's talk to Dawn."

"She's not here, man. But she'll hook you up."

"Get on it, PD. Pronto."

He starts for the road. He needs space and distance between him and this last-minute move by Mr. Dollars & Sense. The most heartbreaking part is knowing the Chinese are only interested in the tennis pic as a vehicle to market a product that is sure to make people even less happy than they already are. What happened to us? When did cynicism become our default mode?

The road is empty but for the maroon hatchback parked in the weeds. Gusts blow up swirls of dust and the trees buck against the wind. Sherman digs his hands in his short's pockets wanting to review the Doppler. Then he sighs, realizing he forgot it. He came halfway across the country for her, for what she represents, the places she might take him, if Sherman trusted her, if he trusted himself. Only the trip's been a disaster. He's overseeing a party that he doesn't want to host for a film that now seems unlikely to see the light of day. And now the front moving in will make the concert a washout?

Something else is amiss. He crosses the gravel road. His security guard lies in the shade of a tree. "Asleep?"

The young man's up fast. "No, Boss. I was resting my eyelids. It helps with nocturnal vision."

"I don't pay you to sleep, Keegan. Even if it helps nocturnally."

Sherman sizes up his security guard. The Brewers cap that looks like it went through a washing machine. The exposed belly bulge underneath a size too small T-shirt. The duct-taped Teva's. "You need to take this gig seriously."

"You can count on me, Boss."

"You don't need to be a hero. But if a man shows and he's got a gun, you let him pass through. Then you get on the horn with Van Doorman. And you follow the son-of-a-bitch. You understand?" Sherman starts back across the road. "And stay the fuck awake."

In no time he's back in the master suite. He pokes his head in the bath. Kimberly is all limbs and slick skin behind the blurred glass. "Be out in a minute," she says. "Shaving my legs."

Sherman paces back and forth. There's only one person with the know-how and reversals of fortune who'll understand. He sits on the floor in that tiny space between the bedframe and wall then places the call.

"What?"

"Don't hang up. Please." His voice is thin and high. "I need help, Ethereal. You're the only person I can trust."

"You've got some nerve calling."

He hears the shower turn off. "I'm going to lose the film. And I need this. I really do."

"What's in it for me?"

He wipes a tear away. "Are you serious?"

"I'm fucking with you."

"You're killing me."

"All that's holding the picture back is the buddy/buddy thing?" she says. "Even if you cede control, it's not the end of the world."

"Shower's open," Kimberly calls out.

"There's one more thing." He tells her about the stupid-shaped phone with the stupid name and how the stupid idea will ruin everything the stupid picture stands for.

"Ha! Those sneaky bastards!"

"I'm fucked," he cries. "The film is fucked."

"You're overreacting. A good writer will figure something out. This is Hollywood, remember?"

He runs a hand under his leaky nose. "I wish I had your optimism."

"How's Minnesota Nice? You know what that means, right? On the surface everything is peachy-creamy. But underneath all that politeness is a passive-aggressive bitch."

"Things are… well, they're okay."

"… Oh?"

The door opens followed by a wall of steam. Then Kimberly emerges wearing a bathrobe. "Thanks, man," he says, pushing himself up. "Let's talk later, dude." Then he hangs up.

She brushes out her wet hair in the full length mirror. "Who was that?"

There's a book on trees sitting on the nightstand. Sherman sits on the bed's edge and thumbs through it. "The sheriff wanted to talk security."

"Security?"

"Standard protocol, you know, for a party this big."

"Are you expecting problems?"

"Problems? No, no problems at all." He tosses the book on the bed then moves for the bathroom. "Wow, it's late. Better take that shower."

He feels better afterwards, though his hands shake while shaving. He's seeing the situation like a conundrum he's slowly figuring out. Ceding control. Having faith in a new writer. He can do that, right? When he reenters the bedroom Kimberly wears a dress he doesn't recognize. It's infinitely tight and made of a flesh-colored shiny latex material. If that's not bad enough, the dress has a grapefruit-sized hole centered over the breast area.

"What do you think?" she says. "Heather let me borrow it. It's from the 90s."

He smiles through a bit lip. "Very festive."

"What's wrong. You seem distracted."

Is this his chance to fess up? Confessing is the last thing he wants to do, but he can't hide anymore. His eyes find hers in the antique mirror hanging on the wall.

"I fucked up, big time."

"That doesn't sound like you. Tell me what's going on."

"Remember how you said keep my cool around Blanco? Well, in defending myself, I challenged him to a tennis match."

Her hand is deep inside the dress's cleavage hole, positioning right and left breast. "There's no disgrace in losing to a guy who was once #20 in the world. Do you have any tape?"

"Tape?"

"To secure everything in place."

"Oh, I see," he says, glancing at her cleavage hole. "Um, I don't know. Maybe. What were we talking about?"

"Playing Blanco."

He walks over to the dresser and opens the top drawer. Inside is the $500 vintage Bob Marley concert T he had overnighted from an eBay vendor. "There's this tiny part that involves you."

She's now shimmying the taut fabric over her hips with pinched fingers. "Me?"

"If I lose I'm to fly you to LA," he says, slipping the shirt over his head. "I'm to introduce you to Ethereal as the woman I'm sleeping with behind her back."

She stops snaking the dress over her curves. "But you broke up with her. That's what you said." A terribly long two seconds goes by. "You mean you lied to me?"

"I wouldn't call it a lie, per se."

"Oh, I get it," she says, prickling with anger. "You can't beat Blanco, at anything. And now you're playing both sides? How fucking cowardly of you."

He keeps busy by tossing his jeans on the bed then spraying cologne on his neck. "I didn't tell her because it slipped my mind. I've been swamped with this film. You know that. The pressure is enormous."

She walks up to him and gets in real close. "What do you get if you win?"

"Huh?"

"The match, Sherman."

He takes a step backward. His eyes keep finding her cleavage. "Oh that. I can't say."

"You can't say because you don't know? Or you can't say because you don't want to?"

"It's bifurcated."

"It's what?"

Sherman grabs the jeans off the bed. "The bet has two components. The first has to do with control of the film."

"And the second?"

He has one foot in the jeans, the other leg hops around the room. "Let me preface this by saying...that this wasn't... my...idea."

"Would you stand still?"

He finally gets the second leg in. "Heather has a yoga studio. There's this room, this private office or something," he says. "With a two-way mirror that looks into the women's shower."

It only takes a moment for Kimberly to catch on. "You mean he?" Her mouth draws in like she's sucking on a lemon. "He watches women? In the shower? Does Heather know about this?"

"Of course not."

"And your prize was jerking yourself off to that shit?"

Sherman dabs his forehead with the T. "The film, Kimberly. My prize was the film."

"You said that already."

"This is what I mean. I don't know what I'm saying anymore."

"Get out," she says. "I don't want to see you right now."

It's only after he'd closes the bedroom door that he remembers he's forgotten to tell her about Solberg. But it's too late for that now.

***

Marley is good live. They make "Waiting in Vain" sound as if old Bob himself has risen from the dead for one final blowout performance. Smoking helps. To be clear, Sherman isn't a pot smoker. Weed feels like a crutch that alcohol isn't. He knows this argument is full of more holes than the line in "A Day In The Life" about Blackburn, Lancashire. He's pretty sure there's conclusive evidence that drinking has a greater negative impact on internal organs than smoking a bowl a few times a week. What he doesn't like about weed is losing control. One second you're nodding along to the dub beat and the next the world is crashing off its axis. Though the stuff Dawn cooked up is fuzzy mellow. Like a tactile coating over everything Sherman sees, feels and tastes. He's relaxed like he hasn't been in years. And his problems have melted away. Yeah, reality isn't so bad when you're high.

For example. He doesn't give a rat's ass that the camera lady is pointing *her thing* his way. She can document his process all she wants. He's high and the reggae beats are seeping into his bones. He feels light enough to float into space. Or stick his entire head down that hole in Kimberly's dress. And right now she's talking to the man in the yellow anorak. He's younger than Sherman and fit like a yachtsman who does biathlons in his spare time. They haven't talked since the argument. He hasn't spoken to Jonathan Lin, either, who waltzed onto the back lawn to the opening sequence from "Natural Mystic" as if it were the scene in a movie that introduced the cool ass motherfucker who blows the bad guys away. His getup—motorcycle jacket, selvage jeans, and black boots he failed to tie the laces of—stands out the way the entire team stands out on Madeline Island. He sees that now. Spaced out on weed, so many things are clearer.

The one silver lining is the weather. The front that was stalled off the coast drifted south. Only the high winds remain. His gaze goes back to where it's been nearly all night. On Jonathan Lin and the movie star. Practically every guest has wandered past the beautiful couple for a gander or photo op. They're getting fucked up. Which he doesn't understand. He's not the only worried party. Sensei Yamaguchi showed up forty-five minutes into their shot-fest. Words were exchanged. Then the actress shooed her personal assistant off like the hired help she is. Right then the stage lights up like a star. Bliss floods every blood vessel in his brain. Cerebrally speaking, Sherman is barely hanging on. The stage is too bright, the guitars too shrill. Tabitha is coming around his flank, filming his weaker profile. A weed-induced panic comes over him. Sweat breaks across his forehead. He needs to do something. Like get a beer. Yeah, he should top off his IPA. But then the stage shines like a bright white angel. And he's transfixed again.

Other things are happening, not bad things in itself... just things. Ethereal's flooding his phone with messages. Her holding a Labrador puppy in her arms. *His name is Stan. Isn't he adorable? And don't worry. I'll give him away before you get home.* Her wearing a tight sweater with her nipples pushing through the fabric. *I forgive you, you schmuck. Let's plan a strategy with the film. We're from the same mold, Shermy.* All the while, Marley plows through "Buffalo Soldier," "Redemption Song," and "Satisfy My Soul."

Sherman's eyes find Kimberly again. She and Anorak Guy are dancing like a couple dorks at a Billy Joel concert. He should apologize. He should come clean. Maybe she could reach her husband before it's too late. There's only so much ground Van Doorman and Keegan can cover. The Hideaway is vulnerable to attack by land, sea or air. Well, Ken Dog swooping down in a jetpack ala *Thunderball* is highly unlikely. But how easy would it be to enter the property through the woods? Or run a boat onshore? Meantime a fat spliff is making its way around the stage. The talented guitarist with the rasta chunks is puffing on the smoke without taking his hands off the frets. Sherman's eyes land on his supplier, who's upfront and perched on Alexander's shoulders, toking on the whacky weed herself. Out on the lawn her oblivious parents dance with the twins. His phone tremors in his pocket. He picks up on the first ring. "Yo, Daddy-O. What's shaking?"

"What's that noise?"

"Life, Dad. That noise is life."

"You don't sound like yourself, Sherman."

He takes several steps away from the stage. "What can I help you with?"

"Just felt like calling."

"You and Henrique aren't in trouble, are you?"

"I feel like what happened between your mother and me, our marriage difficulties, I shouldn't have burdened you with that."

Sheriff Dennis is approaching in a flannel, Wranglers and scuffed boots. "Dad? Can we continue this conversation tomorrow?"

"Sure, son."

"And Dad? It's not a burden. I love that you called to chat."

Sherman hangs up and offers the sheriff a handshake. They turn their attention on the stage, now the joint is being passed among band members. "Wholesome group, that band."

"This isn't good for my reputation," Sheriff Dennis says.

From his back pocket he produces his own tightly rolled marijuana cigarette. "Then I shouldn't show you this."

"Who's your contact? Steve's girl?"

He drops a shocked gaze the sheriff's way. "How can you even insinuate that?"

"She's sliding down a slippery slope and you know it."

Marley is between songs. Roadies switch out guitars. The musicians towel off or sip cocktails. Over at the bar, Lin and Shinkan take selfies. Sherman thinks of the scene early in the script where Shinkan's character strides into the men's locker room at Wimbledon because that's the kind of bold shit her character does. In the scene Blanco's agent unveils the world's first generation of cellular phones. Now, the audience will never be in on the joke. They'll never comprehend what Sherman in his stoned state sees so clearly—as a species we're doomed.

"Whatever happened to the husband?" the sheriff says.

"Mystery Theatre, Denny."

"The wife and I are skedaddling. Shut her down by midnight. And encourage designated drivers. I don't want my men pulling over drunk, stupid-high people."

And the sheriff leaves.

He watches Kimberly and the guy again. He hates his thoughts just then. The way he sees her like his property. She broke from a man whom he feels superior to—culturally, socio-economically, even spiritually. But is he any different than Ken Solberg? He's wrestling with the idea of being a better version of himself when a young couple moves past, toking on a weed cigarette. Feeling lonely, Sherman leans in with a gigantic smile on his face.

"Can I get a hit off that?"

The young woman has large inviting eyes and wears a dress that's long and flowy yet offers up the make of her body. Their hands touch when she offers him the smoke, something he finds mildly erotic.

"Enjoying the party?" he says, inhaling like a pro.

"The band is right on." Her guy's get up fits the island vibe—baggy hemp pants tucked into cavalier boots, a ruffled long-sleeve shirt opened at the collar, this velvet hat with a feather sticking out of it.

"You an actor?" he says, passing him the joint.

"Hey, honey. This guy thinks I'm a movie star."

"Your outfit."

The young man takes a big hit. "This is how I dress, man."

"Legit?"

"I like you," he says, smiling. "You got panache. Doesn't he, honey?"

The joint gets passed around again. "Your house is amazing," she says.

Sherman catches her gaze in the semi-darkness. He wants so many things in that instant. To be twenty years younger. To not only dress like an extra in *Pirates of the Caribbean* but have the panache to pull it off. To have a less complicated life. He's also beginning to feel the high's surge. It's more powerful than the stuff he'd inhaled earlier. "Woah, shit."

"You okay?" the young woman says.

The rush comes and it comes without mercy. Like a dark cloud of voodoo clamping its fangs into his body and soul. He feels his limbs shut down.

"Yo, dude." The boyfriend grabs Sherman's upper arm. "He don't look good, hon."

Then everything goes black.

# DANCING IN THE DARK

He feels like the Boss with his black outfit and work boots, an imaginary guitar strapped over his shoulder. Like he's playing for tens of thousands. He's drunk on the night. Tomorrow is his last day on the island. The decision came to him this afternoon. He'll break down camp, call his boys, apologize to Cal, then send his wife a text wishing her well. And he'll turn himself in. It's him the dead sheriff was chasing. If he'd pulled the F-150 over, a boy wouldn't have lost a father or a wife her spouse. From this night forward he'll accept responsibility for his actions.

Ken parks on the grassy shoulder outside Garrity's place. He can hear the music as he reaches behind the seat for the Glock. Dimley, sitting shotgun, gives him a disappointing look. "What? It's the last time, okay?" He hops down from the rig and sticks the gun in the back waistband of his jeans. That afternoon he'd had a final bath in Lake Superior's baptismal waters, shaved with water he warmed on his stove, and put on the black dress shirt Kimberly got him the night they saw Springsteen play Madison Square Garden. What is he after? Is it love? Is it the fevered yes between consenting adults? Is Kimberly the woman in the songs? Yeah, he's in a peculiar place. He feels pretty wonderful, like he's found the fire within.

It takes only a couple minutes to thread his way to a spot where he can hangout unnoticed. There he watches the band. The reefer stench gives the music a legitimacy it probably doesn't merit. He isn't keen on forced nostalgia. You see Springsteen to hear him bang out "Born to Run" as if it's the last time he'll play the song live. Springsteen moves him. So does Petty and Prince and Bob Marley. But watching some Bruce Springsteen look-a-like in a workingman's shirt with rolled up sleeves belting out "Thunder Road?" That's not his scene.

"Watcha doing?"

Ken whips around fast, his hand instinctively reaching behind his back. In his daydreaming he hadn't heard the young woman with her film camera entering his hiding place.

"Hey," he says nonchalantly, though his insides are thumping.

She moves to the wood's edge, facing the stage and party vibe.

"You work for Garrity?"

"For the weekend," she says, filming the scene on the lawn. "Documenting the process."

"Do you like these people?"

The young woman gives him a bemused look. Then she eyes the stage again. "It's a job like any other." She swings her camera around and films Ken for a beat or two. "See you around." And she exits the woods and heads toward the music.

## PLEASE, PLEASE, PLEASE LET ME GET WHAT I WANT

He lies on a cot in the medical tent like a prisoner at his own party. Five empty water bottles are strewn on the grass. He's been held captive nearly an hour and frightened with words like rapid heart rate and hypotension. A nurse kneeling next to him checks his pulse for the tenth time.

"Can I go, please?"

The man undoes the blood pressure band around Sherman's arm. "Take it easy the rest of the night."

He exits the tent sheepishly and looks around. The band is taking a short break. People mill around the property like it's a Dead show. No one seems to have seen him pass out, well, other than the young couple. Maybe he dodged a potentially embarrassing predicament. Then his eyes find the power couple of the weekend as they toss back another shot. Anxious, he texts his assistant. *How things?*

*Too quiet, sir.*

Sherman looks up from the screen and sees Gil standing in the keg line. He walks over and joins him. "What do you think?"

Gil eyes the empty stage. "The band? Not bad."

"Not Marley." He puts his hands on Gil's gargantuan shoulders and positions him so he's facing the bar. *"Them."*

The line shortens and they take a step forward. "Haven't given it much thought."

"I think Lin's got motives of the insidious kind."

Gil lands a weird look on his producer. "I think you've smoked a little too much weed."

"She's loaded, man."

When it's their turn Gil holds two cups between his fingers then shoves the tap into the mouth of one. With his thumb he presses the knob that controls the flow. "Any husband sightings?"

"No," he says, as if that's a bad thing.

"The dude's nervous. You never drank too much because of a pretty face?" First cup full, he starts on the second. "Did something happen between you two?"

Sherman unclips his Persols from his shirt collar and puts them on. "Maybe."

The second cup is filling fast. "Care to elaborate?"

"No."

"Got a text from your girlfriend. She sent me a couple video clips." Gil shakes his head, chuckling. "She's got pluck. I'll give her that."

He hands Sherman his beer. They turn to see they're being filmed. "Mr. G?" Tabitha says, looking through the viewfinder. "Is there anything you'd like to share with your fans? Any medical conditions? Was it the heat? Dehydration?" she says. "Heard there's a doctor of geriatrics in the crowd. Want him summoned?" Then the camerawoman saunters off.

Gil smiles like he's in on the joke then leaves Sherman high and dry. Who does he talk to? His co-producer, who then casually looks over his shoulder like he must see for himself if Sherman has lost his mind.

Then Blanco walks over. "You baked, Sherm?"

"Maybe I am. And maybe I'm not."

"Heather says you're in the doghouse."

"Might have fucked that up, yeah."

"We're good, otherwise, right?"

Sherman doesn't like how Blanco stares at him, so sincere and direct. "We're not friends."

"Will you take off those sunglasses," Blanco says. "Is this about your collapse?"

"Does the whole fucking world know?"

"Gil says there's a problem with Lin."

"Gil doesn't know shit."

The band is back onstage. Guitars are being slung over shoulders. The drummer is stepping behind his kit with his sticks. There's a noticeable spirit on the lawn, an anticipation for the evening's last set. And Sherman wants everyone to go home. He's done with everything—the messiness and his guests, with trying so hard. He just wants the Hideaway to go back to how it was. The party is interrupted by a heartfelt, not bad rendition of "Is This Love." The singer stands on the narrow bar, serenading a beer bottle with eyes closed. Most everyone in the crowd has their phones pointed in her direction, even members of Marley. Celebrities have that something extra. They're bigger than life. Well, until they lose their balance and fall. Though Shinkan is up in quick time, showering the crowd with kisses. Lin, who's sitting at the bar, howls into his drink. Then Marley kicks into what? You guessed it.

"This is what I'm talking about," Sherman says. "She's wasted."

Blanco's only half listening. For his woman is motioning him toward the dance pit. "Let me know if the shit's hitting the fan."

"You'll be the first to know," he yells after him. He gives Blanco's backside the middle finger. "NOT."

Of course, Kimberly's watching. She sees him and his sunglasses at night. Shaking her head, she leads the man in the yellow anorak into the swirl of bodies. "I'm such an idiot."

"You? Say it isn't so." Steve-O stands next to him in a short-sleeve shirt he completely fills out. The pocket in his lower lip is plugged with tobacco.

"You chew?"

The carpenter shrugs like the question bores him. He's double-fisting, one cup of brew, the other with an inch of dark liquid swishing around the bottom. "Don't tell the twins."

"Because they'd want a pinch themselves?"

He spits into the chew cup. "Because it's not the parental example I'm going for. Now, why are you an idiot? Is this about blacking out? Because there's a doctor in the crowd, geriatrics, I think."

Sherman's gaze falls on Kimberly. "I fucked up. This entire weekend is a bust."

"Dude, you're too hard on yourself. This party kicks ass."

"Hey, Steve-O? You ever sell yourself short?"

His friend doesn't answer. His gaze is preoccupied by something he sees through the throng of head bobs and singalongs, the great inertia of bodies. Then Sherman sees what causes his friend so much distress. His daughter is slow dancing with the leading man in this tight, achy way. Like the world is ending in two hours.

"Hey, big fella. Like chill."

"I'm going to kill that son-of-a-bitch."

"And you'll get arrested. That's Dennis' deputy over there."

"Fuck Norton."

"The kid will sue you, man. I'm not saying your feelings aren't warranted. I'm not saying I wouldn't be pissed, either. But violence is not the answer."

His friend drains his cup then smushes it in his hand. "And I was having such a good time."

Steve-O starts stomping off, nearly bumping into Sensei Yamaguchi, who's walking toward Sherman with purpose. She sticks her phone in his face. "She's exploding!"

"The term is blowing up, Sensei."

"What are you going to do about this!"

# WALK LIKE A MAN

Springsteen stirs inside him. Lyrics steal across his imagination like shooting stars. *"I'm dying for some action, I'm sick of sitting 'round here trying to write this book. I need a love reaction, Come on now, baby, gimme just one look."* His take on sin and atonement, his spirited pursuit for a just meaningful life. His songs have taught Ken so much—about being a better father, about being a bigger participant in mankind. With Springsteen, how you live life matters.

He holds his plate out when it's his turn in the food line. The chef spooning him jambalaya has a tattoo of a spiral shaped shell on the little peninsula of flesh between her thumb and forefinger. The ink reminds him of the people he's encountered since being up north, from the girl at McDonalds to Spicoli riding out the storm. He's done it, hasn't he? He's ridden the dark wave and come clean out on the other side. He pours himself a beer then sits on the lawn. He can't remember food tasting so good. He sees her then. She wears this sexy-hot dress and fuck if his dick doesn't wake in his trousers. She looks radiant and like his wife of old and this sadness leaches from his heart. How did he get so lucky? She was there and the rest was history. Is it that simple? Are they bound somehow? *"Oh, will you walk with me out on the wire, 'Cause baby I'm just a scared and lonely rider. But I gotta find out how it feels. I want to know if love is wild, I want to know if love is real."* More than anything he wants Kimberly to see he's trying to be a better man. If the union between two people is like a great opus that's never quite finished, then we're tinkerers doing our best to make the damn thing rhyme and flex and move.

Then he gets a crazy idea. What if he devotes his life to trees? He'll be the Tree Guy, the Tree Whisperer, the man who moves among trees. Aren't the boys always telling him climate change is the biggest threat their generation faces. It will get ugly. Millions will be displaced. People will die. One man alone can't save the planet. But he can try.

His life is far from over. He knows how quickly a life can be cut short. Like Andrew's had. Or the sheriff from Bayfield County, Wisconsin. If the church taught him anything it's that God forgives those who are truly repentant. So, that's where he'll begin. He finds his wife again. He sees her in all her beautifully flawed ways. He loves her. He's always loved her.

Ken slops up his food with cornbread. He swallows some beer. This is his life. This dancing in the dark. It's time to step back into the world again.

# CRAWLING BACK TO YOU

From his hiding place Sherman sees the brightly lit stage and happy party people. He fingers out the joint from his jean's back pocket and brings it up to his nose. It smells like an elixir that will send him away. And he wants a zombie-apocalypse, shit falling from the sky, it's the end of the world as we know it, sort of stupid-high. He lights up then takes a hit. The music penetrates the woods—its beat steady and melodic. Like the music has no beginning or end. *"Exodus... Movement of Jah People,"* the backup singers chant. They sing and the music speaks to him like nothing has in a long time. He finds himself moved and sways with the rhythm. But then an emotion he can't control surges up and he holds back a sob. *Sport* was to be his *Raging Bull*. Sherman put so much effort into the weekend, into the idea of Kimberly being a proxy for Juliet, into the film fulfilling his hopes and dreams. All that is gone now.

The Hideaway glows like something in a fairy tale. Kimberly dances on the lawn's perimeter. He feels a closeness to her now more platonic than anything else. Maybe Ethereal's right, they should stick to their own kind. The stage lights up like a supernova. His eyes sweep past the bar like he's done all night. Only he doesn't see the beautiful couple. He searches the jamboree and the hundreds of arms swaying in the air like waves of love. But no world-famous actress. Where are they? Then he hears what sounds like a woman's scream. He walks to the wood's edge like a father might hearing a noise in the dead of night with his family fast asleep. He listens hard. There it is again. He's not the only person looking in the direction of the yurts like they heard something, too. Then he's joining the group running around the house. *Not the actress, please God, please not her.* The noise ends at Alexander Field's yurt.

The door bursts open—it's not the movie star—it's Steve-O with his daughter slung over his shoulder like a sack of seed. Like everyone else, Sherman smiles. Dawn is his little girl. She's the sack and they're playing the potato game. Then he sees that she's topless and wearing a thong. And she's beating her dad's back and screaming that she hates him and wants to fucking kill him. Joanie's there with the girls. She's pleading with her husband to stop. But Steve-O's not having it. He's in his own terrible hell, listening to nothing and no one. Then he sees Alexander in close pursuit. It's the actor who gets the most camera views since he's butt-naked and trying to reason with him, saying things like he's scaring Dawn's sisters, that if he's mad at anyone it should be him.

Steve-O comes to a stop. "You know something, you're right."

And he starts after Alexander with Dawn hanging on best she can. By now Joanie is using a voice reserved for a dog who's gotten into the garbage, the twins are balling, and the camera crew has set up a tripod in the drive and thrown the switch on a muscular light. All the while the sure-footed Alexander Field is two steps ahead of the middle-aged carpenter. It's near comical and it's very sad. Finally, Steve-O pulls up to suck in some much-needed air.

"Steve," his wife calls out. "Put Dawn down. You're being a moron."

"Let me go, Dad."

Someone kindly hands Alexander a twig to use like a fig leaf. "Please, Mr. Larson."

Steve-O's facing the port-a-potty with his daughter thrown over his shoulder. He's like the bandit in an old movie with nowhere else to turn. Sherman makes his way over. "Put your phone's away," he says to the bystanders. "And delete whatever you recorded. This is a private moment between father and daughter. And Steve-O?" he says. "We need to put Dawn down, okay? She needs to be safe. I know that's what you want to."

The big man lets out a bone deep sigh then bumps his daughter off his back. Alexander rushes in and puts his arm around Dawn's shoulder.

"Can we get a blanket?" Sherman says. "And a diaper for the kid here."

Then he sees Kimberly. Their eyes meet and she nods like he did okay. And a little of that good he was feeling earlier in the week seeps into his heart. But then he's thinking about the actress again, that she's gone missing, that she might be in danger. The crowd is dispersing when he finds Blanco. Sherman tells him his suspicions. The two men check Lin's yurt but its empty. They peek in Shinkan's room, same thing. Then they look at each other like they'd done earlier that afternoon and were worried about the safety of a woman at the hands of a potentially dangerous man and start running for the lake as if the great body of water holds all the mystery and sorrow of the world. Past the jam session and the party people then down the hill in the dark Sherman has known his whole life. They stop to catch their breaths—the surf is violent and loud— and scan the shoreline in both directions. Then Sherman points to a dark object closer to his neighbor's place north of the Hideaway. "Is that—" They take off again, sprinting the last forty yards over the marsh. The closer they get the more he realizes that Lin's on top of Shinkan and they appear to be having sex. Lin has an arm high in the air, which strikes him as odd and out of place. It's a detail that Sherman will grasp only later, after what happens next, as he tries to make sense of what he's seeing—wondering if Shinkan's lucid; if she's a willing participant.

Before they reach the beach another figure appears from the area north of the property. Then Lin's being yanked to his feet and up go his jeans and then Solberg holds a gun to his head and backs Jonathan Lin into the trees.

And the moment they disappear the two men run for the movie star. She's unconscious and paler and more naked than she deserves. Blanco checks her pulse then covers her body with her clothes best he can. Then he lifts her into his arms and they walk up the hill. Sherman feels in a trance walking past the party people and their obtrusive phones, past the bright lights and music soaring over the trees. They're spotted by Sensei Yamaguchi. Then Kimberly and Heather. They surround Shinkan like moms protecting their own. Only then does Sherman wake from his stupor. Only then does it come to him—Lin was filming himself fucking the passed out actress. He gets out his phone and calls Van Doorman.

"Code Red," he spits into the receiver. "Code fucking red."

***

Twenty-three minutes later the search party stands around the kitchen table as Sherman's assistant lays out a crude drawing of the property, including Grant's Point. Marley's set is over. The band is breaking down their equipment, most guests have left to party on at Tom's Burned Down Cafe, and Kimberly has made numerous attempts to contact her husband. Keegan had found Solberg's truck with the keys in the ignition and his dog inside, so they figure he's nearby. Most everyone wants to call in the sheriff. In the minority is Sherman, arguing for more time.

"Two witnesses saw Solberg on the lawn. He was eating barbeque and listening to the band," Sherman says. "Does that sound like a killer to you?"

"Killers get hungry," Gil says, scowling. "They probably like music."

"My proposal is thus—" Sherman says.

"—thus?"

"We break into search parties like we talked about. If we don't find Solberg we call the sheriff."

Round and round they go. His director doesn't like the idea of hunting down a man "packing heat." Van Doorman is beginning to think Lin is a decoy, that Solberg is using him to get to everyone else. Blanco says this is a matter for the police. Period. And Sherman wants to yank his hair out. No one knows what Solberg has planned but he feels that if the sheriff and his deputies are called in then Solberg dies. And he can't do that to Kimberly. Or her boys. Especially since it was him who'd withheld the information. All because of his stupid movie.

"Solberg's too much of a wildcard, sir."

"We have no idea what he's thinking," Sherman says.

"We know his kind," Gil says.

"And what kind is that?"

"The kind who lashes out first and asks questions later," Blanco says.

"Just because Solberg was violent when he was younger doesn't mean he's the same guy now."

Is he really defending Ken Solberg? The man who'd been stalking them? Who put a gun to Lin's head then took him into the woods?

"Anyone ask what Kimberly thinks? Oh, that's right," Blanco says dryly. "She's only talking through an intermediary."

This is true. When she found out her husband was on the island, and she was the last to know, she did two things in quick succession. She slapped Sherman so hard his eyes watered. And she flat out wouldn't speak to him.

"I want to do this for Kimberly," Sherman says in a low steady voice. "She deserves better than this. And if the sheriff shows up my gut tells me it's going to be bad."

There's a drawn out, unsettling quiet in the kitchen.

"Fine," Blanco says, breaking the silence. "Thirty fucking minutes. And I hope you're right."

"And if he harms Lin, sir?"

"Then the asshole fucking deserves it."

And so it's begrudgingly decided. Keegan and Van Doorman will traverse the largest area south and west from Old Fort Road to the lagoon then over to Grant's Point, Blanco and his son the shoreline down from the neighbor to the north, and Gil and Sherman the woods from the hill to the water. The groups will meet at Grant's Point at the designated time.

"Unless you come across Solberg," Blanco warns. "Then stay put and call the rest in."

Flashlights are distributed and the group chat tested. On the way outdoors Sherman tells Gil he'll meet him in a few minutes. He pokes his head in the porch where Kimberly and her intermediary are hanging out.

"Heather?" he says. "Please ask Kimberly if she's heard anything?"

Solberg's dog, lying on the rug between the women, lifts his head hearing Sherman's voice. Both women have changed into casual clothes and drink coffee in the chairs underneath the Tiffany floor lamp. Heather sets her cup on the table then leans in. "Have you had contact with your husband since last time it was asked?"

"Tell him to fuck off."

Heather looks across the room. "She says to fuck—"

"Heard her loud and clear," he says, chuckling.

Kimberly turns her blue eyes on Sherman, her glare cold. "God, you piss me off."

# THE TIES THAT BIND

*Andrew… you out there, man? I bet you're with Dad and the two of you are fishing that spot on Rainy where the walleye roam. I miss you, brother. I miss our conversations. I miss your presence. I miss all the good in you, man, all the good you could have passed on to Brandon and Jeremy. Who knows where you'd be if you hadn't taken Ellen Enzler to old man Gleeson's that night?*

*I've come a long way. I can feel it, you know? It's like those nights on the ice when there's a flow, when the game hums. It's like everything you touch and feel is elevated. I miss those days. I miss those conversations after games, in the dark of the bus, the boasts and bravado, or just talking about girls or what our dreams were.*

*The pretty boy's drunk, and a little off in the head, nothing I can't handle, don't worry, brother, I got this—I'm not going to hurt him. I'm not that guy anymore. Though I scared him good when I told him we were going for a walk. He cried like a little kid and said he was sorry and didn't mean any harm to the woman.*

*I have an affinity with this place. Madeline Island is in my soul. It's like you and me, Andrew. I can't explain it except to say it feels right and true. It's like I've been lost, but now I'm found. Who wrote that song? Shit, it doesn't matter. I'm just happy to have found this place. Will you look at that tree leaning toward the water? It's like a child reaching for its mothe—.*

# WHEN DOVES CRY

They hear a gunshot.

It's close by and has that punctured, hollowed out sound that's manmade and foreign. A sound like few other things on earth. Sherman searches his director's face in the darkness when they hear two more in rapid succession. Then they're running through a cluster of balsam fir toward Grant's Point.

They see a light flickering in the dark up where the teepee of driftwood stands like a skeletal horse. They are still a long way off and their shoes keep slipping in the sand. This is the barren flat area a couple hundred yards from the island's most southern point and at night it's like the surface of some dying planet, a lifeless sprawl of bone-white stones, driftwood of the same eerie color, and crosscurrents of surging water. Out the corner of his eye Sherman spots others running where the water breaks the shore. It's Blanco and his son. The athlete suddenly cuts across the point at a higher spot and halves the time to where the light flashes.

By the time he and Gil reach the teepee he sees that it's Keegan flagging them down with a flashlight. They're catching their breaths when Bjorn sprints back toward the house. Van Doorman is on his phone, giving the authorities the coordinates. Blanco locks eyes with Sherman, then they both look in the direction of the lagoon. About twenty yards up, on a sliver of sand, stands the silhouette of a man. Jonathan Lin.

## BLINDED BY THE LIGHT

*In that moment all ceases… it is like passing through a slipstream… lost in depths you can't explain. Images flicker here and there… Andrew lacing his skates… the boys smiling faces… the love of my life.*

*Everything is fading, Andrew.*

*Then something is penetrating through the blur… a rip in the dream… then nothing.*

## LIKE A PRAYER

A body lays slumped on the shore. So close to the water's edge the waves hit his face. Jonathan Lin stands beside him, a gun resting by his side. Sharp winds break across the exposed point, sending sand and sprays of mist swirling in the air. The cramped stretch of land where Solberg lies feels confined—on the one side, the lake, and on the other, trees crowding the embankment. The men are spread ten or so feet apart with their flashlights casting stark beams on Lin and the lifeless body.

"Hey, Jonathan," Blanco says. "Can you put the gun down?"

"So you can jump my ass? Fuck that. And turn those fucking flashlights off."

One by one the men lower their lights.

"Can we check to see if he's alive?" Sherman calls out.

Lin steps up to the body and kicks Solberg in the chest. He doesn't move. "I don't know. I think he's dead. What do you think?"

Sirens ring out in the night. In the vast open space, the sound carries, fading into the distance before coming around as if its suddenly overhead.

"Here comes the calvary," Lin says, taking a seat on the body.

"What happened?" Blanco asks.

"He was babbling about love and sex and magic, blah, blah, blah. What a fucking chatterbox. I was like 'shut the fuck up, old man.'" The gun lies low between Lin's legs when he runs a hand through his stringy hair. "The bastard walked over to a tree and held his palm against the bark like it had a heartbeat." Lin shakes his head, chuckling at the recollection. "I saw the gun in his waistband, so I grabbed it. Three shots. Boom, boom, boom. You should have seen the look on his face."

They hear her then. She comes from over the sand in a run. The noise she makes is primal. Like she can read the future. Like this is how her stories end. She's turned the bend where the land is higher from years of wind blasts and storm surge. Her foot catches on a rut and down she goes. The men stand and watch. They say nothing. They offer no help. It feels like life being played out in slow motion. Lin gets up off the body and moves several feet away, still landlocked between the trees and water.

Kimberly runs the rest of the short distance and collapses on her husband. "Why!" she cries out. "Why!"

The sirens are louder now. Down by the lagoon police flashers wick across the darkness. Kimberly sits up suddenly as if she's consumed by a spirit. "It was ordained," she says in a voice not her own. "He saw it in a dream, a death on the beach. But it wasn't his mother's he saw. It was his own." Then she makes the sign of the cross and lays her head on the body and weeps.

Lin faces the men again. He's twitchy crazy and has gotten into a power stance and levels the handgun like he thinks they might charge. The men take a step backward with their hands up in surrender. Behind Lin, they can see the sheriff and deputies' flashlights bouncing off the dark ground. Lin's voice shakes when he says he's sorry. "I never wanted to hurt her. She was my dream girl." Then Lin sinks to his knees. "Chinko phones, Sherman. Ha ha."

Lin puts the gun to his temple. And he shoots himself in the head.

# PART THREE

# TUNNEL OF LOVE

It's a new year with a new president and his new agenda. Though in Kimberly's estimation nothing feels right about the direction the country is heading. She grew up in a conservative household, and other than a radical turn in her college days, she was loyal to party lines. Until this election. This year she's seeing politics in sharper contrast. Hasn't she been paying attention or is the Republican Party comprised of mostly bitter old white men? As for the newly elected president, she's no fan. There are so many things she finds intolerable about him. That he got conservative women like herself to cast a vote for him, with all the abhorrent things he said and did on the campaign trail, is what troubles her most. Have we fallen that far as a nation that words and deeds don't matter?

She's driving through Kansas with its rolling hills and gray vistas. Clouds cast huge slabs of shadow over the nut-brown land. The view is almost incomprehensible in its flatness, its immensity. Here's a land she doesn't know, foreign as a second language. The highway deteriorates at the Oklahoma state line. There, the shoulder's nonexistent, the road crumbled and pock-marked. Kimberly passes mass-incarcerated cattle farms, slaughterhouses with tens of thousands of animals in tightly congested pens, all standing in mud and feces up to their knees, waiting for their next meal. She doesn't get modern farming. How a man of good conscience can look his family in the eye when his work centers around preparing animals for slaughter in such climates. She isn't against eating beef. But the conditions we subject other living things to? Where is our sense of duty? And don't tell her it's the only way to make meat affordable. Human beings are better than that.

A couple hours later she crosses into New Mexico. The ranches she passes are the size of small towns, nothing but grassland, tumbleweed, and driveways a mile long. There's a desolateness to this country that splits her wide open. Her mind drifts to better days and she slips an old CD into the player. And if that doesn't make her smile. She sings along, especially on the refrains. Old Dimley sits up in the backseat. "Is this what it was like, boy? You and Ken on the road?"

Naomi and David offered up their condo in Santa Fe. Two weeks on her own, no contact with the outside world, no responsibilities, just her and the burnt-red desert and distant mountain ranges. She brought her road bike and skis. Her therapist encouraged the trip. She thought a break from the boys would be healthy. Six months in, therapy is like a sucker punch to the gut. During sessions Dr. Lederman leans in whenever a sensitive subject comes up. It's like she's picking a scab. She wants to hear the things Kimberly doesn't want to say for fear of what they'll unfold. Her therapist picks and picks until she's a heap of quivering goo. Until it feels like she doesn't walk out her office afterwards but is dragged heels first down the hallway and onto the sidewalk where life goes on in sparkly vividness. Where everyone sitting inside the corner coffee shop seem stable and worry-free. Kimberly feels the opposite— like she's hanging on by her fingernails from a tall building in the sad movie called her life.

There's a word Dr. Lederman proposes, a catch-all for what happened on Madeline Island. *Incident.* But it wasn't an *incident.* It was a nightmare no one would wish on an enemy, something Kimberly will toil with the rest of her life. *Incident?* Jonathan Lin isn't coping with two young men minus a father. Jonathan Lin's selfishness, his petty wants, didn't set in motion what Dr. Lederman calls the incident. The motherfucker Jonathan Lin got off easy.

\*\*\*

The morning after the murder the Wisconsin State Patrol, Bayfield County Sheriff Department and City of Bayfield Police Department were cordoning off the crime scene with yellow tape, interviewing people who'd attended the reggae fest, searching Ken's campsite and truck for clues, confiscating both the documentary and property surveillance footage, and bagging the bodies then taking them to Bayfield by boat transit.

Statements were taken. When it was Kimberly's turn, they quizzed her as if she was a main suspect herself. Did she know her husband was on the island? Did he have a vendetta against Lin? Had she put a contract out on her husband's head? "Are you fucking kidding me?" she'd cried.

She'd walked onto the front porch afterwards, shaken and upset. A glossy black Suburban with tinted windows idled in the circle drive. A man in a fitted suit was loading luggage as the executive producer's family climbed into the car. When Heather saw her standing on the porch she gave her friend a sad wave. A minute later the luxury car drove off the property. Hidden behind it was Brandon's rusty old pickup. She'd known her oldest boy would arrive before his brother since he'd been in the area the past week searching for his father. She was worried about how her sons would react, especially Brandon. He was the one who used to talk his dad off the ledge. Now Kimberly wondered who'd fill those shoes for her son.

She found him sitting near the crime area with the dog. And she let him be, instead walking up the shore where she sat on a dune with her knees hugging her chest. Where did she begin? How did she tell her boys the pain would one day pass? How did she console them when it sunk in that they'd never again hear their father's voice? Or hug him? Or ask his advice? How did she begin those conversations? She wouldn't. She would tell them in as few words as necessary how their father died. And then she'd let the moment breathe. Because this was what a parent had to do. Because children needed space to digest tragedy, senseless though it may be.

A little while later Brandon and his brother walked around the point with the dog. They came over, not saying a word, Jeremy electing to sit on the bank above her and his older brother standing at the water's edge. Then came the questions. *What was Dad doing here? Was he at war with these people? Had they done him wrong?* Kimberly answered best she could. She thought it important to show Ken in a favorable light. Their dad was a hero. He'd stopped an assault on a young woman. People who'd seen him that night said he was enjoying himself. "The man who did this was a *sick, diseased, evil fucking* person." Then she paused. Because Jeremy was crying. There was nothing worse than hearing your own flesh and blood hurting like that. She went down where Brandon was and touched his hair. He leaned into his mother like a dog accepting a caress. Then Kimberly was sobbing and pulling her oldest along with her. The three Solberg's sat huddled together on the beach with Dimley sticking his wet nose in their faces and they clutched one another and wept for the man they called father and husband and friend.     .

The brothers took off after the police gave them the keys to the pickup. They broke down their father's camp then drove to the state park and dove off the red cliffs and lay in the sunshine. It was later in the day when Jeremy showed up alone. He said Brandon went into town to fill up the F-150. But when her oldest didn't return, Kimberly got nervous. She thought he might hurt himself or wrap the truck around a tree and they'd bury not one but two Solberg men on the same day. She and Jeremy left him voice and text messages. She even called Ken's mom. Betty took the news hard.

"I know you're upset," she said. "But Brandon may show. If he does, he needs you to be strong. Okay, Betty?"

A couple hours later she got a call from Cal. "Brandon's with me. And he's okay. I texted Jeremy. They're going to spend some time up here. Hope that's okay. I'm sorry, Kimberly. This has really shaken me up, too."

\*\*\*

Kimberly rides hills on a backdrop of sagebrush and pinyon trees. She catches glimpses of mountain ranges black in the late afternoon light. Fine red sand runs along the shoulder and the desert has no smell. It's open road and houses carved into hillsides up gravel lanes named Mountain Cloud Zen and Raven Ridge. The cycling isn't extreme. Long slow pulls up moderate inclines then a glorious downhill race home. Her first week she clocks in rides of 14.3, 16.5, 18.8 and 21.4 miles with elevation gains around 1800 feet. Her lungs are responding to the thin air. She sees herself retiring in Santa Fe. The idea throws such an energy through her that she finds herself charging like a race is on.

One day, cresting a pass, her phone pings. Thinking it's an emergency, her motherly instincts take over. She brakes, clips out of her pedal, and pulls her phone from her cycling jersey, all in one swift move.

*Santa Fe? Beautiful country. How are you?*

Her gaze finds the slot between the hills. They'd communicated twice since Ken's death, the first time the night she got home from Madeline Island, then a couple days later. Sherman had told her the tennis film was on hiatus indefinitely. His assistant had also written him a letter of resignation. His voice caught telling her as if his relationship with Van Doorman meant more to him than he realized.

"Are you back with her?" she'd asked.

His hesitation said it all. And Kimberly bristled. What had she been thinking? Did she honestly believe a man she hardly knew, who lived a life of privilege and entitlement, who she'd spent two days flirting with on the slopes of Aspen, whom she sexted with!, would lead to something real and permanent? Movie stars! Professional athletes! What fun! What stories she'd tell Naomi! But it was a sham, a show. He'd played her like he played the others. The simple fact was if she hadn't agreed to meet Sherman on Madeline Island then Ken didn't die, Lin didn't take his life, and her boys weren't without a father. She was so preoccupied with payback, with getting what she felt was her due, that she failed to grasp her husband's cry for help.

Dr. Lederman disagreed. "It wasn't you who had an affair. You didn't stalk him or carry a loaded gun. It wasn't you who stopped communicating with the outside world. Your husband was angry, Kimberly. He died, not because of anything you did, but because of decisions he made."

"I should have heard the desperation in his voice," she said. "I should have known."

***

She closed her eyes, and it was there. She ran an errand, and it was there. She looked in her boy's eyes, and *it was there*. She either felt emptied out or her emotions were like a tub overflowing with water. The abruptness got her. Her husband being ripped from the earth like an ugly useless weed? That didn't sit right. The hole that created. The hole she stuffed with pain and misery and rage. "Good riddance," her dad said. "He disappointed us for a long time." Her friends called him unprintable names. They said he'd never been good enough for her. These comments didn't have the intended power her friends thought they might. If other people saw her husband for who he was—a lying, cavorting parasite— what did that say about her? She was like a balloon, a bright red balloon that accidentally slipped from her fingers. Up she went, past the trees and the house, past the neighborhood, up, up, up, above the skyline and the river's thick gleam, up past where airplanes flew, into the thin cerulean air, where it was difficult to breathe. When would the balloon break? What happened when the bright red balloon popped?

***

She rides. And the beauty of riding, of spending hours in the saddle with her legs churning and heart pumping, is how the past washes over her. Pedal over pedal she sees how it really was. What she put up with—what a person puts up with for the sake of a marriage, for their children's wellbeing. She'd always looked unfavorably at failed marriages. Either they hadn't tried hard enough or the partners were stuck inside their own egos. *Buck up*, she'd think. *Put on your adult pants and make it work.* She had no patience for nitpicky sour people, either. The way one person dominated the other, the curt remarks, the lack of love. Kimberly believed in the union of two people with all her heart. Even after hearing those voices in her head. Those voices, warning her, telling her the state of her marriage wasn't right. *Something's up with Ken. Mentally and emotionally, he's left the building. Watch him. Or you'll lose what it is you have.*

She knew her husband. They shared the same bed. He was a great lover. It was easy to get caught up in his spell. But if she could, couldn't another? So, she watched his movements. She watched his words. She listened to his mouth for falsehoods. One day he surprised her. "What do you think of marriage counseling?" And so they went. There were tears and breakthroughs and finding common ground. They'd go back in time so they'd have a future. And it worked. The marriage got better. They took a trip to Florida. Time rolled on. But it was happening again. She felt him pulling away. She felt him letting *them go.* They were empty nesters now. At first Kimberly thought that explained the voices. Ken was simply adjusting to life without his boys around. But the voices were getting louder. She was losing her husband. She felt this in her bones.

That didn't explain Sherman Garrity, not in full anyway. They'd met at the tent bar the summer before. This was the long weekend with Naomi and the girls up north. He was sexy and in good shape. He made her laugh and feel pretty. Madeline Island became her little secret. A crush on the cute guy from the other side of the tracks. She went back to her old life again. She was working for the first time since the boys were born. And she liked the interior design firm. Working had restored a vitality in Kimberly she hadn't known existed. Then, out of the blue, she got a text from Sherman. There began a game that involved her and the dashing man from Bel Air. There was a dangerous edge to the flirtatious back and forths, a titillation she was drawn towards. How far was she willing to go?

Did she regret the trip to Aspen? Yes, in that the covertness felt akin to betrayal. Then she came across the photos on the family computer. And what a tramp she was. Ken was choosing this woman *over her?* This rage shot through her. It was like a wildfire consuming her from the inside out. She wanted to destroy things. *His things.* Then she had to get away from the things that mouth said. She had to prove that he didn't matter. That she could inflict pain, too.

She served divorce papers then placed a call to Los Angeles. "It's over," she said. "When can we meet?" She sensed him hesitating, slowing down the train she saw blowing through the night.

"How does Madeline Island sound?"

"So, it's over?" Kimberly asked.

"She's gone," Sherman said. "She moved out."

***

Her dreams consume her. In one, she runs on a deserted beach, gunshots zipping past her head. Then she's being chased by a man who resembles Lin. She jolts awake, heart racing. In another dream she's a dark angel, seeing nothing, feeling nothing, observing from above. A blast goes off and she wakes, her heart beating like a drum. The clock reads 2:15AM. It's always 2:15. In one vision, she's holding a handgun when it explodes in her hands. She feels something warm and not unpleasant, near soothing, coursing through her body. Sometimes, Ken appears. He looks at her like he knows something she doesn't. Like he's been places and seen things she can only dream of. He extends a hand, but she doesn't trust him, even in her dreams. She opens her eyes and stares at the clock-radio on her nightstand. And guess what? It's quarter past two.

Those nights she can't sleep she brews tea and sits in his chair wrapped in her grandmother's quilt. She listens to a band that Brandon turned her onto. Yo La Tengo's music is like nothing she's ever heard before. Weird droning overtures that remind her of time itself, days gone by, tranquil places. Dreams, maybe. The boys find her the next morning wrapped in the quilt. She's up in no time, pretending she doesn't have a sleeping disorder, pretending 2:15 isn't imprinted on her eyelids.

There are so many things to consider, foremost being the boy's welfare. Her role means 100% accountability. But not in a way that betrays her concern. When it comes to the boys, her movements can't be choreographed. She can't come across worried or showing pity. If Kimberly learned one thing from living with men, it's that sympathy must be earned. So she keeps her ears attuned to the quiet of the house. She's adept at reading facial expressions, what's said and not said, the way bodies steal past another without touching. Overnight, Jeremy's grown into a workout fanatic. Twice a day he lifts with the garage door open and hip-hop cranked to the max. He's equally obsessed with food intake—fat ratio, carb index, his protein consumption. Three times a day he makes these chalky protein shakes so thick you can stand a spoon in it. Jeremy calls it maximizing gains. And Brandon? He sometimes walks in the kitchen and she swears its Ken in the flesh. He spends chunks of time away from home, stopping by at odd hours to do laundry or see what's for dinner. One afternoon she finds him bent over the dryer bin.

"What's her name?" she says, standing in the threshold.

Brandon stuffs sweats into a duffle without folding them. "Chandra."

Kimberly leans against the doorframe. He's letting his beard grow. His forearm displays a beautiful new tattoo—tall wispy pines shrouded in a smudge of nothingness. Like something drawn from an ancient Chinese scroll.

"That's a pretty name." Brandon shrugs like duh, she's pretty. There are a few items left in the bin when she steps inside the room. "Let me fold those." He makes a noise like his mom is a pain in the ass, but he moves aside and leans against the washer. She folds a sweatshirt into a plump square. "You two serious?"

Brandon doesn't break a smile. "It's not like that."

"Is she good to you?"

"That's it. I'm outta here." Brandon pushes himself off the appliance and reaches for his duffle. "I know what you're doing, and it won't work." They both grab the bag's straps at the same time. Kimberly holds on long enough to make eye contact with her eldest boy. His face is filled with the fluster of youth, but also a swagger he inherited from his father. Then his eyes cloud over with tears.

"Oh, Brandon."

And he's gone. Out the side door and storming for the truck. She watches from the window as he backs out of the drive. Tears fill her eyes. Crying never hurts, she thinks. What came before, that hurt.

***

Everything she reads says it's a good time to sell. Truth is she no longer sees herself in the house. She resents what she sees as his junk—the hunting gear and expensive toys in the garage. When she thinks about the kind of place she sees herself living in the vision contains sunlight, trees outside big windows, a space large enough for her easels and canvases, in walking distance of parks and lakes, a shopping area. She holds firm to the long view. *Sell before winter,* that voice says. Anytime she feels a purge coming on she consults the boys. They keep the strangest things… his ice skates and a Rush Limbaugh "Dittohead" coffee mug. They divvy up his albums, hunting gear and tools. Neither boy will sell the snowmobiles even when Kimberly says the insurance premiums are on them. Her focus is selling the house. Broaching the subject is another matter. The house is all the boys know, and after what happened—a source of comfort and safety. They're in the backyard one crisp clear night in October, a fire in the stone ringed pit. Moosehead is being passed around in honor of their dad, dead three months to the day.

"I don't get it," Brandon says, stoking the fire. "I guess my question is why?"

"The market's good."

"Where will we live?"

"Think about me, bro." Jeremy takes a gulp of beer. "At least you got Chandra."

"We grew up here, Mom. This is home."

Kimberly looks up from the crackling flames. The air is cold enough that their breaths shine white against the darkness. "I need a change of scenery."

"Like an apartment?"

"The two of you won't be living with me forever. I see well-paying jobs in your future. I see lovely women."

"Like Chandra," Jeremy quips.

His brother gives him the middle finger.

"I'm forty-six," she says. "I plan on living a long time. That means making smart financial moves."

No one speaks. They watch the fire and drink their beers. "How much do you think it's worth?"

She wishes the question came from Brandon. He's the nostalgic Solberg boy. He more so than his brother holds family tradition aloft. "The realtor thought 325, maybe 340."

Jeremy whistles then glances at his brother, who's finished off his beer and reaching for the twelve-pack lying on the grass. "What do we owe?"

"Around fifty."

Brandon pops the bottlecap off with an opener, then takes a drink. "Then what?"

Here's the difficult part. Imparting her dreams and what they might hold without coming off as selfish or anti-Ken or not sensitive to the boy's feelings. "I'll find a place somewhere, maybe in Minneapolis. I know this is hard," she says. "But the marriage was over. There was no going back."

"You're saying the house was being sold either way?" Jeremy asks.

"That's cold, Mom."

A flash of anger shoots through Kimberly. "What about a fresh start, Brandon? Is that asking too much?"

\*\*\*

And rock bottom? Halloween night.

There's a *For Sale* sign in the yard, been a half dozen walk-throughs, but no offers. Meanwhile it's Halloween. Her life might be upside down, but she can dress up in her witch's makeup and wig. She can pretend life is normal. The doorbell rings at dusk. Kimberly peers out the window in anticipation. Snow falls down in silent sheets. Yesterday it was corn-blue skies and gold leafed trees. Now all she sees through the white blur are grim parents in grim coats waiting grimly by the drive's end for their trick-or-treating children. She feels a sob in her throat. What she wouldn't give to be one of those grim parents. It takes all she can muster to crack the front door open and slide the candy bowls outdoors. "Have at it," she says, choking up.

Thank God the boys aren't home. She doesn't want them to see her so not in control. She's been trying so hard. But it's all fucked. Everything is fucked. She'll be fifty in four years. What does she have to show for it? Where will her life be then?

She cries all week. If the boys are home she locks herself in her room. She survives on Netflix, kettle corn, and white wine. Five days later she emerges a new woman. She builds a roaring fire and makes herself a bourbon. Then she writes messages on Post-It notes she then sticks on the hearth.

It's true. You cheated on me.

It's true. You made love to me while you were having sex with that woman.

It's true. You NOT ME broke our trusted union.

It's true. You lied and lied AND LIED.

It's true. You broke me. You broke us.

It's true. I hate you. Even in death I do.

It's true. You're dead and I'm alive, so ha-ha motherfucker, the jokes on you.

It's true. I wish you were here for Brandon and Jeremy. They need you right now.

It's true. I hope you found peace in death, Ken.

One by one Kimberly plucks the Post-Its from the hearth, reads them aloud, then drops them into the fire. She watches each piece of paper flame, curl and smoke. The act is liberating.

\*\*\*

The house sells in the middle of November, and Kimberly puts down a deposit on a condominium near Lake Nokomis. The boys pitch in with her move, and as a thank you, she treats them to Bruce Springsteen's *The River* concert at Xcel Center. That night, while she waits for them to pick her up before the show, she's filled with nervous energy. She hasn't completely found herself yet, but for the first time since Ken's death, she feels the ground solidly beneath her feet. The boys are finding their way, too. Brandon has moved in with Chandra, whose sweet and utterly smitten with him. And Jeremy's been invited to try out for the Tampa Bay Lightning.

Her text pings. She pulls on her down jacket, locks the front door, then heads downstairs. As soon as she steps outdoors and feels the cold February air, she hears "Dancing in the Dark" blaring from the F-150. "Why is that so loud!" she says opening the passenger door.

Brandon turns down the volume a notch. "So Dad hears it in heaven."

"But I don't understand." She hasn't yet climbed up into the rig. "Neither of you believe."

Her youngest points at the roof of the cab. "But he does, Mom. The point is, he does."

Her boys make Kimberly want to cry. "That is so sweet."

What's the show like? Exhilarating, unlike anything else in life. Springsteen gives you everything he has. He makes you believe in America, well, at least for two and half hours. Throughout the night, her thoughts keep going back to the show he'd taken her to at Madison Square Garden. Bruce was three songs in when suddenly there he was, the man she once knew, the one she fell for. Underneath the ballcap and black dress shirt, underneath the whiskers and beer breath—underneath all that gruff—there was Ken.

The concert feels like a proper sendoff.

*Don't let him fade, boys.*

*Feed yourself his stories, talk to him, dream him, let him reside in you, listen for him in the wind through the pines, in song, in that eruption of noise inside an arena or sports stadium, when you hike or bend down and stroke your dog's neck.*

*Don't let him fade, boys.*

*Don't let his spirit go. Carry him like you'd carry a wounded brother, carry him wherever you go, whatever path life takes you down, no matter the joy or misery or death around you. Let the best of him inside you. Don't let him fade, boys.*

*Don't let him fade.*

END

# ACKNOWLEDGEMENTS

A heartfelt shout out to my dedicated readers for your thoughtful and generous feedback: Elaine Eschenbacher, James Pacala, and Kari Niessink Takai. A special thanks to Tom Boulay, Jillian Coppley and Jake Moosbrugger. Your knowledge and input were invaluable.

A huge thank you to my car expert, Jeff Sweitzer; my screenwriter friend, Karl Gajdusek; my documentarian brother, Robert Trondson; all my friends from International Falls (Charles Casanova!) and Madeline Island, and everyone who read an early draft and encouraged me to keep going.

To *Black Rose Writing*, thank you for taking on this project.

And finally, my family—thank you for letting me do what I do with such unconditional love and support.

# ABOUT THE AUTHOR

Photo by Ann Trondson

Tom Trondson's debut novel, Moving in Stereo, was the winner of the American Writing Awards 2022 Sports Book of the Year. His work has been featured in Glimmer Train, The Under Review, and elsewhere. He holds an MFA from Hamline University, where he's taught creative writing. Twenty-five years ago, he left the corporate world to be a stay-at-home dad, something he wouldn't change for the world. Recently, he and his buddies cycled a Tour de France segment, the famed Colle Dell'Agnello, a category one climb that travels from a small village to the mountains above the treeline. He has lived in six states but now calls the lakes and woods of Minnesota his home.

# NOTE FROM TOM TRONDSON

Word-of-mouth is crucial for any author to succeed. If you enjoyed *Sport & Leisure*, please leave a review online—anywhere you are able. Even if it's just a sentence or two. It would make all the difference and would be very much appreciated.

Thanks!
Tom Trondson

# ALSO FROM TOM TRONDSON

*Moving in Stereo*

We hope you enjoyed reading this title from:

www.blackrosewriting.com

Subscribe to our mailing list – *The Rosevine* – and receive **FREE** books, daily deals, and stay current with news about upcoming
releases and our hottest authors.
Scan the QR code below to sign up.

Already a subscriber? Please accept a sincere thank you for being a fan of Black Rose Writing authors.

View other Black Rose Writing titles at
www.blackrosewriting.com/books and use promo code
**PRINT** to receive a **20% discount** when purchasing.

www.ingramcontent.com/pod-product-compliance
Lightning Source LLC
Jackson TN
JSHW022110160625
86253JS00004B/34